THE
MOTHER'S
PHONE
CALL

BOOKS BY VICTORIA JENKINS

THE MOTHER'S PHONE CALL

VICTORIA JENKINS

bookouture

Published by Bookouture in 2025

An imprint of Storyfire Ltd.
Carmelite House
50 Victoria Embankment
London EC4Y 0DZ

www.bookouture.com

The authorised representative in the EEA is Hachette Ireland
8 Castlecourt Centre
Dublin 15 D15 XTP3
Ireland
(email: info@hbgi.ie)

ISBN: 978-1-83618-056-2
eBook ISBN: 978-1-83618-055-5

PROLOGUE

Monday

'Emergency, what service do you require?'
    'It's my son.'
    'Is he injured?'
    Pause.
    'No... no, he's not injured.'
    'Okay. Is he there with you now?'
    'Uh... yes. Yes, he's here.'
    'Could you tell me what your emergency is?'
    Silence.
    'Caller, are you still with me?'
    'Yes, I'm here.'
    Pause.
    'It's my son... He's killed someone.'

ONE

JO

Two days earlier

Everything she tries on, she hates. She didn't bother to buy anything new for the party, but now it's starting in little under two hours, she wishes she'd treated herself to something she felt good in. Eve had made a point of stating 'cocktail dress' on the invitations, though Jo isn't sure she's ever really known what that means. She ran several internet searches last night, but none of the suggestions looked suitable for a garden party in twenty-nine-degree heat.

'That one's always looked great on you,' Rob chips in from behind her, doing that disconcerting thing of seeming to read her mind. Jo moves to the side, glancing past the mint-green chiffon to catch sight of his reflection in the mirror. He's sitting on the edge of the bed, his skin still wet from the shower.

'I don't know. I just feel a bit... meh. Eve will no doubt be wearing something "designer".'

'It's a good thing you're not in competition with her then, isn't it?'

Jo feels affronted by the comment, though she isn't sure

why. 'What do you mean?' She turns to Rob, who slips his arms into a short-sleeved shirt that could do with ironing.

'I mean what I said. You don't need to compete.'

Still unsure how she's expected to take the comment, Jo turns back to the mirror and assesses herself in the dress. It shouldn't be as important as it seems to her in this moment. It's a garden party, she reminds herself. A glorified barbecue, really. So why does she feel as though she's received an invitation to Buckingham Palace?

Because it's Eve and Chris, she tells herself. Well... Eve, really. She loves her friend, but everything she does has to be just so. Just right. Instagram-worthy, lest anyone should think her life is anything but perfect.

'Do you want me to iron that shirt for you?'

'Does it need it?'

'Not if you don't mind looking like a bag of crisps.'

Rob sighs and pulls the shirt back over his head, rolling his eyes good-naturedly as he hands it to her. Jo hasn't let him touch the iron since 2015, when they'd been running late for a wedding, and he'd singed a hole in his suit trousers. They'd arrived ten minutes late for the ceremony after having to stop at a supermarket to buy an emergency pair of chinos that when they'd looked back on the professional photographs had made Rob look as though he hadn't been quite sure where he was going for the day.

She applies her make-up and pins up her copper-streaked brunette hair before taking the shirt downstairs. Alice is in the downstairs bathroom, the door open, the hallway smelling of citrus perfume. Her daughter is wearing a floral pink playsuit and sandals, looking beautiful as ever.

'You look lovely,' she tells Jo.

'Thank you. So do you. Do you want me to do that for you?' Jo gestures to the bracelet resting on the shelf below the bathroom mirror – a gift from her and Rob when Alice had got her

GCSE results two summers ago. Alice passes her the bracelet and holds out her hand so that her mother can loop it around her wrist.

'Where's your brother?' Jo asks, fitting the clasp in place.

'Somewhere,' Alice says vaguely.

Jo takes Rob's creased shirt into the kitchen and gets the ironing board and iron from the utility room. Once she's finished, she puts everything away and takes the shirt back upstairs to her husband.

'Have you seen Toby?'

'In his room, I think.'

Jo goes to the other end of the landing and taps on her son's bedroom door, waiting for the call that allows her to enter. After the second knock goes unanswered, she pushes the door open. She's lucky he's not like a lot of teenage boys in regard to cleanliness and personal hygiene; she's heard plenty of horror stories from other teen-boy mums, of fur-covered food discovered beneath beds and clothing so stiff with grime it could walk itself to the washing machine. Toby has always been quite particular about his room. Even when he was as young as six, she would sometimes find him tidying his things, liking his toys to be in their right boxes and books to be stored in a certain way on the shelves. The same could never be said about his sister, who was a whirlwind wherever she went.

The thought of the twins so much younger, all those years passed in an eye-blink, stops her steps, and she pauses with the door half opened, as though the past might lie behind it still, set to evaporate as soon as she enters the room.

She finds Toby, eighteen and unrecognisable from the boy she'd just remembered, lying on his bed looking at his phone. He's wearing a set of earbuds.

'I knocked twice,' she tells him as he pulls the bud from his right ear.

'Sorry... I didn't hear you.'

'Everything okay?'

'Yeah,' he says without taking his attention off the screen.

His work T-shirt and trousers are folded in a neat pile on the chair beside his desk, the hardware shop's logo printed in orange lettering on the chest. He hadn't needed to take the job, she and Rob had both told him that. He could enjoy this final summer before university without responsibility: see his friends, go travelling. Yet he'd insisted that he hadn't wanted to live off them – that he could earn his own money, and he wanted to. She's proud of him for that.

He's still wearing the shorts and T-shirt he woke up in this morning, not having showered yet. 'Are you going to get ready? The party will be starting soon.'

Toby locks his phone before turning it face-down on the bed. 'I'm not coming.'

'Toby...' Jo starts.

'I'm not feeling well.'

'Everything okay?' Behind her, Rob is now dressed and ready. He smells good, moving in a mist of the aftershave he's worn for years because she once told him it was her favourite, though she's never able to remember the name of it. And he looks even better than he smells. In their climb towards middle age, Rob has somehow managed to look more handsome every year, the grey flecks at his temples and the laughter lines at his eyes sharpening his features.

'You need to get ready,' Jo says, turning back to their son.

'I just told you, I don't feel well.'

'You can't not come now,' Jo argues. 'They're expecting you.'

'Does it really matter?' Rob says. 'If he's not feeling well, he's not feeling well.'

Jo eyes her son. He never once mentioned this morning that he felt ill in any way, and she's pretty sure it's just an excuse to stay at home. Yet Toby isn't the type of teenager to laze around in his pyjamas until 2 p.m.; he never has been. He's usually up before anyone else in the house, and he always keeps himself busy, whether it's study or exercise or seeing friends. An avoidance of social situations is more something she's come to expect from Alice.

'Has something happened?'

'Like what?' he says defensively.

'Like, I don't know. Anything. I'm just wondering why you suddenly don't want to go over there.'

'Because he's eighteen years old, and spending a Saturday with his middle-aged neighbours isn't likely to rank highly on any teenager's options for the weekend list.' Rob punctuates his comment with a shrug.

'Thanks for your support.'

He sighs and goes back down the hallway to their bedroom.

'Just come over for a bit, even if you don't stay,' Jo suggests. 'For me. Please.'

She waits for a smile, a shake of the head, even an eye roll, anything to show some kind of acknowledgement, but nothing is offered. She pulls the door closed, leaving Toby alone, not wanting to annoy him any more than she probably already has. She goes back downstairs and searches for the suncream she'd used yesterday, her pale skin needing a barrier before she braves the heat of the afternoon.

A short while later, Toby appears, dressed in a light pair of shorts and a shirt. His thick floppy hair has been swept back from his face, and when Jo catches sight of him, she's struck by just how much he looks like a younger version of his dad.

'Thank you,' she says. 'If I tell you I really appreciate your effort, will it mean anything?'

'If you make me a cheese toastie, we'll call it quits.'

'Deal.' Here he is, she thinks, relieved that her son seems to be back from whatever distraction had temporarily gripped him.

She smiles as she pulls the toastie maker from the back of

the cupboard. It's only ever used by her, and only ever for Toby – a comfort food she's made him ever since he was a little boy. Whenever he was upset or feeling unwell, life could be made better with a cheese toastie. But as she plugs in the machine, she realises that the excuse about feeling unwell was just that: an excuse. She wonders what's really the matter with him, but she doesn't want to annoy him by pressing the subject any further. When he's ready, he'll tell her; he's always done so before, eventually.

'Is there going to be food over there?' Rob asks as he comes into the kitchen and sees Jo sliding Toby's toastie onto a plate.

Jo pulls a face. 'This is Eve. There's going to be a banquet... no expense spared.'

Rob goes over to Toby and musses his hair before stealing a bite of his toastie. 'Well done, mate,' he says, putting a hand on his back. 'Let's just get this over and done with, shall we?'

TWO

ALICE

The sun is too hot. Even in the smallest playsuit she owns, the sweat still rolls off her; she can feel it running down the centre of her back in a thin line, tracing her spine like a wayward fingertip. The drink in her hand tastes like a holiday hangover, the ratio of alcohol to mixer measuring heavily in favour of the former. With her free hand, she adjusts her sunglasses. This vantage point at the far end of the garden has proved the perfect place for people-watching, a pastime she engages in frequently. And where the Harris family are concerned, there's always plenty to witness.

Alice watches Eve flit around the carefully tended lawn like a butterfly trapped in a suburbia-shaped bottle, darting from this neighbour to that, offering thanks for gifts and compliments on the other women's dresses. Above the chatter and laughter of the forty-odd people gathered in the garden to soak up the sunshine and the free champagne, Eve's tinkling voice stands out, a knife tapped against a glass to gain everyone's attention.

'The flowers are just beautiful, thank you... You really shouldn't have gone to all that trouble... You made it yourself? God, you're so talented... Those shoes are just amazing.'

It's all as fake as a February suntan. Alice feels pretty sure the only female here Eve considers worth celebrating in any way is Eve. She watches the guests fawn over her, the women gazing upon her admiringly, the men barely attempting to hide their lingering looks from their wives. Everyone is so quick to offer congratulations and compliments. And why would they behave any differently when she's passing around champagne like water?

Alice's dad has already had too much. As she scans the garden, she sees him at the summer house, leaning precariously on the wooden veranda that surrounds the raised decked area at its front. He's talking with Chris, Eve's husband; he raises an arm in gesticulation, revealing the sweat patch that has formed at his left armpit. Alice can always tell when her dad's been drinking, because he doesn't stop talking. Without alcohol, he's the silent kind, not one for saying more than needs to be said. He's a listener. She supposes that's where she gets it from, this tendency towards quiet but intent absorption. But she's also learned from her father that drinking doesn't suit their temperaments, which is why the cocktail in her hand is now as warm as the metal frame of the sunlounger.

'Hey.'

She leans to the ground and places her glass on the lawn before tilting her sunglasses down from her nose. Freya Harris appears haloed by sunlight, her summer-blushed body the shade of milky coffee. The spaghetti straps of her barely-there dress hang loose at her collarbones, where her recently bronzed skin dips into prominent valleys. She was never this sharp before, Alice thinks. Never this angular. She's been running. Dieting. She wonders whether the effort is for herself or someone else.

'You as bored as I am?' Freya asks. She perches at the end of the sunlounger without being invited, Alice having to draw her legs in to avoid having her feet sat on.

'I'm enjoying myself, actually. People-watching is my kind of entertainment.'

'You and Scarlet kissed and made up yet then?'

Alice bites the inside of her cheek, holding back the response she's tempted to give. Freya is fishing for gossip; she doesn't really care whether she and Scarlet are on speaking terms or not.

'I don't have a problem with her,' she lies.

'Then please make up. For me. Pretty please. How am I supposed to plan a girls' holiday if you two aren't speaking?'

There's been talk of a long weekend to Marbella, but Alice can't think of anything worse. Scarlet is Freya's friend, and she's never made much secret of the fact that she doesn't like Alice. Jo calls it jealousy, but Alice doesn't see that Scarlet has anything to be jealous of. She just enjoys making her look stupid at every available opportunity, and the worst of it for Alice is how intensely Freya is influenced by her whenever the two of them are together.

'It was just a joke,' Freya adds.

Alice gives her a thin smile. There was nothing funny about the text message Scarlet had sent from Alice's phone a couple of weeks earlier, when Alice had been careless enough to leave it sitting unlocked on Freya's dining table when she'd gone to use the bathroom. She'd wondered why the two girls had been so quiet when she'd come back into the kitchen, and it hadn't taken long for the strangeness to be explained. Not long after she'd got home, a WhatsApp message had pinged up on Alice's phone. It was from one of the boys in their year group, asking when she wanted to meet up. To her horror, when she scrolled back, she found that a message had been sent to him offering him a blow job. Whichever of them sent it, Alice could be certain Scarlet had come up with the idea.

'It wasn't funny.'

Freya pulls a face, widening her eyes like a baby deer, her

lips curving down slightly to try to make herself appear vulnerable. Alice has seen this expression plenty of times, usually worn for men when she wants to manipulate them for something. The maddening thing is, it nearly always works.

'Where's Dylan?' Alice asks, wanting to move away from the subject of Scarlet and that text. 'I thought he was coming home this weekend?'

Freya's brother moved to London for university the September before last, but he's due home for the holidays, as usual. Alice knows his course ended weeks ago.

'Don't mention his name in front of my mother. She's furious with him. Apparently one of his flatmate's comedy gigs is more important than today.' Freya pauses to scan the garden for Eve, who she spots near the house, whispering something into Chris's ear. 'He had the right idea,' she adds.

'Must be costing him a fortune, staying in London longer than he needs to.'

Freya shrugs. 'That's what the Bank of Mum and Dad is for.'

Alice wonders at the nonchalance with which this is said, and the ease of Freya's assumption that her parents will see her and her brother through life for as long as is needed. It's true that the family has plenty of wealth. No one on this street is short of money; they couldn't afford to live here if they were. But unlike Freya and Dylan, Alice recognises her privilege.

'You're so hot.' Freya leans over Alice, and for an awkward moment, Alice thinks she's about to kiss her. Instead, she props herself on one hand as she hovers over Alice's prone body, raising her free palm to the hot spot of skin at her bare shoulder. 'You're burning. There's suncream in the house – shall I get you some?'

'Thanks.'

Freya glances at the glass beside the sunlounger. 'What are you drinking?'

'Margarita. But I'm not drinking it.'

'Pass it here then.'

Alice reaches for the drink and passes it to Freya, watching with an expression of undiluted disgust as she sits up to down it in one.

'What?' Freya says, her face breaking into a coy smile as she runs the back of her hand over her mouth. 'I need something to get me through this shitshow.'

Alice gets the feeling of eyes upon her, and when she glances towards the house, she sees Toby watching them from the patio table. When their eyes meet, he doesn't bother to pretend he isn't staring.

Eve passes by in a flurry of sky-blue silk, now with a tray of canapés in her hand, ever the attentive hostess. Despite the fact that a catering company has been hired to provide the food and wait on guests, she can't relax, always needing to maintain control. Alice and Freya watch as she tries to encourage one of Freya's young cousins to try something, at which the child turns his nose up, his features shrivelled as though his aunt has just suggested he sing a solo for the grandparents.

Alice is grateful for the distraction when Chris's voice rises above the chat and gossip around them, calling for everyone to gather at the top end of the garden, where the food arranged on trestle tables earlier this afternoon now sits dry and curling in the heat. Someone turns down the music that comes from the speakers by the kitchen doors.

'Eve!' he calls, waving an arm for her to join him.

With mock self-consciousness, Eve smiles coyly, abandoning the tray of canapés on the closest table to join her husband on the patio. Freya grabs Alice by the ankle and shakes her leg. 'Come on, we'd better be seen to be making the effort.'

Alice follows her across the lawn, where the rest of the guests have gathered as though assembling for a photo shoot. Chris stands with his arm around his wife's slim waist, holding her close to him. Too close, Alice thinks, like someone hiding a gun to keep a hostage silent.

'I just want to thank everyone for coming today,' he begins. 'It means the world to both of us. It's not often we get opportunities to have all our favourite people in one place, which is a shame really – we should make this an annual event.'

A couple of people laugh, but the general reaction, it seems to Alice, is one of silent dread, the proposal of a yearly gathering hanging over them like a death threat.

'Some of you were at our wedding twenty years ago today. There'd been a fair amount of bubbles already consumed by this point. It rained, if you remember – the only rainfall we'd had all week. It didn't matter, though. My beautiful new wife brought the sunshine.'

There are a few aahs among the listening guests. Alice feels a roll of nausea in her stomach, the small amount of margarita she consumed earlier spinning a flip in objection to the sickly show of affection. At her side, Freya blows air into her cheeks as though stopping herself from being sick.

'As many of you know,' Chris goes on, 'the past couple of years haven't been the easiest for us. First, we sadly lost Eve's mother, and then there was the break-in. To be honest, for a little while we weren't sure whether we'd be able to stay here after it happened, whether this place would still feel like home. But where else would we find friends and neighbours like you guys?'

There's a cheer from Freya's uncle, who raises a glass to the comment. The rest of the guests are quick to follow his lead.

'Eve,' Chris says, turning to his wife once the toast has subsided, 'I know that what was stolen last year was irreplaceable. I can never get back the things you lost, but I'd like you to have this as a gift, as a memory of today.'

He produces a jewellery box from his pocket. Eve looks from it to Chris, eyeing him questioningly. From where she stands, Alice is too far away to see what's in the box when Eve opens it. But there's a collective gasp at the front of the crowd as she pulls out a necklace.

'Oh Chris,' she says, turning the piece of jewellery in her hands. Her eyes glisten with tears. 'It's beautiful.' She holds it to her throat, and he reaches around her neck to fasten the clasp.

'Thank you,' she says, before kissing him. 'Thank you so much.'

'To the friends and family who've been with us over the years, through everything,' Chris says, raising his glass, 'thank you. To those we've gained along the way, thank you also. There have been highs and lows, like any marriage, but we've come through them all together, and that's only possible with support. To friends and family.'

'To friends and family.' The phrase is repeated as everyone holds up their own glasses.

'To Chris and Eve!' someone shouts.

There is cheering, laughter, more alcohol consumed. The music is turned up again, and the gathering crowd disperses back to their separate conversations, yet for Alice the sound shrinks and fades, leaving her alone with the noise of her own thoughts.

'I need to use the bathroom,' she says to no one in particular, and she leaves Freya's side to make her way to the house.

By the time she reaches the patio, Toby has left the table and is nowhere to be seen. She goes through the kitchen, a glossy, sparkling showroom of a place that's somehow managed to stay looking immaculate despite the afternoon's festivities; she's near the door that leads to the hallway and the downstairs shower room when she hears voices coming from near the staircase, lowered and urgent.

'I don't want to talk about it,' she hears her father say. His words are slurred, strung slippery over champagne and cocktails. Alice stops where she is and presses herself to the wall. At the bifold doors behind her, a conversation about the potential cost of the afternoon's catering continues between a couple of Chris's relatives, but she manages to block it out, her attention fixed to the dialogue developing in the hallway. She has had a lifelong ability to drown out sounds she doesn't want to hear, a bit like wearing a device she's able to alter for tuning in and out. When she was younger, it used to cause her problems in school, her teachers often accusing her of failing to pay attention. But she always knew what she was doing. She absorbed what she needed to.

'But what if I do?' she hears Eve reply. Alice feels a knot form in her throat. She hadn't noticed Eve come into the house. As far as she was aware, she was still outside with her husband, fawning over the necklace he'd lavished upon her.

'It's not always about you, Eve.'

Alice could applaud her father for that if she was able to make a sound. Instead, she holds her breath and folds herself into the gap behind the kitchen door, waiting to hear what is said next.

'Don't do this,' Eve says, desperate in a way that makes Alice cringe. 'Please.'

She waits for her father to say something else; instead, there is a noise just the other side of the door. Panicked, she coils like a snake and slips into the walk-in pantry, sliding the door to shut herself in.

There are three different styles and sizes of house in the street: a fact of which Eve has always been keen to remind Alice's mother. The Harrises' house is, of course, the largest of them all, renovated and redecorated just a few years ago. Now, standing amid the shelves expertly stocked with various beans with strange names and health foods she can barely pronounce, everything stored in clear containers and labelled with the precision of a medical clinic wary of the possibility of one day confusing patients' samples, it occurs to Alice that everything in

Eve's life is for show, whether for her own eyes or those of others.

She holds her breath when she hears footsteps passing by the pantry door: the click-clack of high heels on the kitchen tiles. Moments later, she hears Eve's voice from beyond the bifold doors, someone laughing in response to something she says, her performance turned back on for her audience like the flicking of a switch. Alice waits a little longer, wondering whether her father has left and gone home. What's she supposed to say to him when she sees him next? She can't just come out with it and ask him what's going on, because then he'll know that she'd been standing behind that door, listening in on their conversation. But she can't just say nothing. She must do something.

Alice realises she hasn't seen her mother in a while. The last time she did, she was standing near Toby, talking with one of the older women from the other end of the street; the one who recently lost her husband to a younger woman, although to hear her talk about him, anyone would think he'd died of an incurable disease. The husband might be gone, but the house stayed with her, and it seems to Alice that all in all she had the better end of the deal. She wonders what might become of her mother if it turns out her dad and Eve have been having an affair. It won't matter to her and Toby too much – they'll be gone to university by mid September – but her mother won't ever be able to afford their house on her own, and what would she even do with all those empty rooms and no children left to fill the spaces recently vacated?

She tastes bile in her mouth, acidic and sickening.

She's got it wrong, she thinks. Her dad would never do that. He's not like that. And definitely not with Eve, of all people.

She has her hand on the door handle when she hears a second set of steps. Someone stops just outside the pantry, and once again Alice holds her breath, this time for so long she starts to fear she might pass out and send Eve's glass jars crashing to the tiled floor in a shower of lentils and pulses.

She can't hide in here for ever. She waits for silence before opening the door and stepping out.

'What the hell were you doing in there?' Freya is standing by the kitchen door, arms folded across her chest, a bemused expression on her face. She's been there for a while, Alice realises, waiting for her to come out so she can mock and then question her.

'Just studying your mum's herb collection.'

Freya laughs. She sounds like Eve, high-pitched and frantic, a wind chime on a blustery night.

'Alice, my little oddball.' She comes closer and puts an arm around Alice's waist, and it's only after she's let go that Alice berates herself for holding her breath as long as she did, not wanting Freya to feel the fold of flesh at her side of which she has grown self-conscious. Freya is looking more like her mother as she gets older: long-limbed and lithe. Alice waits for the lump of jealousy that's formed in her throat to rise before holding it on her tongue and letting it dissolve like a cloud of candy floss.

Your mother and my father were having a weird conversation, she thinks, knowing she'll never speak the words aloud. *Something's going on.*

Freya smiles, one eyebrow arched as she studies Alice's distant expression. 'Come on,' she says, taking her by the arm and leading her back through to the garden. 'There's cake to be eaten.'

It's only after she returns home later that evening, the cake cut and distributed on sparkly disposable plates, the sun now dipped beyond the roofs and replaced with the glow of string lights and warm-lit windows, that Alice wonders where Freya had been before she'd stood waiting at the kitchen door. She assumes that both her father and Eve had left the house to return to the garden, though they must have been careful to have reappeared at separate times. As far as she's aware, no one else came into the kitchen after that, which means Freya must have been inside the house while her mother and Rob were talking in the hallway. The house is big, with plenty of space for her to have been ignorant of the conversation. Yet Alice wonders how much she might have heard. She wonders just how much Freya might know.

THREE

JO

By nine o'clock, the sun is setting. The food has been cleared away and the drinks are only now beginning to flow at a slower, more sedate pace. Jo has had enough. She wants to go home. The sandals she's wearing are cutting into her left ankle; she's grateful she didn't opt for heels, or she would by now have had to borrow a pair of flip-flops from Eve, if she even owns some – or worse, go barefoot.

For over twenty minutes, she has listened to Sue from number 3 tell the rambling tale of her decision to take early retirement. She imagines it must have come as a relief to the other people in her office; it's a wonder anyone managed to get anything done with Sue working in the same room.

'Do you know what I got?' she says, pulling Jo's focus back to the conversation. 'Twenty-seven years I worked for them, and you know what they gave me?'

'What?'

'One of those carriage clocks, you know the ones that used to get given away with subscriptions to magazines. You're probably too young to remember them.' She puts her empty glass on the table beside her. 'I mean, what do you think they were trying to say? Here you are... you can watch the time tick by until you die?'

Jo is grateful for an interruption from Rob, although less so as soon as he opens his mouth. 'You seen Alice anywhere?' he slurs.

Sue raises an eyebrow, and Jo feels her body tense. 'No, not for a while now. I think she's gone back to the house. I'll go and check on her. I was ready to call it a night anyway.'

'No,' he says, putting a hand on her arm, needing her solidity to keep him standing. 'I'll go. You stay and enjoy yourself.'

He almost stumbles over the step as he makes his way into the house. Jo wishes she knew what was going on with him. Rob has never been much of a drinker, but recently, whenever they've been invited out anywhere, he's seemed to rely on alcohol to get through social situations.

'Just leave it, I said!'

The night air is splintered by the sound of smashing glass. At the opposite end of the patio area, beneath the string lights and the shadow cast by the summer house, Freya and Toby stand apart, broken glass lying at their feet. Even from this distance and in the fading light, Jo can see her son's face flushed pink, an uncharacteristic flare of anger illuminating his cheeks.

'Everything okay?' Eve rushes over to help clear up the broken glass, though Freya stoops beside her, telling her to leave it.

'I'm sorry,' Jo hears Toby say. 'I'll do it.'

'It's fine, really.'

'Do you have a dustpan and brush I can get?' Jo offers. She goes over to her son. 'Everything okay?' she asks him quietly.

He dismisses her with a shake of his head, avoiding eye contact. 'Sorry,' he says to Eve. 'It was an accident.'

'It's okay,' Eve says breezily. 'No harm done.'

Chris appears with a dustpan and brush, and the remaining guests return to their chatter.

'I'm going home,' Toby tells his mother.

'Good idea. Can you hang on just a minute while I find my bag? I'll come with you.'

But by the time Jo retrieves her bag from where she left it in the kitchen, Toby has already left. In the garden, she sees Freya sitting alone on one of the sunloungers at the end of the lawn, a thin blanket pulled over her legs.

'You calling it a night?' An arm snakes around her waist, pulling her in for a hug. Eve smells of expensive perfume and buttercream. Her mascara is smudged at the corner of her left eye, but even with champagne-fuzzy eyes she looks as beautiful as ever.

'Thanks so much for inviting us,' Jo says. 'It was such a lovely afternoon.'

'Did it go okay, do you think? I was worried there wouldn't be enough food for everyone.'

'There's still enough to feed the street for the next week,' Jo says, gesturing to the kitchen. 'Would you like me to stay and help clear up?'

'Absolutely not.' Eve hiccups and puts a hand to her chest. 'Oops. Might have had one too many glasses of bubbly.'

'This is beautiful,' Jo says, putting her fingertips to the necklace Chris presented Eve with earlier. It glistens even in the fading light of the evening.

'Antique green tourmaline and diamond,' Eve tells her, her mouth falling into a sad smile. 'The same as Mum's. He tried to find as close a match to it as he could.'

Jo puts a hand on her arm and gives her a gentle squeeze. 'He's a good one.'

'He is.'

'Is Freya okay?' she asks.

Eve glances down the garden, briefly registering her daughter. 'Seems to be.'

Jo doesn't mention Toby, or what happened with the broken glass. It was just an accident, she tells herself. Yet she wonders what he and Freya had been arguing about before it happened. *Just leave it...* hadn't that been what Freya had said?

'Let me know if you need anything tomorrow,' she offers. 'A hand clearing up, or whatever.'

Eve puts a hand on her arm. 'You're a gem. Thank you.'

'Hey. You heading home?'

Chris holds out his arms to her, and Jo moves in for a hug. But rather than the usual friendly but brief gesture that might be exchanged between them, she finds herself ensnared within his arms. They slide down around her waist, a hand roaming precariously close to the base of her spine. His face moves towards her neck, breathing in her perfume. She pulls away sharply, wondering whether anyone else noticed his strange behaviour. Eve is standing right behind her; she must surely have seen everything.

'Toby okay?' Chris asks, as though nothing untoward just happened. 'He looked a bit flustered when he left.'

'Tired, I think,' Jo tells him, unable to make eye contact. 'He's been putting in a lot of extra hours at work.'

Eve looks at her husband with thinned lips. She noticed, Jo thinks. 'I wish ours had the same motivation,' she says, rolling her eyes. 'I think Freya might have an allergy to work.'

Jo says nothing. It isn't her place to point out that Freya's laziness might be the product of her parents' overindulgence in her sense of entitlement. Chris and Eve are both intelligent people; they must realise for themselves that to an extent their children are what they've allowed them to become. Freya isn't an unpleasant girl, but the older she's got, the more noticeable her privilege has become.

'It's the summer of freedom,' Chris says casually. 'Let her

enjoy it. What were you doing the summer before you started university? Or had we best not ask?' He winks at Jo before squeezing Eve's waist affectionately. 'She'll be fine. Dylan as well.'

Eve rolls her eyes at the mention of their son.

'Look, I'd better be going,' Jo says, suddenly desperate to go home. She doesn't want to get inadvertently dragged into a conversation about the Harrises' son. Dylan's problems in London have been well documented to her by Eve over coffee and occasional tears. Jo would have the same outlook on the situation if it were Toby, though Chris seems far more casual about everything. She knows if this were one of her children and Rob were so relaxed about it all, she would feel as frustrated as she knows Eve does.

But it's not just that. She can't stop thinking about that strange and inappropriate embrace, the way Chris held her in a manner that was almost predatory. He's never looked at her before today in the way he did tonight. She's pretty sure he's never been interested in her, and he's never been that kind of man. She can't make any sense of it, and just recalling it makes her feel uncomfortable. She doesn't want to find herself unwittingly involved in any awkwardness in Chris and Eve's relationship.

She says her goodbyes to the few remaining family members and neighbours as she passes through the garden. Outside, she stops on the pavement and looks across the road to her own house: a five-bedroom detached a million miles from the home she had grown up in on the other side of Cardiff. Sometimes, when she pulls into the quiet cul-de-sac after returning from the supermarket, or when she's tending to the shrubs in the front garden, she still pinches herself at how lucky she is. Last year, Rob modernised the front of the house, adding the glass porch she'd seen on another house and had mentioned in passing.

She'd come home from a weekend at her sister's to find he'd had it installed while she was away.

When she goes into the house, she expects to find everyone in bed, but Rob is in the kitchen, drinking coffee and looking at his phone.

'Hey,' he says as she walks in. 'Everything okay?' He notices her limping, looks down at the dried blood that stains her foot. She hadn't realised until she'd left the party just how much her sandal had been cutting into her skin.

'What happened to your foot?' he asks, getting up from his chair.

'Cheap sandals.'

He rips off a piece of kitchen roll and folds it into a square before dampening it slightly. 'Come here.' She sits beside him at the table, and he gestures to her to raise her foot onto his knee. He dabs gently at the dried blood until the cut is clean.

'Did you enjoy the party?' she asks.

'Yeah, it was okay. Glad it's over, though.'

Less than an hour ago, Rob had seemed too drunk to balance on his own weight. Now, Jo watches as he tends to her foot, the alcohol apparently soaked up by a single coffee.

'What do you mean?'

He shrugs. 'Gets a bit much, that's all, watching people flaunt their wealth.'

Jo hadn't thought that was what they were doing at all. Eve is her friend, and as such, Jo knows what she is. She loves attention. She enjoys having fancy things. But at no point today had Jo thought either she or Chris were being boastful.

'Is that what you thought? I thought they were just celebrating. It was incredibly generous of them.'

Rob raises an eyebrow.

'What?'

'Nothing.' Her foot still resting on his leg, Rob's hands move to her ankle, and he starts to carefully massage her skin. She allows herself to relax, lying back in the chair and closing her eyes for a moment. But as soon as she does, she remembers what happened just before she left the party. She wonders what went on between Toby and Freya in the moments before that glass was dropped. She wonders what was said.

'Did you see Toby when he got home?'

'No. He went straight upstairs.'

'Something happened between him and Freya. They were arguing about something.'

Rob's hands move to her calf. 'Jo. Just try to relax, will you.' They work their way further up, and he leans forwards to pull her to him. 'I love you in this dress,' he whispers into her ear. 'But I love you even more out of it.'

Jo laughs. 'Nice line.' But she reciprocates when his hands move to the back of her neck and find the zip that runs the length of her spine.

'The kids...'

'They're in bed.'

He kisses her harder, his hands moving to her hips as the dress falls from her shoulders. Despite the warmth of the night air, goosebumps pimple her skin as his mouth moves down her throat and his attention shifts to her breasts. He pulls away, stands, and directs her to the island in the middle of the kitchen. Jo's instinct is to worry they might be glimpsed through the patio doors by a neighbour, but she lets the thought go easily, allowing herself to go with the moment and be led by Rob.

Later, as her husband takes a late shower, Jo sits sipping peppermint tea at the open kitchen doors, the late-night air still as warm as it was hours ago. She breathes in this moment of silence, wishing that all of life could be this peaceful. A sense of calm rests upon her, settling over her shoulders like a comforting embrace. She is lucky, she thinks. This life, this home, this family. They are so very, very lucky.

FOUR

ALICE

Alice can't sleep. Though it's gone midnight, the temperature is still past twenty degrees, and the open window does nothing to help with the humidity. She lies on top of the duvet, her phone screen lighting up the corner of the bedroom. She scrolls TikTok and Instagram, trying to keep her brain from what she saw and heard this evening over at the Harris house. The thought of her dad and Eve together makes her feel sick. It's disgusting.

It's not true.

Her father would never have an affair. Her parents are one of those weird couples who seem to like each other. Alice knows it's not the norm. Half the people she went to school with have parents who have separated, and for the half who are still together, most don't seem to spend enough time in the same room to even know whether they're still able to tolerate each other. She's seen it first hand at plenty of her friends' houses. And never more so than over at Freya's.

As far as Alice can make out, Chris seems to think every-thing is fine. Better than fine. If his speech at the party this afternoon was anything to go by, he thinks his marriage is made of the good stuff, the enduring kind of friendship and familial resilience that sees a couple able to survive for decades. But Alice sees through it. Eve might perform the role of doting wife and perfect mother, but even with her Instagram-perfect life, she isn't happy. And Alice has always seen the way Eve looks at her father.

She drops her phone onto the duvet and sits up. Her head feels thick with the onslaught of a migraine. In the street, a car door slams. She gets up and goes to the window, leaning on the sill to watch the sleeping world outside. A set of headlights flings a glow onto the road outside the Harris house, someone only now leaving a party that started over eight hours ago. She wonders whether the person who's just got behind the wheel of the car has been drinking.

On the bed behind her, her phone pings. She turns and sees the WhatsApp message lit up on the screen.

Hey shithead.

She smiles. Dylan has called her this since she was about nine years old, and it's stuck. He's always been like a second brother to her, and sometimes she wonders whether he envies Toby's close relationship with her. It's different with twins, she knows that without having any other experience. She's been sure so many times in her life that she could feel Toby's pain, and that he too had a sixth sense to know when she was upset or needed help. Anyone who spends time with them can see the connection they have, and no one has spent more time with them than Dylan and Freya.

She taps out a reply.

Hey arsewipe.

As a child, this had been the best response to his insult that she'd been able to come up with. Dylan had laughed, and their respective nicknames for one another had been born.

So how was the party of the century?

Like nothing else, Alice types, a wry smile on her face. Then she sends another:

If salmon vol-au-vents and small talk are your thing.

Dylan responds with a series of laughing emojis before adding, *Mum's not happy with me.*

So I heard. Comedy set worth it though?

Awful. But he's a mate so I didn't tell him that.

Toby, Freya and Alice went to visit Dylan in London a few months ago, before their exams started. They found a relatively cheap Airbnb for the night and went out in Brixton with a group of his university friends, first to a rooftop bar that was decorated like the Amazon rainforest, then to a club that was so poorly lit Alice had had to grope at everything and everyone to get her bearings. She remembers the music ringing in her ears, her heart tripping with the thrill of the place: the heat of strangers dancing around her, the feeling of being without time or rules. She could have been anyone, anywhere.

She'd got lost on her way back from the toilets, unable to find the rest of the group. She'd taken a wrong turn and ended up by a fire escape, and it was there that Dylan had found her. Even in the darkness, she could see there was something off about him, his eyes not quite right; some kind of vacant glaze shadowing his enlarged pupils.

She can't recall now exactly what he'd said to her, but she

remembers him reaching into his pocket before pressing something into her hand. It was small and yellow. A pill.

Alice had been around drugs before, though she'd never taken them. Classmates with affluent parents meant easy access to recreational drugs for some, though no one had ever offered them to her outright before that night. Their town was such a small place, with everyone knowing everyone else, that no one had bothered because they all knew it wasn't her thing. But that night, Dylan had decided differently.

She'd told him she didn't want it, expecting him to accuse her of being boring. Instead, he took it from her with a shrug, then led her back into the club. When they found the rest of the group, it became quickly apparent that whatever had been offered to Alice had also been offered to Freya, only Freya had made a different choice.

Alice remembers the evening changing after that. Hours later, as she lay on the Airbnb sofa listening to Freya throwing up in the nearby bathroom, things had already started to look a bit different. Maybe London wasn't everything Dylan had made it out to be. Perhaps he wasn't as happy as Alice had assumed.

When will you be home? she texts.

Next few days at some point, he replies, vague as ever.

Alice starts to tap out a response, but changes her mind and deletes it. She'll see him when he gets back, and they've then got the whole summer to catch up.

She puts her phone on the bedside table and lies back against the pillows, knowing she should try to get some sleep. Her phone vibrates on the table beside her. Dylan again.

Can we meet up when I get back? There's something I need to tell you.

FIVE

JO

In the early hours of Sunday morning, Rob snores softly beside her, the purring of a contented cat. But Jo can't sleep. Despite the late hour, the air is still warm. The bedroom window is open; somewhere a dog barks insistently, its yelps a metronome against the black midnight sky. She pushes the duvet away from her body, desperate to feel the coolness of a breeze from somewhere. She goes downstairs to get a glass of water, and on her way back up notices that Toby's bedroom light is still on.

She taps at the door, and when there's no response, she pushes it open gently.

'Sorry,' she says, finding him wide awake and lying on top of the duvet, scrolling his phone. 'I thought you'd fallen asleep with the light on.'

She stands there awkwardly for a moment, wanting to talk to him. 'I'm sorry I made such a fuss about you going to the party.'

She waits, but he says nothing.

'Did something happen tonight?'

Did something happen between you and Freya? is what she

really wants to say, but she knows if she does it will only push him into further silence.

'No.'

This isn't like him. The one-word answers, the lack of eye contact. Toby has never been this teenager, the sullen type who shuts himself away and won't speak to her. She's not naïve enough to believe he's always told her everything, but they're close, and she's respected his right to privacy when he's made it clear he needs it.

She can't stop thinking about the anger she saw on his face in the garden at Eve's house. How it was so unlike him.

'You know where I am if you want to talk,' she reminds him. 'Do you want a cup of tea or anything?'

'No thanks.'

She pulls the door softly and clicks it shut. On the opposite side of the hall, Alice's light is off. Jo doubts she's asleep; like her brother, she is probably glued to her phone, catching up on whatever she's missed during the party. She wishes she hadn't made such a fuss about it with either of them. If it had been her and Rob's anniversary, would she really have cared if neither Freya nor Dylan had turned up? As ridiculous as she knows it is, she was insistent upon her children being there for Eve's sake. She wanted to make a good impression. She supposes now that was as much for herself as it was for Eve.

Back in the bedroom, she drains the glass of water, then goes to the bathroom, knowing she'll probably need the toilet again before dawn if she doesn't go now. When she gets back into bed, she turns off the lamp on the bedside table before pressing herself to the warmth of Rob's body. It's then she hears it. A voice in the darkness.

Her body freezes, her heart pausing for a moment at the sound. Her hands grip Rob's T-shirt, clinging to him as she waits to hear the voice again. But nothing comes. There's someone at the door, she thinks, not wanting to turn towards it.

She can sense it there, this unseen presence. There's someone just behind her.

She moves a hand to her husband's arm. 'Rob. Rob... wake up.'

She knows there's no one else here. The rational part of her brain tells her that she was out on the landing just moments ago, and if there had been anyone else in the house, an intruder or a burglar, she'd have heard him when she was coming back from the bathroom. But it happens, she reminds herself. Eve had thought her home was a safe place, too.

She waits to hear the voice again, her body rigid at the expectation of it, but there's nothing more. She couldn't make out what it said. She turns to the bedroom door, expecting to see it swing slowly open in the darkness.

'Rob,' she says, putting a hand on his arm. 'Rob.'

She shakes him, but the alcohol and the sex seem to have wiped him into an oblivion.

She reaches over to put the bedside lamp back on, then slides from beneath the duvet and goes to the door, her body braced for an attack despite knowing there's no one there. But she knows she didn't imagine it. She heard a voice.

She taps at Alice's bedroom door, suspecting her daughter will still be awake. She sticks her head around the side of the door. In the darkness, she can make out the shape of Alice's back turned to her, curved beneath the duvet. She pulls the door gently closed but hears her voice just before it clicks shut.

'Mum?'

'Sorry, love. I thought you were asleep.'

Alice sits up in bed. 'Is everything okay?'

Jo goes into the room and closes the door behind her. 'Did you hear anything?'

Alice looks at her blankly. 'When?'

'Last few minutes or so.'

'Like what?'

She doesn't want to tell Alice she heard a voice, not wanting to scare her unnecessarily. It's probably the drink, she tells herself. She doesn't really drink alcohol very often any more, but she lost count of the glasses of champagne she had this afternoon.

'I don't know. I thought I heard something, that's all. I must have been dreaming.'

Even in the darkness, she can make out Alice's scepticism.

'It's fine, love. Sorry if I woke you up.'

'Mum,' Alice says again, before Jo pulls the door closed.

'Yes?'

'I love you.'

A sad smile twitches at Jo's mouth. She can't remember the last time she heard those words from her daughter, uttered in the way they used to be when she'd been so much younger.

'I love you too, sweetheart.'

She clicks the door shut and tiptoes to the staircase, not wanting Alice to hear her go downstairs. She checks every room in turn, making sure the windows and doors are locked. When she's satisfied there's no one there and that the house is secure, she goes back upstairs and gets into bed, moulding herself to the shape of Rob's sleeping body prone beside her. She wonders whether Alice is okay. She seemed vulnerable tonight somehow, the 'I love you' seeming to represent so much more than the words alone suggested. Now she has both twins to worry about.

She lies in the darkness questioning what she heard, because she knows she didn't imagine it. She hasn't drunk *that* much. That voice came from somewhere.

SIX

ALICE

On Sunday morning, Alice stays in bed until the sun has pushed its way above the tops of the houses opposite, the pale curtains hazy with persistent daylight. She lies beneath the duvet and scrolls social media, ambivalent in the face of her peers' desire for attention and public validation. Everything is meaningless, she thinks. Fake. One of the girls from her year at school has just started dating a local footballer who's been tipped to make Premier League within the next year. Her social media is now filled with photos of them together, in expensive restaurants and at parties with Z-list celebrities – the kind chasing fame by appearing on every reality television show and envelope-opening that will accept their desperate interest – but behind the scenes, Alice and everyone else knows that he's already cheated on her twice. To look at this girl's photos, anyone would be forgiven for thinking she was living a dream life: the kind of life she'd hope her friends would envy. All a show, Alice thinks. All meaningless.

She throws her phone on to the bed and slides from beneath the duvet, arching her body into a cat-like stretch. It's already warm; her bedroom window has been on the catch overnight, and the air has that balmy summer feel that usually takes until midday to arrive. She pulls the curtains open, allowing daylight to slice through the bedroom. From her window, she can see the Harrises' house, its perimeter bordered by an always immaculately tended privet hedge. Chris is outside, tipping rubbish into the recycling bin at the side of the driveway; she watches as he grapples with cardboard boxes, hears the smash of a champagne bottle as it crashes on the ground and splinters glass across the block paving. He leans on another of the wheelie bins and puts a hand on his forehead as though holding his brain in place, and Alice wonders how bad his hangover is.

She hears her mother's piano from downstairs, hears her dancing fingers playing one of those haunting tunes she seems to favour: the kind of sad-key music that makes you nostalgic for something you've never experienced. Some people eat their feelings: food for depression, food for celebration; consumption for the sake of boredom. Some people develop an addiction to exercise: miles run to retain some sense of control over a life slipping from its owner's grip; sweat spilled and calories burned in the face of something heartbreaking, unexpected, exhilarating, anything. For her mother, music is the means through which she manages her moods. She plays when she is sad, she plays when she is happy; she plays every morning with the same familiarity of routine in which other people flick a switch on a kettle.

When Alice goes downstairs, her father is sitting at the kitchen table, his laptop opened in front of him. It still feels strange to see him here in the house like this so early in the morning, even at a weekend. He spent so much time away from home while she and Toby were growing up that his presence came to feel like an event, as though he was holidaying with them rather than being a permanent fixture. As a child, she never considered how it must have felt for her mother, to be left with the responsibility and the loneliness of parenting in the regular absence of a partner. He'd promised her an empire, though, and an empire he delivered: a portfolio of properties that now earned a six-figure salary without him needing to leave the house. By the time she and Toby turned fifteen, their father was back, the decade slog of his endeavours proved in the privileged upbringing they'd both been gifted. But by then, it sometimes felt they barely knew each other, and Alice often wonders whether any of it was worth the price that was paid.

'Good afternoon,' Rob says teasingly, glancing at the clock.

'It's ten fifty,' she responds. 'It's still morning.'

She goes to the coffee machine and turns it on. When her mother comes into the room, she makes one for her before taking her own out into the garden. As she sips her drink with the sun on her face, Alice feels grateful for not drinking. She can think of nothing worse right now than having a hangover in this heat.

She' s just finished her coffee when she gets a message from Freya.

Free to pop over? I'm bored.

Alice rolls her eyes. Freya is always bored, even when she's surrounded by people and opportunity. She texts back, *I'll be over in ten.*

After she's gone back upstairs to dress and brush her teeth, she heads over to the Harris house. Freya is waiting for her in the hallway, the front door open. She sits at the bottom of the staircase scrolling her phone, barely looking up from it when Alice says hello.

'Do you want a drink or something? Urgh...' She puts a hand to her head as she slips her phone into the pocket of her pyjama shorts. 'I shouldn't have had so many cocktails last night.'

Alice follows her to the kitchen, where Eve is loading plates and cutlery into the dishwasher. 'Hey, Alice. Did you enjoy the party yesterday?'

'It was great, yeah.' She catches the look Freya throws her, the lazy roll of the eyes. 'I hope you like the gift,' she adds. 'It was actually my dad who chose it.'

This is an outright lie: Alice's father wouldn't know a restaurant voucher from a box of bath bombs. She doubts there's been a single birthday or Christmas on which either she or Toby unwrapped something for which their dad had been involved in any way in the selection process, and he was probably clueless yesterday about the contents of the box that Jo placed on the table next to all the other presents left by the guests. Alice just wants to test Eve's reaction to the mention of him.

'Do you know,' Eve says, straightening as she shoves the dishwasher door closed, 'we've not had a chance yet to open anything. It's taken until now to get the house back in order. We wanted to open them together once everything's finished, so we can enjoy it properly.'

She is an actress, Alice thinks. Well rehearsed. Convincing, too. There wasn't a shred of a reaction to the mention of her father; at least not one that was visible to an outsider. But not yesterday. Alice saw the way Eve looked at him. Surely she can't have been the only one who'd noticed?

But there could be another explanation, she thinks. Another secret between them. Not necessarily *that*.

Freya waves an orange juice bottle in Alice's face, and she shakes her head, refusing the offer.

'I heard someone mention Barbados,' she says casually. 'Are you having a second honeymoon?'

Eve laughs, the sound sharp and tinged with resentment. 'I wish. Not likely, not with the amount of work trips Chris has got coming up. Still, a girl can dream, right?' She smiles as she returns to her chores, but the expression is empty, no warmth reaching her eyes. 'What are your plans?' she asks, as Alice follows Freya to the kitchen door. 'You can't be intending to stay cooped up in that bedroom all afternoon? Look at the weather!'

'We had our quota of vitamin D yesterday, thank you, Mother.'

The girls head upstairs. 'Is your mum okay?' Alice asks, once they've reached the landing.

Freya shrugs. 'Yeah. Why wouldn't she be?'

'I don't know. She just seemed... distracted.'

Freya pulls a face. 'Probably just a hangover.'

Alice wants to ask her, but at the same time, she doesn't. The more she's thought about what happened inside the house yesterday, the more she's convinced herself Freya must have overheard something, because she would have had to have passed Eve and Rob to come downstairs. Perhaps she'd lingered on the landing after hearing them in the hallway, or maybe she'd been in the living room, neither parent realising she was behind the closed door. Either way, it seems to Alice that Freya must have been within listening distance of the two of them. She needs to know exactly what she heard.

'Look at this,' Freya says, taking her phone from her bedside table and opening TikTok. She plays a short reel of some of their friends from school on a night out, a row of them performing the dance routine of a Beyoncé song. 'Urgh... they give me the ick.'

These girls are her friends, Alice thinks, although she says nothing. Freya is supposed to be Alice's friend, but she still let Scarlet send that text from her phone. Friendship seems to have a different set of rules for Freya than it does for Alice. It's probably got Freya's back up that she wasn't invited on the night out.

'Like, grow up.' She clicks her phone locked and throws it onto the bed before getting up and closing the door.

'Are things okay between your parents?' Alice asks.

Freya eyes her suspiciously, and Alice wishes she'd found a way to get onto the subject a bit more casually. Last night is bothering her. That conversation between her father and Eve keeps replaying in her head like last-song syndrome.

'Fine,' Freya says defensively. 'Why?'

'I just wondered. With the break-in and everything. Like your dad said last night, it's been a tough year for them.'

Freya rolls her eyes. 'Yeah, so tough. Just imagine, a few jewels go missing... oh no.'

'It's not just that though, is it?' Alice says, playing down Freya's insensitivity. 'I suppose it's the thought of a stranger being in their home. It must feel violating.'

Freya shrugs. 'They had insurance. I'm sure they didn't do too badly out of it. Anyway, it worked out well for him in the end.'

'For who?'

'My dad. Look, if that jewellery hadn't been stolen, he wouldn't have been able to make his grand gesture last night, would he? He's happy, Mum's happy... everyone's a winner, I suppose.'

Alice smiles, thinking there must be a punchline to Freya's analysis of events. But there's not, she realises. Her attitude just sucks.

'My dad loves an expensive gesture,' Freya adds. 'I suppose it compensates for a lack of everything else. Not like your dad.'

'What do you mean?'

'Well, Rob's a bit more... I don't know. He doesn't need to make so much effort to impress. It comes more naturally for him.'

Alice isn't sure whether Freya's saying what she thinks she's saying. For both their sakes, she hopes not. 'Impress who?'

Freya shrugs nonchalantly, but glances at Alice with a wry smile. 'Anyone he wants to.'

She checks the door is shut properly before returning to the bed to sit beside Alice.

'There's something I need to tell you,' she says, lowering her voice to little more than a whisper. 'I've wanted to talk to you about it before, but...' She trails off and glances to the door. 'I can trust you, can't I, Alice?'

Alice feels her heart drop a little in her chest. She was right: Freya did hear something at the party last night. And now she's about to confirm Alice's suspicions.

'Of course you can.'

'I—'

'Girls,' Eve voice calls out, as she crashes into the room without warning. 'I've got some of these left over from yesterday.' She brandishes a Tupperware box filled with an array of miniature cupcakes. 'Would either of you like one?'

Alice doesn't miss the look Freya gives her mother. 'Any chance of knocking or something next time?' she says.

'Oh Freya,' Eve says with a laugh. 'Don't be silly. I pay the bills.' She laughs again, high and tinkly, but the atmosphere becomes so suddenly tense that Alice has the amusing thought that the cupcakes might be laced with arsenic, and Eve is willing her daughter to take the item she knows to be most densely saturated. You watch too many true-crime documentaries, she tells herself. She reaches to take a cake from the box.

'No thank you,' Freya says sharply, and she grabs her mobile from the bed before getting up and heading to the bathroom.

'Daughters,' Eve says casually. 'Who'd have them?'

Alice assumes she isn't meant to respond to this, so she doesn't. Eve leaves the room and goes back downstairs, leaving Alice alone in Freya's bedroom. She sits on the side of the bed, near to Freya's bedside table, and it's then that she notices it. The letter is just sitting there on top of a pile of books, the logo printed on its corner instantly recognisable to Alice, who feels a wave of nausea crash in her chest.

She picks it up, her hand shaking as she reads it, the words blurring in front of her. When she looks up from the page, the first thing she sees is the collage of photographs above Freya's desk: photos from concerts and beach days and nights out; even one from their recent prom. Alice is in at least half the photographs, the two girls always side by side as they pose for the camera, an arm flung over a shoulder; faces pressed together as they share an in-joke.

She hears the toilet being flushed along the hallway and shoves the letter back where she found it. They're supposed to be friends, she thinks. How could Freya do this to her? The pain in her chest is physical, as though she's just been punched in the ribs. She hears the click of the bathroom lock, and stands from the bed as Freya returns.

'Everything okay?'

Her heart is beating too loudly; she feels sure Freya must be able to hear it. She wishes it wasn't the case, but her vision is starting to blur with tears. 'No,' she says, reaching for her phone from the duvet. 'Actually... I've got to go.'

Freya pulls a face. 'What's going on?'

'It's my mother,' Alice lies. 'She just messaged me. Said I need to get home. Something's happened. I don't know what it is.'

Freya's mouth twists: she doesn't believe her. The girls have grown up together; they know each other well enough to know when the other is lying. Or at least, Alice thinks, Freya knows when *she's* lying. Clearly, Alice can tell nothing about this girl she'd thought was a friend. The closest thing she's ever had to a sister.

She hurries to the door, mumbling that she'll text Freya later. Grateful when Freya doesn't try to follow her, she almost bumps into Eve as she heads out through the front door. Freya's mother is at the side of the house, emptying a recycling box into a wheelie bin. Alice darts to the pavement and hides behind the hedge before seeing Eve go back into the house. She doesn't want to say something she might regret.

SEVEN

JO

When Jo goes to the kitchen to prepare lunch, she finds Rob at the table, his laptop opened in front of him. The amount of time he spends looking at his laptop and his phone continues to be a source of resentment between them. She had hoped that once he was able to work less and spend more time at home, his attachment to his devices would decrease. He had promised her that the long hours and the weeks away from home would be confined to setting up his business, and that once it was established, he would have more free time. If anything, he's become increasingly addicted to his phone. His argument has always been that the business can't run itself; he still needs to be present, even if remotely. She knows he's right, but at times she feels herself competing with technology. Time has slipped away from them, the twins' childhoods gone in what seems to her a heartbreakingly short space of time.

'Look at this,' he says, turning the laptop towards her.

Jo only needs to glance at the screen to see what he's looking at, and the website resurrects a host of old arguments. Rightmove has proved both a blessing and a curse in their relationship: the place where Rob's career change was born, yet later, the source of an obsession that has caused confusion and frustration, mostly from Jo.

'Not this again,' she sighs. She goes to the fridge and takes out a bag of carrots and some parsnips. Last night, things had been so good between them, despite his earlier excess at Eve and Chris's. She can't understand why he would choose to dampen the atmosphere with all this again now.

'This is a brilliant buy for the price,' he tells her, ignoring her reaction. 'Three-bed detached, still with a lovely size garden but more manageable, and look at this. A ten-minute drive to the beach. You always used to talk about living near the coast.'

In a different life, she thinks. Twenty years ago. And then they'd made choices. Choices that had brought them here, where they'd agreed to raise their family. This place, where they'd agreed to settle. For the last year or so, Rob has been fixated on the idea of moving. Jo dismissed the idea as soon as it was first mentioned, not understanding why, after years of working so hard for what they had, he now wanted to walk away from it.

'I used to talk about touring as a concert pianist as well, but you know... things change.'

'Don't they just,' he mumbles.

She drops the peeler on the chopping board and turns to him. 'What's that supposed to mean?'

'Nothing. I'm agreeing with you.'

But she understands his tone and the insinuation that came with the words. He thinks she's changed, and not for the better.

'I wish you'd just consider it,' he says. 'We've never had a proper conversation about it; you've always put an end to it before it's had a chance. The kids are going to be gone soon – do we really need all this space when there's just the two of us?'

Jo bites her lip. Despite Rob's claims, they *have* had this conversation, too many times now to mention. It isn't just about them. This will still be Alice and Toby's home, no matter where they choose to go.

'Kids come home, Rob. They'll probably be home for the summer holidays. And Christmas.'

'For three years or so. And then they'll move on with their own lives, which is as it should be. But we still have ours, Jo. We could live for another forty years. Fifty, even.'

'And our lives are here, where they've been for the past twenty years. Say we move somewhere else... what then? We won't know anyone – we'd be starting from new. It isn't easy to make friends in your forties.'

Rob sighs. 'Exactly. We're in our forties, not our eighties. You should see the opportunity as an adventure.'

Jo sits down at the table. 'We can have plenty of adventures. We can travel when we want to, to wherever we want to go. I just don't see why we need to sell this place to do it.' She reaches out and puts a hand over Rob's. 'We're lucky enough to be able to have the best of both worlds. Isn't that a blessing?'

It's difficult to keep her resentment quashed. She wouldn't change a thing now – she's loved the life they've lived here, in this house and this town – but years ago, before the twins had been born, it wasn't what she'd imagined for herself. She'd wanted to travel, and she'd pursued a musical passion she'd hoped would become a career that would enable her to see the world. Her pregnancy hadn't been planned, although when it happened, she'd been ready to embrace the changes. Quickly, though, she'd felt herself being pushed towards suburbia, destined for the kind of domestic life she'd never seen for herself, but she'd loved Rob and she'd trusted that the decisions they made together would be the right ones.

The children have been happy here. They have a lovely, lucky life. Why would he want to leave all that behind?

'All that money you spent on the porch last year,' she reminds him. 'Why do that if you wanted to leave?'

'It isn't wasted. It'll have added value, if anything.'

She pulls her hand away from his and sighs, not sure when he started to look at everything in monetary terms.

'Why are you so scared of change?' he asks.

'Why are you so intent on it? You wanted this life,' she reminds him. 'If you remember, it was you who pushed for this place.'

'I didn't realise I wouldn't be allowed to change my mind.'

The chair legs scrape across the tiles as Jo stands. 'I had to change mine, remember?' She returns to the chopping board and takes her frustration out on the carrots, which she chops into chunky circles. Has he forgotten the sacrifices she had to make? The change of mind that was forced upon her by circumstance. The news that they were expecting twins had come as a shock. There was no history of twins in her family or Rob's, and the enormity of having two small lives to care for was a prospect to which she had needed to quickly adapt. There would be no chance of pursuing her dream of becoming a concert pianist now, though her tutors at music college had claimed it to be more than within her capabilities. No chance for the travelling she had imagined for them before they'd considered the idea of starting a family.

Fear of the unknown was quickly replaced by excitement. Two little lives to love instead of one. A tiny hand to be held in each of hers. Both their children would have a best friend for life from the minute they entered the world. She placed to one side the dream that had been born when she was just a child, carried throughout her teenage years. She could return to it later; it would wait for her. But while her ambitions were replaced with bottle sterilisers and nappies and sleepless nights, Rob's were starting to take shape amid the chaos of those early baby years, somehow managing to find time and space to flourish.

It seems unfair to her now that he wants to pull this life

from beneath her when she's done so much to build it and sacrificed so much to make space for its existence.

'I never realised you saw it that way.'

'Really?' Jo says, unable to keep the sarcasm from her voice. She finishes preparing the vegetables, grateful when Rob makes no attempt to pursue the conversation any further. Once she's done, she leaves the kitchen without speaking to him, needing some time alone. But she doesn't get it. As she heads into the hallway, Alice comes clattering through the front door, her cheeks red and stained with black streaks of mascara.

EIGHT

ALICE

Alice's heart hammers so hard in her chest that it hurts. She feels every beat like a punch to the ribcage, and when her mother puts a hand on her arm and asks her what's the matter, what's happened, she can't help but burst into tears.

'Freya,' she sniffles, but the rest of her words get choked.

Her mother takes her by the hand and leads her through to the living room. 'What's Freya done?'

'Loughborough,' Alice says, dropping onto the sofa. 'My rejection letter.'

'What about it?'

Her mother knows just how disappointed Alice was not to get a place at her first-choice university. The fashion and design course at Loughborough is considered one of the best in the country, and Alice had done so much research on the place she'd set her heart on. She'd looked at places to stay before she'd even completed her application, as well as places to visit while she was there; she'd familiarised herself with the transport routes and had looked at part-time job opportunities. Her predicted grades were good, and there had been nothing to suggest she wouldn't achieve what her teachers believed her capable of.

The rejection had arrived soon after she'd submitted her application, and her enthusiasm towards her schoolwork had been sliced in two as a result.

'Freya's been made an offer there. Unconditional.'

Jo's face creases, confused. She sits beside her daughter. 'I didn't know Freya had applied there. Which course?'

'The same course,' Alice says, exasperated. 'The fashion and design one I didn't get onto.'

Her mother reaches gently to push away some stray hair that's fallen into Alice's face. 'I don't understand. I didn't realise she had any interest in fashion.'

'Exactly,' Alice says, the word fired from her like a gunshot. 'She's doesn't. She's done it just to piss me off.'

She sees the scepticism on her mother's face, etched into the lines around her mouth. She knows what she's thinking: applying for a three-year degree in a subject you've never shown any interest in is an elaborate way to get someone's back up. It involves a lot of effort. But that's what Freya can be like, and Jo must know that as well as Alice does. Anything Alice has ever had, Freya has to have it too. Freya must win. She must come first. Always.

And the worst of it for Alice is that Freya manages it without even appearing to try.

'Are you sure about this?'

'The letter was on her bedside table, just sitting there. I swear, Mum, she must have left it there on purpose for me to find it. Wouldn't she have kept it in a drawer or something otherwise? She knew I'd see it.'

Alice runs a finger beneath the neckline of her T-shirt, her fingertip wet with sweat. It's not just the temperature that's causing her to sweat, she thinks. It's adrenaline. Rage.

'Have you two talked about the course a lot? I mean, you've

always been so close. You grew up together. Maybe she wanted to go with you. It's kind of flattering in a way, I suppose.'

Alice can't hide her disgust at Jo's suggestion there may have been anything innocent in what Freya has done. Her mother might think she knows the Harris family, but she doesn't know Freya, not really. Freya's an actress, good at showing what she wants to be seen and hiding the parts of her character she knows will make her look shitty to others. She's learned from the best when it comes to being disloyal. Just look at what her mother's doing to her supposed best friend.

'Then why wouldn't she just have said so?'

Alice sits on her hands to stop them shaking. She can't look at her mother. She wants to tell her; she wants to tell her what she heard between Eve and her father at the party last night, but without evidence she knows there's every chance her mother just won't believe her. Worse still, she could end up resenting Alice for it.

She needs to speak to her father first, though how she's supposed to bring up the subject without admitting she was snooping on him and Eve from the pantry, she isn't sure yet.

'I don't know,' Jo admits.

'She told me she wanted to go into theatre. That was all she ever talked about. That's what she said she'd applied for. Why would she do this to me, Mum? She knows how much I wanted a place on that course.'

Alice doesn't want to cry again, but she can't help it. All the work she's put in over the past couple of years feels for nothing, and she can't avoid the fact that Freya manages to pull straight A*s even when she seems to do next to no work. Every good result Alice has ever had in her life, she's had to put in the time and effort for. Everything with Freya is handed to her on a gold tray, gift-wrapped.

She wonders if Eve knows about the letter. Of course she knows – she's hardly likely to be unaware that her daughter's been accepted on a course. She has no doubt badgered Freya about it for the past year, trying to push for the most prestigious courses at the most respected universities. Alice wonders what she makes of Freya's choice. She knew it was what Alice wanted. They both knew, because until a few months back, that was all she had talked about. It was the only university she had wanted to go to.

'There's still clearing, love,' Jo tries to reassure her. She puts a hand on Alice's knee. 'You might get in once your results come through.'

Alice knows she won't. She knows enough people who were in the year above her at school to know that no one gets their first choice of university through clearing. She'll end up at some second-rate college on a course with zero prospects, and all her hard work over the past few years will be for nothing. Freya will go on to get an apprenticeship at some designer fashion house before landing a job there, because that's what happens for girls like Freya. She'll work her way up and become known for something she's never really had any passion for, and just the thought of it makes Alice sick with anger.

'I don't think Freya will have done this intentionally to hurt you,' Jo says, though even she sounds as though she doesn't really believe this.

'No? Why not? Eve's the same.'

'What do you mean?'

Alice shrugs. 'Competitive. Always wanting to one-up people.'

'Does she?' Jo muses. 'I hadn't noticed.'

Sometimes Alice finds it difficult to gauge her mother's tone. She can't tell whether she's being sarcastic or not. She needs only to think back on details of the party yesterday to see how much Eve loves being the centre of attention. And being the centre of attention means being better than everyone else:

more athletic, slimmer, prettier, wealthier. Perhaps a daughter can't avoid becoming whatever her mother is.

'Look,' Jo says, 'I'm sure there's an explanation for it all. You and Freya are like sisters – I just can't imagine her doing this to spite you.'

Alice raises an eyebrow.

'Do you want me to speak to her?'

'No,' Alice says quickly. 'It's fine.'

It's not fine at all, but she doesn't need her mother to fight her battles for her. What she really means is, she'll deal with Freya herself.

NINE

JO

There's a strange atmosphere at Sunday lunch. By the time Jo has managed to prepare and cook it – wondering why she's bothered when the temperature is in the high twenties – Rob has declared he hasn't much of an appetite, Alice is red-eyed and pale-faced from crying, and Toby has still said barely more than two words to anyone all day. Jo knows it's irrational and irrelevant, but she wishes none of them had gone to that party yesterday. The mood in the house seems to have been dictated by the Harris family, and she feels a resentment towards them that she knows is unfair.

Toby clears the table, while Alice rinses the plates and pans before stacking them in the dishwasher. They've always had the rule that whoever has cooked doesn't have to do the dishes, and she's lucky that the kids have never made a fuss about chipping in and helping out. Usually, the kitchen is filled with playful banter while they work, but today there is silence.

Jo is standing at the open fridge when she feels a hand on her waist.

'Can we talk?'

She and Rob haven't had a chance to finish the conversation
that was interrupted when Alice returned from Freya's. Perhaps
it's better that way. Jo doesn't have the energy for a second
round of argument with him. Where the subject of moving is
concerned, she fears they're always going to have a difference of
opinion.

'Not now.'

'I don't mean now.'

She closes the fridge door and sees Alice checking her
phone. She wishes she could throw it away. Before social media,
her daughter had been happy. Some of the girls at school had
always been an issue, but when they started to communicate
online, there was no longer the cut-off of a 3 p.m. school finish.

'Are you okay, Alice?'

Her daughter shoves her phone into the pocket of her
summer dress. 'I'll live,' she says, unable to keep the bitterness
from her tone. Jo feels a rush of sympathy for her. Everything
Alice has ever achieved, she's worked so hard for. It must smart
to see a girl like Freya steal her dream so effortlessly.

Toby glances at his sister. 'Has something happened?'

'No,' Alice answers quickly. 'It's nothing. I'm going
upstairs.'

Jo thinks about stopping her and trying to get her to talk, but
she knows there's no point until Alice has had time to process
things alone. She'll go up and find her in a while, see if she's
ready. Until then, she still has Toby to worry about.

'Has Freya said anything to you about Alice?' she asks him,
trying to make the question sound casual. It occurs to her that
maybe Toby already knows about the university place, and
perhaps that explains the tension between him and Freya last
night at the party. Toby has always been protective of his sister.

'No. Should she have?'

Jo shakes her head. She feels Rob's hand on her arm, and

she reads what it means. She needs to stop probing. The kids are eighteen now; they have to work things out for themselves. They'll both talk to her when they're ready.

'Do you need me for anything else?' Toby asks, once the dishwasher is running.

'No,' Rob says. 'Thanks for your help, mate.'

Jo would have answered differently. She would have found an excuse to keep Toby in the kitchen, because she knows that all Rob wants is to get her alone so he can resurrect their conversation from earlier.

Toby has barely made it onto the landing before Rob makes a start.

'About earlier—'

'I don't want to talk about it again.'

'I know. That's why I'm not going to. I'm sorry.'

Jo waits for the catch, but there doesn't seem to be one.

'Come here,' he says, and she goes to him, allowing herself to be pulled to his chest. He puts a hand in her hair, tilts her face towards his to kiss her.

And then they're interrupted by the doorbell.

'I'll get it,' Rob says.

Jo goes into the utility room to start folding the clean washing that's still sitting in a basket on the top of the machine. She wonders what's caused Rob's sudden change in attitude. Perhaps Alice's disappointment has made him realise that now isn't the time to be focusing on their own future, not when there's so much of the twins' lives still to be sorted out. Whatever it is, she's grateful for the respite.

She's folding one of Toby's work T-shirts when she hears Eve's voice. She pauses for a moment, thinking perhaps she's mistaken. But she isn't. Eve is crying.

She isn't sure why she does it, but the side door is open, and she knows the gate has been left unlocked since she went there earlier to take out the recycling bag. She'd been planning on doing some gardening if the weather cools a bit this afternoon, so she'd left the gate open, needing access to the bins. She abandons Toby's T-shirt and slips outside. Rob would usually invite Eve into the house – certainly rather than let her cry on the doorstep. So why hasn't he done so now?

She stands at the side of the house and listens to snatches of conversation as it plays out between Eve and her husband.

'Can't stop,' she hears Rob say, half his sentence stolen in a whisper.

Eve responds with something equally incoherent, but amid whatever is said, she hears Freya's name. Eve is still sobbing, her voice choked by tears.

'Not here,' Rob says, the clearest words he has spoken as clarity rises with his anger.

Eve replies, but once again, it's inaudible.

Then Jo catches the tail end of what sounds like a threat, the phrase 'or I will' following another she can't make out.

She hears the click as Rob closes the front door, and she waits to catch a glimpse of Eve as she leaves the driveway. She is wearing a floaty summer dress, looking more like she's off to another party than about to spend the day recovering from one the night before.

Jo darts back into the house, but Rob is already in the kitchen. 'Everything okay?'

'Yes. Just took some washing out.'

She realises the basket is still on top of the machine and hopes he doesn't notice it there.

'Who was that?' she asks conversationally.

'Just a parcel.'

She feels a sting in her chest, a tightening that wraps itself around her heart. 'On a Sunday?'

'Amazon.'

Rob goes to the worktop and retrieves his phone from its

charger before leaving the room, apparently having forgotten now about the conversation he'd so desperately wanted to have just minutes earlier. Jo stands at the door of the utility room, staring at the empty space her family has left, wondering at how easily things can change. Wondering at how casually she and her husband have just lied to each other.

TEN

ALICE

Alice has never thought of herself as a vengeful person, but the more she thinks about everything that's happened over the past few weeks, the more it seems an appealing route to go down. She thinks back to when she'd received that rejection letter from the university, and how she'd sat and cried on Freya's bed later that same day, drinking tea with her as Freya had silently absorbed her disappointment. She'd thought then that Freya had been listening to her when she'd spoken, and maybe she had. But not because she cared about her. It occurs to Alice now that she was probably revelling in the upper hand that she knew she had, laughing inwardly at Alice's ignorance and her blind faith in their friendship.

If they hadn't grown up in houses across the street from one another, and if their parents weren't so close, Alice is sure she and Freya would never have been friends. Their relationship has been forced by Eve and Jo, by Rob and Chris, and she feels a resentment towards her parents that feels alien and unpleasant as it settles in her gut. But she can't blame them entirely. She's known for a long time what Freya really is, yet she's kept going back, enduring the abuse like a spouse in a coercive marriage holding onto the hope that the other will one day change.

Does she hate her? She thinks she might. Alice has never felt hate before. She's never had her heart broken. She's never had a parent who abandoned her. Her life has been blessed in a way she recognises so many aren't, and yet this seething, burning resentment feels now as though it might always have been there, buried a little beneath the weight of better things, just waiting for an opportunity to push through.

She knows that sitting in her bedroom with just her phone for company is only going to make her feel worse, so she turns it off – something she hasn't done in as long as she can remember. She knows that the best place to be when you're feeling an extremity of any emotion is usually outside, something her dad had taught her and Toby from a young age. Excited? Run around in the garden. Frustrated? Dig a hole in one of the flower beds. Sad? Go and sit under the beech tree until your head feels clearer, and then come back and talk about it.

But Alice is past the age of being able to run around the garden or sit under the tree without drawing unwanted attention to herself, so she decides to do the next best thing: go for a walk to try to clear her head. She puts on her trainers and slips out of the front door without telling anyone she's going. She won't be long; it's too hot to go for a walk of any length. She just needs to be away from the street and away from the house for a little while.

She finds herself crossing town and walking towards the school, her legs taking her in that direction on autopilot. From there, she crosses over to the playing fields, passing the park where children with water pistols run and scream as they try to cool off in the now-baking sun. She goes to a bench by a tree and takes out her phone. This isn't what she'd planned to do, but she can't help herself. She turns it on. A succession of messages and notifications ping through, though she only really sees one. A WhatsApp message from Freya.

Everything okay? What did your mum want? Let me know x

For a moment, Alice doesn't understand the message. Then she remembers what happened earlier, and the excuse she'd given to leave Freya's house. She locks her phone, not wanting to be drawn towards the temptation to respond.

Why is Freya telling her to let her know what her mother wanted? What business is it of hers? None, and yet she always seems to think she's owed an explanation, as though the whole world revolves around her even when it doesn't.

Unless this is to do with Eve and her father, and Freya suspects that Jo knows something.

The thought strikes Alice like a slap. And then she realises her skin is burning.

She stands from the bench, thinking now that she didn't put on any suncream before she left the house. Her skin is fair; she'll be blistered within no time if she stays out much longer, even in what little shade is to be found. She heads back home the way she came, cutting across the playing fields to get back to the school. By the time she reaches the cul-de-sac, her hair is wet with sweat against the back of her neck, and she can feel the skin across her shoulders tightening with sunburn.

She doesn't make it as far as the driveway. Before she gets there, she sees Freya standing by her dad's car. Rob is beside her, one hand resting on the wing mirror. She's wearing a pair of shorts that are tiny even by Freya's standards, and a boob tube top that barely stretches to the bottom of her breasts. Her bare flesh is shiny in the sunlight, oiled and slick, and her hair is pulled back in a long, tight ponytail. She throws her head back as she laughs, and as she straightens, she leans towards Rob and puts a hand on his arm.

Everything that Alice had felt earlier returns, that feeling of vengefulness twisting once again in her chest. What the hell is Freya playing at? She thinks of the comment she'd made earlier in her bedroom, about Rob managing to impress without having to try. Alice feels sick. Not her dad.

The conversation from last night starts over again in her head, the words sounding different now they're played to a different tune.

I don't want to talk about it.

But what if I do?

Could she have got it wrong? What if Eve hadn't been referring to her and Rob? What if she'd been referring to Freya?

Alice feels a lump in her throat at the sound of Freya's tinkling laugh. Rob hasn't responded to her touch, yet he hasn't moved away either. Alice watches Freya arch her back in a way that pushes her breasts forward, exaggerating every curve. And then she looks up at Alice's bedroom window and smiles.

'Dad!'

Alice rushes up the driveway towards them as they both turn at the sound of her voice.

'Alice,' Freya says, putting her hand to her mouth in a faked expression of concern. 'That looks painful.' She gestures to Alice's shoulder before placing a cool hand on her sunburned skin.

'Can you help me with that thing?' Alice asks, ignoring her.

'What thing?'

'That thing you said you'd help me with.'

Rob pulls a face. 'Yeah... I mean... okay.'

When Alice goes through the front door, her mother is at the top of the stairs. She's clutching an armful of dirty washing, and Alice recognises the items as those she left on the floor in her bedroom, meaning to bring them down and put them in the basket. Jo has just been in her room. A silent exchange takes place between mother and daughter. Alice thinks of Freya smiling up at her bedroom window as she flirted with her father. She must have seen Jo there. She'd seen her watching them together, and she'd mocked her with it.

She goes into the downstairs toilet, where she takes a tub of her mother's moisturiser from the cupboard above the sink. She applies it liberally to her face and shoulders, trying to erase the thoughts that taunt her as she rubs at her burned skin.

She barely recognises herself in the mirror. She sees a darkness behind her eyes, something she's never noticed there before. Perhaps it has always been there, silently settled beneath the girl-next-door exterior. All that's needed to push a light through the darkness is the tiniest sliver of a gap. Maybe the same applies in reverse.

She finishes applying the moisturiser and stands with her palms pressed to the sink. Her heart races in her chest. From the hallway, she can hear her parents' voices. Freya had told her there was something she'd wanted to talk to her about. Alice had assumed it was to do with Eve, but what if she was wrong? She feels a knot tie in her gut. She doesn't want to think that whatever Freya had been prevented from saying had been about her and Rob.

ELEVEN

JO

Alice and Toby are in their bedrooms, and Rob has gone up to the office to do whatever it is he does up there. Jo suspects his claim that he has work to do is an excuse. Since Eve came to the house earlier, and since Freya made an appearance on the driveway dressed like a ring girl at a boxing match, Rob has been strangely quiet. Of course, he doesn't know that Jo is aware of either of their visits.

She takes a glass of iced water up to the office and taps on the door before going in.

'Thanks,' he says, taking the drink from her.

'Everything okay?'

'Yeah, fine.'

She waits a moment. 'What did Eve want earlier?'

She sees a flicker of panic behind Rob's eyes at the knowledge that he has been caught out in his lie about an Amazon parcel.

'She was crying. I heard her.'

'It was about Freya.'

'What about her?'

Rob exhales noisily through his mouth. 'I had a word earlier, after Alice came in crying. All that crap with that bloody text message, and now this.'

'Alice asked us not to get involved.'

'Which is why I didn't tell you.'

'Eve was crying, though.'

'Wouldn't you be, if Freya was your daughter?' Rob reaches out and takes her hand. 'I'm sorry, okay, I shouldn't have spoken to her about it. But something needs to be done about that girl. She's out of control.'

Jo thinks about what she saw from Alice's bedroom not so long ago. Rob's right: something needs to be done about Freya. But it's not for them to deal with her. Chris and Eve need to do something to manage her behaviour before it really is too late.

'You said "not here",' Jo says. 'Something about not doing something here.'

'You were listening in on us?'

She doesn't bother to deny it.

Rob lets go of her hand. 'I told her I didn't want to talk about it on the doorstep. I didn't want Alice to know she was here.'

'I thought you were the one who said we shouldn't get too involved?'

'I've just said I'm sorry. It's just that girl...' His hand tightens its grip around the pen he's holding.

'That girl what?'

'She's got away with too much for too long.'

Jo thinks about mentioning Freya on the driveway earlier, but after just admitting to listening in on him and Eve, she can predict the fallout it'll cause. Rob already thinks she doesn't trust him. It's not that, though. She's always trusted him. There's something bigger going on, but she just can't see what it is yet.

'Is Alice okay?' he asks.

'She's in her room. I'll try to speak to her again later.'

'Are *we* okay?'

'Why wouldn't we be?'

He puts the pen down and gets up from his chair. 'Everything's going to be all right. We'll work something out for Alice. She'll get another uni place. It might even end up better for her in the long run. And it'll do her good to be away from Freya.'

Jo can't disagree with him there. She's thought it for a while, but never admitted it to herself. Her friendship with Eve and Chris has kept her from truly acknowledging the type of character their daughter has become.

'Maybe,' she says. 'Anyway, I'll leave you to it.'

When she goes back downstairs, she stops in the kitchen doorway. Toby and Chris are sitting at the breakfast bar.

'I was just heading out,' Toby says, standing. 'I won't be back late.'

'Okay,' Jo says absently, wondering why Chris is here. She still hasn't erased that awkward hug at the party from her mind, and it makes her sad to think that in all the years they've known each other, this is the first time she's felt uncomfortable alone with him.

'Recovered from the party yet?' she asks casually, as she hears the front door close behind Toby.

'Started to feel human again about an hour ago. I'd forgotten I can't drink bubbles. Did you enjoy?'

'It was lovely,' Jo says. 'And very generous of you both.'

'So long as everyone enjoyed themselves. I think Eve did. I hope so, anyway. It's been a difficult couple of years. She deserved it.'

'She seemed more than happy yesterday. And that necklace... good touch.'

'Well, like I said yesterday, it could never replace the original, but you know...' His words trail off as he stands from the breakfast bar stool. 'Everything okay between you and Rob when you got back?'

Jo feels affronted by the strangeness of the question, which she feels borders on rude. She's still had no explanation as to why he's here. 'Fine,' she says defensively. 'Why wouldn't it have been?'

She remembers the way Sue from number 3 had looked scornfully at Rob when he'd come over to them and slurred his way into the conversation before leaving the party. Then she recalls how he'd been when she'd got home, as though nothing had happened. The attention he'd shown her. The sex that had followed. Everything between them was more than fine.

Or it had seemed so at the time, at least.

She thinks of Rob upstairs, oblivious that Chris is here. She wonders whether she should call him down, but perhaps it's better that she just tries to get Chris out of here as quickly as possible.

'No reason. I'm going away tomorrow,' he says. 'With work.'

'Abroad?'

'Unfortunately not. Leeds. Not quite so exotic.'

'How long for?'

'A week.'

'I'm sure Eve will miss you. Absence makes the heart grow fonder, and all that.'

Chris's lips stretch into a thin smile. 'Something like that.'

He looks past her shoulder into the hallway, his gaze lingering there too long. 'Is everything okay?' she asks.

'Yes. I mean... Look, I've come to say sorry.'

'What for?'

'For what happened at the party.'

Jo doesn't want to talk about it. She doesn't want him to explain why he did what he did, and she doesn't need an apology. She's got enough problems to be dealing with already.

'When I... I just—'

'Everything's fine,' Jo says quickly. 'How's Eve?'

'Eve? She's okay.'

'She was here earlier, with Rob. She was crying.'

'Crying?' Chris repeats. 'What about?'

'I wasn't there, but something about Freya, apparently.'

Jo knows that what's she's doing is sneaky and underhand, but she also knows she's being lied to. She's just not sure who by. Chris's hands on her at the party... Eve crying at the door... Freya turning up and flirting with Rob.

'Is Rob in?' Chris asks.

'Yeah. Upstairs.'

'Okay. Look, I'll leave you to it. If you ever need anything, Jo, you know where I am, okay?'

'Of course.' She smiles past the strangeness. 'Thank you. And the same applies to you and Eve as well, you know that.'

When she follows him to the door, he stops and looks up the stairs.

'Is everything okay, Chris?'

'I'm sorry,' he says, tearing his attention away from the staircase. 'It's after the break-in, you know. I'm just paranoid about safety.'

'Understandably.'

'I'll go and see if Eve's okay.'

'Say hi from me.'

Jo closes the door and goes into the living room, careful to stay to the side of the window, where she won't be seen. When she glances out, Chris is on the pavement, turned back towards the house, just standing there staring.

TWELVE

ALICE

Its 3 a.m. and Alice can't sleep. She lies awake in the stifling heat of her bedroom. The window is open, but with no breeze to cool the place, she feels like she's lying in a hot bath, near drowning in her own thoughts. Her eyes are stinging from hours of screen time spent scrolling through Freya's social media pages, hating her so-called friend more and more with every post and every photograph. She can't get her brain past what she witnessed on the driveway. Freya couldn't have been doing it to wind Alice up, not this time, at least. She hadn't known Alice was there.

With her phone gripped in her hand, she cries hot tears. Freya was taunting her yesterday morning with those comments about her dad, trying to prompt a reaction from her. This is madness. If it's Freya's idea of a joke, she's even more sick than Alice realised. She's seen the way Freya behaves around any boy she wants something from. She's even played a toned-down version with some of the male teachers at school. This is not her father's fault, she tells herself, the mantra repeated over and over. Freya is the problem.

Eventually she drifts into a disrupted, broken sleep, and

stays in bed until mid morning, when she hears Toby leave the house for his Monday shift at the DIY store. She goes down to the kitchen. Her parents are in there, her mother's voice strained. Alice stands in the hallway behind the closed door, listening to them talk.

'What time did you say your meeting with the builder is?'

'One.'

'Do you need lunch before you go?'

'No. Thanks. I'll grab something while I'm out.'

She listens as someone goes into the fridge. Her parents' words are sharp, their sentences clipped during the strained exchange. She wonders what's happened between them. Whether anything has been said. When they fall silent, Alice goes into the room. Her father greets her with a grunt and her mother tells her there's still coffee in the pot if she'd like one.

Her phone pings in her pyjama pocket as she's taking a slice of bread from the bag to make herself some toast. A message from Dylan. She hasn't heard from him since yesterday, after she asked him what he needed to tell her. She'd presumed that whatever it was, he wanted to wait to speak to her in person.

Hey. I'm so sorry I have to show you this, but I thought it would be better coming from me.

There's a TikTok link below the message, which Alice clicks on. She recognises the username instantly: @harlotscarlet.

She remembers asking her mother a couple of years earlier what the word meant, and her mother giving her a brief definition, adding charitably that Scarlet probably didn't realise when she'd chosen the rhyming username, although Alice was sure that neither of them really believed that to be true.

The image is blurry before the reel starts playing, just a flash of ruby red and a darkened background.

When your vajayjay comes out to play-play, the caption reads.

Alice knows straight away what she's watching. She realises what the ruby red is now, and she recognises the prom dress as soon as she clicks to start the reel playing: the one she'd picked out with Freya when they'd gone shopping together during the Easter holidays. She'd felt different when she'd put it on. Special. Her father had commented on the length of the split, but her mother had defended her choice. It wasn't too bad when she was standing up; she just needed to be careful when sitting down. It hadn't caused an issue until they'd been getting into the limo at the end of the night, and this was exactly the moment Scarlet had caught on camera.

That annoying song used in so many TikTok reels plays over the top, with the screechy-voiced woman repeating the words 'oh no' on a loop. Alice watches herself get into the limo, awaiting the moment she knows is coming, when a brief but sharp gust of wind catches the bottom of her dress and yanks at the split, revealing her underwear. She and the girls had laughed about it in the car, Freya assuring her that no one had seen anything. But when she watches the reel for a first and then a second and third time, she knows that wasn't true. Everyone saw everything, and in place of the nude-coloured seamless knickers she'd been wearing that night, Scarlet has superimposed a cartoon beaver with an enormous pair of front teeth.

'Alice. What is it? What's the matter?'

Jo comes up behind her, and when she reaches for the phone, Alice lets her take it. She says nothing as she watches the short reel play out.

'Who's put this up?' she asks.

'Scarlet.'

Jo rolls her eyes. 'Why doesn't that surprise me?' She's never liked Scarlet, and Alice has always known that. Her mother has made frequent comments on the inappropriate posts Scarlet used to post on social media long before Alice had even been allowed a phone. As young as twelve, Scarlet was ahead of her time, getting involved with boys and making no secret of the fact. Alice can still remember Scarlet's mother laughing it off when a comment was made by one of the other mums at a birthday party; the way she joked about her daughter's antics as though it was all perfectly normal and to be expected. Alice's parents had always referred to Scarlet as Code Red when the twins were younger, thinking Alice and Toby too naïve to know who they were referring to.

And of course, she knows about the message Scarlet had sent to that boy from school from Alice's phone.

'What is it?' Rob asks, getting up from the table. He peers over Jo's shoulder. 'For Christ's sake. I told you the bloody split in that dress was too long.'

'Is that really the issue here?' Jo says sharply, turning to him.

'Well, if she'd listened and chosen something more suitable, no one would have had this footage, would they?'

'Wow. Sounds like a casual bit of victim blaming. I suppose young girls who get raped should be more covered up too, right?'

Alice thinks of Freya on the driveway yesterday, the way her body had been on show for him. She wonders if her mother is remembering the same, whether this is now clouding her reaction to Rob's response.

Rob's jaw tenses. 'What the hell has got into you, Jo?'

Her father was angry when he'd found out about the university letter; now she knows he'll be furious. Although Freya may not have uploaded this, Alice has no doubt she probably knows about it. If Dylan's got hold of it, there's no way Freya can have missed it. She should have been the one to let her know. She should have tried to put a stop to it.

'This isn't Alice's fault,' Jo says pointedly. 'These girls are supposed to be her friends.'

Alice is grateful to have her mother's support, though she wonders whether Jo's outrage is now more a stance against Rob than it is a defence of her.

'"Supposed to be" being the key phrase there,' Rob says. 'Some bloody friends.'

Alice goes to the front door and pulls a pair of trainers from the shoe rack.

'Where are you going?' her mother asks.

'To see Freya.' She doesn't care that she's still in her pyjamas. This can't wait.

'I don't think that's a good idea, love.' Jo tries to deter her. 'Wait until you've had a bit of time to think.'

'There's nothing to think about.'

She hurries across the road to the Harrises' house, aware that both her parents are following her. She bangs a fist on the front door, and when Eve answers, she barges past her. 'Where's Freya?'

'Alice—'

'Where is she?' Alice walks through the living room and comes back into the hallway. There's no sign of Freya in the kitchen, but then she notices the bifold doors are ajar. She hears her mother talking to Eve in the hallway, Eve's voice already thick with indignation.

Alice goes into the garden, her phone clutched in her hand. Freya is on a sunbed at the end of the lawn, catching the midday heat behind a pair of designer sunglasses.

'How could you?'

'How could I what?' Freya sits up and pushes her glasses to the top of her head, squinting as she looks at Alice.

'I'm guessing you knew about this.'

Alice holds out the phone in front of Freya and plays the

reel. She's sure the faintest shadow of a smirk plays out on Freya's lips.

'I told her not to upload it.'

'So you knew about it? For how long? Do you know how embarrassing this is? My dad's seen it, for fuck's sake.'

Freya does nothing to withhold a laugh. 'Oh God,' she says, just as their parents join them. 'Poor Rob.' She looks him up and down as the corner of her mouth quirks into a wry smile.

Alice's hands ball into fists, her nails digging into her palms. She reminds herself that Freya is doing this to wind her up, that everything is designed to provoke a reaction.

'Freya!' Eve stands beside Alice, arms folded across her chest. 'I told them you didn't know anything about this. You didn't, did you?'

'Not before this morning.'

On Alice's other side, her mother mutters something inaudible beneath her breath.

'Get it taken down,' Rob says.

'I didn't upload it,' Freya objects, getting up now from the sunbed. 'It was Scarlet, and she's not going to take it down just because I tell her to.'

'You don't get it, do you?' Rob says, and Alice can hear the threat in his tone; she hasn't heard him like this since the last time she and Toby got themselves into trouble for misbehaving, years ago. 'Things like this stick for life. Once they're online, they're available for anyone to see. Haven't you caused enough damage already?'

'You can't speak to me like that,' Freya says, eyeing him defiantly. 'You're not my father.'

'And would you flaunt yourself at him as well?' Alice says flatly. 'Or is that just reserved for *my* father?'

She can almost feel the rage radiating from Eve beside me. 'What did you say?'

'Ask her,' Alice challenges. 'Ask her about yesterday, when

she came over to the house with her shorts up her arse and her tits hanging out, thrusting herself at my dad like a cheap hooker.'

Freya swings a fist at Alice, but Rob intervenes and stops the blow before it connects. He grabs Freya by the wrist and yanks back her arm, and when Freya cries out in pain, he drops his grip and lets her go, looking at his own hand as though it doesn't belong to him.

'Get out,' Eve says, her voice trembling. 'Before I call the police and have you arrested for assault.'

Alice notices that Eve makes no move to go to Freya's aid.

'Assault?' Jo repeats. 'She was just about to punch my daughter.'

'Get out!'

'Deal with her,' Rob says, turning his words on Eve. 'Because I swear if you don't, I will.'

He reaches for Jo's arm, leading her back to the house. Alice follows. She wonders why she ever allowed herself to be pushed towards Freya. They're not the same; they never have been. Freya has a mean streak running through her like a stick of rock. Yet now she sits there sobbing quietly, acting the part of victim.

Before she follows her parents into the kitchen, she looks back to see Freya arguing with her mother. Rage snakes through her, twisting in a knot in her stomach. She could kill her.

THIRTEEN

JO

'What do we do now?' Jo asks as they go back inside their own house.

Rob slams the door and kicks his shoes off, leaving them where they land by the radiator. 'Can you contact Scarlet's mother?'

'Don't do that,' Alice objects.

'I don't think you realise how damaging this could be,' Rob reminds her. 'Universities can search people out online. Employers do it all the time these days. That reel makes you look...'

Jo sees her daughter's face harden.

'Oh please.' Alice folds her arms across her chest. 'Don't stop on my account. Do go on. Makes me look what?'

'It says far more about Scarlet than it does about Alice,' Jo says.

'But it's not Scarlet's...' Once again Rob cuts his sentence short. His face is flushed, anger bubbling beneath the surface. Jo hasn't seen him like this in a long time, but she feels in this case it's justified. Freya has been causing trouble for Alice for a while. She loads the bullets before getting someone else to fire the gun, and it seems that person is usually Scarlet. Now she has brought trouble even closer to their home. Her behaviour on the driveway yesterday was a crossed boundary they can't come back from.

'Can it even be taken down now?'

'It's been shared,' Alice says. 'So no. Not unless everyone who's shared it deletes it.'

Rob's jaw tightens. 'She thinks everything's one big joke,' he says, jabbing a finger towards the door.

'Who?'

'Bloody Freya. She takes no responsibility for anything, thinks she can do whatever she likes. She acts like a spoiled brat.'

'Freya didn't do this,' Jo reminds him.

He's about to respond when the front door is flung open. It swings into Alice and knocks her sideways. She cries out in pain, holding her arm as Jo helps her to her feet.

'Careful,' Rob snaps. 'What's the matter with you?!'

Toby slams the front door and glances at his sister. 'Sorry,' he mumbles.

Jo checks her watch. Toby's shift isn't due to finish for another couple of hours. 'What are you doing home?'

'Work was quiet.'

She looks at him questioningly. She knows this is a lie: there have been plenty of occasions when Toby has complained how bored he's been at work, yet they've always been able to find something for him to do, whether watering plants or restocking shelves when there have been few customers.

'Are you okay?' she asks Alice, who's still rubbing her arm.

'Fine.'

Alice might be, but Toby certainly isn't. When Jo looks back at him, she notices his tensed jawline and watery eyes. 'What's really happened?'

'Nothing.'

Jo sighs. She's so fed up with these recent one-word answers from him. 'Your shift doesn't finish until four. Why are you home?'

'I was told to leave early.'

The way he says it suggests he definitely wasn't sent home early because the store was quiet.

'Why?' she says, stretching the word into three syllables as she tries not to lose her patience.

'No reason.'

Toby veers around Rob to get to the stairs, escaping to his bedroom before he receives any further questioning. Jo hears his bedroom door slam, and wonders how things have managed to get to this. She thought they'd bypassed this phase: the teenage sulks and the sullenness. Perhaps where the twins are concerned things have just been delayed slightly.

'What the hell was that all about?' Rob asks.

'No idea. Are you okay, love?' Jo puts a hand on Alice's arm. She feels her trembling, her run-in with Freya still raw in her memory.

'I shouldn't have said what I did.'

'Oh love,' Jo says, pulling her in for a hug. 'We've all got a breaking point.'

'She was laughing at you,' Rob reminds her, not particularly helpfully.

'Rob—'

'I'm just saying! She had every right to say what she did.'

Rob's mobile starts ringing, vibrating on the hallway table beside them. 'Shit,' he says. 'Dan.'

He answers the call from his brother and takes it into the kitchen, leaving Jo and Alice alone in the hallway.

'What do you think has happened with Toby?' Alice asks.

'Don't worry about Toby for a minute,' Jo tells her. 'Listen to me – you've done nothing wrong. You're not to blame for what just happened over there, okay?'

Alice nods, but Jo knows her well enough to know she doesn't believe her. Alice will go up to her bedroom and spend the next few hours dissecting the encounter, taking it apart piece by piece and putting it together in a hundred different ways. And in each of those ways she will end up somehow responsible or to blame for it all.

'Shall I make you something to eat?' Jo offers.

Alice shakes her head. 'I'm not hungry. Let me go and see Toby before you do. He might speak to me.'

The implication stings Jo a little, that her son might not want to speak to her. Yet she knows Alice is right. The twins have always been closer to each other than to anyone else.

'Give me a shout if you need anything.'

When she goes to the kitchen, Rob is just ending his call with his brother.

'I forgot all about tonight, didn't I. I told him I can't make it, there's too much going on.'

Every Monday evening he plays squash with his brother in a leisure centre a half-hour drive away. It's a regular commitment between the brothers, ensuring that no matter how busy their family or work lives become, they also make time for each other. After the game, they usually go for a drink or something to eat, and Jo has got used to having these evenings to herself, appreciating the time alone. She usually takes the opportunity to clean the house or catch up with the ironing so that she doesn't have to do these things during the time she and Rob get together at weekends.

'Please don't do that. Call him back.'

She realises she sounds a little too keen for him to be out of the house. Perhaps she is. She just wants some time to herself. The argument in Eve's garden has raised a niggling doubt that has gnawed away at her. When she thinks of Rob's anger, it seems disproportionate somehow. He was protecting Alice, but she can't escape the feeling that he was also protecting someone else in some way. Himself.

'I'm not going to do that.'

'Please, Rob. It'll be good for you. You're wound up—'

'I'm not wound up.'

She raises an eyebrow, her point proven by his interruption.

'We all need a bit of space to breathe. I'll sort the kids out, speak to Toby. Alice is okay. Come on,' she says, putting a hand on his arm. 'What was it you always used to tell the kids? Feeling angry? Run around in the garden.'

Rob smiles sadly. His hand slides into hers. 'I'm sorry if I overreacted. I just see how much all this is hurting Alice, and it isn't fair. She deserves better. People like Freya shouldn't get to win all the time.'

'Is that all life is, a competition?'

'For the most part, yes.'

'So which one of us is winning and which is losing?'

'That's not how it works. We're a team. We take the wins and the losses together.'

'Okay, teammate. So maybe I deserve the truth.'

Rob's eyes narrow. 'The truth about what?'

'Why didn't you tell me about Freya being here yesterday? About how she behaved out on the driveway?'

His hand falls from hers. 'Because it was nothing. She's a silly little girl who thinks she can play grown-up games. I knew what she was trying to do.'

'What do you think she was trying to do?'

Rob sighs and pushes a hand through his hair. 'I don't know... Wind me up. Intimidate me in some way. Who knows what goes on in that messed-up head of hers.'

Jo studies him closely, searching for clues to a lie. She has known him for over twenty years. She knows him better than anyone else does, or ever could. She would know if he was lying... wouldn't she?

'What are you accusing me of, Jo?'

'Nothing.'

'Good. Because she's eighteen years old and she grew up alongside our own kids. I've been like an uncle to that girl. I might be many things, but I'm not a fucking pervert.'

She sees the hurt in his eyes, just how pained he is at the thought that she might have considered him in this way if even for the briefest of moments. And then he notices it – that there, for that slightest slice of time, she had.

'Fucking hell, Jo.'

He brushes past her as he leaves, slamming the kitchen door behind him.

Jo stands in the kitchen alone and tearful. She feels a surging resentment strong enough to make her feel she might hate Freya for what she's managed to do to her family. She hates that she's allowed Freya to make her think of her husband in this way.

FOURTEEN

ALICE

When Alice goes up to her brother's room, he's lying on his bed with his earbuds in. The room is a mess, completely out of character for Toby, who is usually neat and tidy to a degree Alice sometimes finds annoying. There are dirty clothes on the floor and leftover food sitting on a plate on the bedside table. An empty crisp packet has been dropped on the carpet.

'What?' he snaps.

'I just came to see if you're okay.'

'Fine.'

'What happened at work?'

He sighs and pushes his head back into the pillow. 'Has Mum sent you up here?'

'No.' Alice sits in the swivel chair at his desk. 'Do you want to talk about it?'

'No. But it looks as though you're not going anywhere until I do.'

She smiles, but it's met with another sigh as Toby heaves himself up to sit against the pillows.

'Did you try to sell someone tartan paint?'

He casts her a glare, unamused by her attempt at humour.

'I called some bloke a dickhead. He was arguing with me over a discount on a lawnmower. I muttered it under my breath, and he heard me.'

Alice laughs, but it's more from the surprise of it than at what's happened. She can't imagine Toby reacting in the way he's just described, not when he's always so polite to everyone. As kids, he had set the bar for good manners, and Alice was often told to 'say thank you, like your brother' if she hadn't been quick enough to do so. It sounds so unlike him to call someone a dickhead, although when she thinks about it, he hasn't really been himself recently.

'Have you been sacked?'

'Probably.'

'From golden child to bad boy with a single insult,' Alice muses, but Toby isn't in the mood for banter, not today.

'Are we done now?'

She stands from the chair and goes over to him, taking the plate of abandoned food from the bedside table.

'Freya was flirting with Dad yesterday.'

'What?'

'Outside on the drive. She came over here wearing those ridiculous shorts she loves. You know the ones. She was all over him. It was embarrassing.'

Toby laughs bitterly. 'Sounds about right.'

'What do you mean?'

'Well, I doubt anyone's surprised by that. What did he do?'

'Who?'

'Dad. When she was flirting with him.'

Alice doesn't know how to answer this. She was too far away to have heard anything that might have been said, and he didn't seem to do anything. He didn't show Freya attention in any way, but at the same time, he didn't seem to discourage her either.

'Nothing, really.'

'Nothing?'

'I was across the street. I couldn't really tell.'

Toby swings his legs over the side of the bed and sits with his elbows on his knees. His pale face has flushed. 'What was she doing then?'

'Sticking her tits out at him. She kept touching him on the arm and laughing.'

'And Dad just stood there letting her?'

'He probably didn't know how to react.'

'He could have just told her to fuck off.'

Alice laughs. 'Maybe not.'

'Why not? That's what she needs.'

'Toby,' Alice says, her tone reprimanding. She's still feeling guilty for what she said to Freya in the garden earlier.

'What? Everyone knows she's a slag.'

'Toby!' She feels heat rise in her face. This isn't her brother speaking; she's never heard him say anything like this about a girl before. It's the kind of language other boys use, but not Toby.

Yet hadn't she herself called Freya a hooker not long ago? Like her mother had said, everyone has a breaking point.

'What? You don't really like her, you never have. You just tolerate her because you're expected to.'

Alice knows he's right. More and more recently she has realised that she would never have chosen Freya as a friend. Freya was chosen for her, pushed upon her by their parents. But she's not a child any more. She doesn't have to tolerate Freya for anyone.

'Was there anything else?' Toby asks, reaching for his earbuds.

Alice sighs. She takes the plate to the bedroom door, but before she closes it behind her, Toby calls her back.

'Last thing,' he says. 'I don't want to hear anything about Freya any more.'

FIFTEEN

JO

After Rob has left to play squash with his brother, Jo goes up to Toby's room.

'Do you want anything to eat?' she asks.

'No thanks.'

'What happened today, love? Do you want to talk about it?'

Alice has already told her, but she doesn't want Toby to know that.

'If I'd wanted to, I would have. So no.'

His attitude takes Jo aback. He never speaks to her like this. 'When you're ready then,' she says, trying not to sound defensive. 'You can always tell me anything, you know that. There's nothing we can't work out together.'

She sees his jaw tense, but he says nothing. Something's happened to him, she thinks as she pulls the bedroom door closed behind her. Not just what happened at work today. He hasn't been himself for a week or so now.

She can't be bothered catching up with housework tonight. She's managed to stay on top of most of it anyway, so after finishing off a bit of admin she's been putting off for weeks, she makes herself a cup of tea and takes it into the living room, where she makes herself comfortable on the sofa.

She's not normally one to watch much television other than the latest Netflix series she and Rob sometimes get hooked on, but tonight she fancies scrolling for something mindless and inane, something she won't have to concentrate on. She flicks through the channels and settles on a documentary about a missing woman, but before long, her attention has moved to her phone. She scrolls through her Facebook newsfeed, skimming over birthday wishes and photos of people's meals and self-congratulations on weight loss results, wondering as she does so why she would care about any of these announcements. Yet for some reason, she keeps scrolling, her mind tuning out from Toby's strange behaviour and Alice's disappointment over university, escaping for this short time into other people's lives, where nothing can hurt her.

After a couple of minutes getting distracted by a reel of cats apparently doing impressions of their owners, Jo sees Eve's face looking back at her. The post was uploaded just a couple of hours ago: Eve curled in the big snuggle chair in her living room, her blonde hair styled in a way Jo supposes is meant to look effortless; the strap of her loose summer dress falling from her shoulder. With her head tilted to one side, the caption of the photo reads: *Two-day hangover – still recovering from all the weekend's fun.*

Eve loves Facebook. Her profile reveals so much of herself and her life that Jo marvels at just how easy it would be to become a stalker, for anyone who might find themselves persuaded by the inclination. She posts details of her family and her children's achievements; she marks the times and days of fitness classes and appointments, using the platform as an online diary upon which to track her schedule. She makes it so easy for others to do the same.

The post irritates Jo. Eve has made no attempt to contact her since Alice confronted Freya in the garden this morning, and to look at this, it seems she's barely dwelled on what happened. It's not her daughter who's been publicly ridiculed and humiliated, but Jo thought Eve had greater empathy than this. She thought she would at least reach out to check that Alice is okay.

She doesn't think she's ever seen Eve post something quite like this. The way her long blonde hair is swept over one shoulder, her head tilted to the side while she smiles for the camera: there's nothing unusual about the pose, in a different context. It's what she's wearing that causes surprise, that somehow smacks of a desperation level even Eve has never reached before. The flimsy summer dress has a low scooped front, Eve's right breast pushed up so that her nipple sits just beneath the seam line, precariously close to exposure. The hem is high, revealing the tanned flesh of her thigh. Jo saw her in this dress yesterday when she was outside speaking to Rob, but she doesn't think she's worn it before, and she wonders if she's borrowed it from Freya's wardrobe. It certainly looks something more suitable for a teenager than a middle-aged woman. But it's the look on Eve's face as she poses for the selfie that takes Jo aback, unashamedly and intentionally provocative.

The broken pieces of conversation she overheard between Eve and Rob at the front door yesterday play out again on a loop in her head. *Can't stop... Not here... or I will.*

When she'd asked him, Rob said the conversation had been about Freya, but what if he was lying? Jo can't think why Eve would come here to discuss her daughter dressed like that, not unless she felt she had some point to prove.

Without thinking, she screenshots the post. She'll show Rob later, to gauge his reaction. Perhaps when he sees it, any guilt he might have about an earlier lie will be visible in his reaction.

She can't imagine Chris would be too happy about the photo, though he's not on Facebook so he's unlikely to see it. Besides, Chris behaved strangely over the weekend too. Perhaps that's why Eve has done it, Jo finds herself thinking. She was sure Eve must have seen the way Chris touched her before she left the party on Saturday night. Perhaps she mistakenly believes something is going on between Chris and her, or that one or maybe both of them would like there to be. Is this why she came to the house dressed the way she did, and why she's uploaded this post? Perhaps she's trying to make him jealous. Maybe she's trying to make a point to Jo.

A wave of guilt washes over her. She loves Eve. She's been her friend for as long as she's lived on this street, a neighbour and confidante she quickly found herself able to rely on. When they'd first moved to the area, Jo had known no one. Eve was kind and helpful; she'd been everything Jo had needed at the time, and they'd navigated their pregnancies together, Eve offering a much-needed and otherwise missing voice of experience. In so many ways she was the mother figure Jo had never had, despite being a similar age. It would crush Jo to think Eve might believe her capable of involving herself with her husband in any way.

But there's something about the post that makes her cringe. It's so attention-seeking. The selfie is embarrassing. It strikes her that it's the kind of photograph a woman would use to advertise herself on an adult website, and as soon as the thought crosses her mind, she feels guilty for thinking it, wishing it could be erased. It feels unpleasant to think of Eve in this way, and Jo isn't this person; she's not normally so judgemental. Yet she can't escape the feeling that this is why Freya is the way she is: a product of what her mother is, and what she's allowed her to become.

She's still staring at the photograph on her phone when the

screen changes and Toby's name appears, accompanied by the tinkly piano music of her ringtone. She wonders why he's calling her from his bedroom.

'Toby?'

'Mum,' he says, his voice barely audible, little more than a whisper. 'I'm at Freya's house. I need you.'

SIXTEEN
ALICE

Alice is on the landing, just leaving the bathroom, when she hears a voice. A male voice. It's not her father's: he isn't home, and anyway, it sounds nothing like him. The sound stops her, and she lingers outside the bathroom, listening. When she hears it for a second time, she's pretty sure it's coming from her parents' bedroom. It doesn't sound like a human voice, more like it's coming from a laptop or a phone. She goes into the room tentatively, half expecting to find someone in there. At the doorway, she waits, and then she hears the voice again. *Batteries low.* She follows where she thinks the sound came from and slides open the wardrobe door, wondering what her parents own that might have made such a noise. Scrap that, she thinks, maybe she doesn't want to know.

She sits on the end of her parents' bed and opens the internet browser on her phone. When she taps in the words *batteries low heard in bedroom*, she's not quite sure what results to expect, though what she finds hadn't been on her bingo card of potential offerings.

Found a hidden camera in my bathroom.

Should I call the police about a hidden camera.

What to do if you find a hidden camera.

She scrolls the page, skim-reading the key details from each result. Then she sees something that catches her eye, with advice on apps that can help you detect whether a hidden camera has been installed in your home. There really is an app for everything now, she thinks. She goes to the app store and downloads the recommended suggestion. It's quick and easy to use, and within no time she has run the programme that promises to find any devices in the room. In no time, it has led her back to the wardrobe, alerting her to something near the top.

It's small but visible, though only, she thinks, to anyone actively looking for it. Alice can't think of a reason for her mother to have put it there, and she can see how Jo would never have noticed it, tucked away in the corner but presumably offering the viewer a decent view of the room, providing the wardrobe doors are open. The furniture in the room is minimal, with most of her parents' belongings hidden behind the sliding doors. She imagines that anyone looking for somewhere to place a camera might have had difficulty doing so elsewhere in a way that would keep it concealed for long enough.

She takes the camera out onto the landing and waits at the top of the stairs for a moment, listening for any sound from the ground floor. It's quiet, so she presumes no one will know she's been snooping around. She wonders how this thing works. Is it livestreaming to someone's device, an iPhone or a tablet? The thought makes her nauseous, and she turns it over, flat on her palm so that anyone who might have been watching or recording these past few minutes will now be greeted with a blank screen.

In her bedroom, she places it face-down on the bedside table and gets her phone to text her friend Amy. They were supposed to be going to a late showing at the cinema tonight, but she can't face it now. She was already fifty-fifty about the idea, but the camera has made the decision for her. It's just too weird.

Sorry Amy, been sick – think it must be something I've eaten. Can we do the cinema later in the week? X

She throws her phone onto the bed and lies back on the pillows, distracted by the camera on the bedside table. Maybe she should have just left it where it was. Now it's been moved, someone will notice it's gone. It just bothers her who that someone might be. The thought of her parents filming themselves having sex makes her feel sick. She baulks at the idea, feeling nausea roll in her gut. It's not an impossibility, though. Is this what happens in middle age, when people get bored in their marriages? She supposes that twenty years is a long time to be with the same person. Maybe they do it to stop their partner from being tempted by an affair. Or to stop themselves. No way, she thinks. Her parents are way too conservative for that. And old, she thinks. Far too old.

But it just doesn't ring true anyway. She can't see her mother agreeing to something like that, even if her father had wanted to. Urgh. She tries to shake off the idea. She doesn't know what to do with the camera now, or if she's done the right thing removing it from where she found it. She retrieves her phone and runs a search on what to do if a camera is found hidden in a bedroom. According to the results thrown up, the police should probably be notified – if someone living in the house is ignorant of the camera's presence there, at least.

And yet she still knows what she heard at that party. For the first time, Alice wonders whether her mother already knows about Eve. Maybe something has happened, and this is her mum's way of trying to keep her dad from straying again. It just seems so unlikely. She knows her mother. Is she trying to catch them out, trying to gain evidence of an affair? Alice can't imagine when her father would be able to bring Eve here without anyone in the house finding out. There's always someone home.

Her phone beeps with a text.

No worries. Hope you're feeling better soon.

No kiss at the end, and a full stop – both signs that Amy is annoyed with her. It's not the first time her texts have revealed her frustration, although it's not the first time Alice has bailed out of a catch-up at the last minute.

Her thoughts return to what's happened this evening. She can't bring herself to believe that her dad would put a camera there to film her mother without her knowledge. The idea is sick. If something *has* happened with Eve, it makes her dad weak. Selfish. But she doesn't want to consider that he may be worse than those things. But if neither of her parents is responsible, that means someone else is. Someone else who's had access to their home. Yet that doesn't seem possible. There's a downstairs toilet, so anyone who visits has no need to come upstairs to use the bathroom. Alice and Toby haven't had friends over to the house for a while now: the weather has been so lovely that everyone has been outside, making the most of it. Besides that, she doesn't think either of them has any friend strange enough to want to install a camera in their parents' bedroom.

Except, of course, for Freya.

Images of her flirting with Rob on the driveway skitter through Alice's mind. Whatever she was playing at – whether trying to make Eve jealous or trying to wind Alice up – her actions were meticulous and calculated, as they always are. Freya is devious enough to plant a hidden camera, and she has easy and regular access to the house. But why? The only reason that makes any sense to Alice is that Freya might have hoped to blackmail one of her parents.

Alice continues to scan the search results on her phone, reading posts from people who've had cameras installed secretly by family members. It makes her sick to think a person could violate someone's privacy in such a way, though it occurs to her that people are capable of anything. The thought that Freya might be responsible brings a resurgence in the anger she had felt so intensely yesterday. The recorded voice must be what her mother had heard on Saturday night, just before she'd come to Alice's room.

She takes the camera from the bedside table again and turns it in her hand, at once disgusted at and in awe of how easily this thing has remained hidden until now. She wonders how long it's been there. She wonders what might have been done with the recordings. There are so many questions, many of which she probably doesn't want the answers to. But there's one thing she feels sure of, if nothing else: her mother has no idea this thing was there.

SEVENTEEN

JO

The side gate is open at the Harrises' house, and Jo goes in through the utility room. There's an eerie silence about the place, and if she hadn't received that text from Toby, she would believe there was no one there.

'Toby.'

There's no reply when she calls his name. She goes through to the kitchen and then to the hallway, stopping sharply at the sight that meets her there. She wants to look away, wants to see anything other than the sight of Freya lying on the floor at her son's feet, but she can't tear her eyes from the girl. There is a wound on the side of her head, long and deep, the flesh split so that the white shine of her skull is exposed beneath the river of blood that has flowed from the injury. Jo needs no forensic experience to see what's happened here: a child could work it out. An ornament lies just feet away from Freya's body, the white elephant that Eve was gifted by a relative during her first pregnancy. Jo had once asked about it, years ago, as she'd stood near the doorway ready to leave the house. She had marvelled at the pretty mosaic pattern of the elephant's body, strangely beautiful in its mirror-like quality. Eve had told her how it was a symbol of energy and good fortune, and how if placed facing the front door, it was believed to protect the house. The irony of all this now cuts through the detachment that has momentarily seized her.

'Toby,' she says quietly, standing just behind him. 'What happened?'

Because despite the fact that a child could work it out, she still needs confirmation from her son. She needs to hear him say the words that what happened here this evening was exactly as it looks to her now, having just walked in to find him like this. She needs to hear him say it, because she doesn't want to believe it.

Toby says nothing. She reaches to put a hand on his arm, but finds herself clinging to him, using him for balance. She hears her own blood in her head, feels her heart racing as she tries to make sense of a scene that is incomprehensible.

And then it seems she rejoins the present, a sudden alertness pushing her into action.

'Freya.' She moves past Toby and drops beside the girl, reaching for her wrist to try to find a pulse. She isn't sure what she's doing exactly; she did a first-aid course years ago, but it was when the twins were little, so long ago now that she's forgotten the details of what she'd learned. It isn't rocket science, she tells herself, trying to slow her own breathing and focus on what needs to be done. Find a pulse. Just find a sign she's still alive.

She moves her fingertips to the girl's throat, pushing gently where the skin indents with the dip between bones. There is blood on her fingers now, but she doesn't care. She just needs to know that Freya is still breathing. That she hasn't arrived here too late.

'Toby,' she says again, looking up desperately at her son. 'What the hell happened?'

But Toby is rigid, unmoving. His face is so pale he might be a ghost, and he stares blankly ahead of him as though unseeing, unable to bring himself to look down at Freya. Not prepared to look at what he's done. The thought hits Jo like a fist. Her boy, she thinks. Her baby boy. Not this. Not him.

She moves her fingers around Freya's neck, desperate now to find a pulse. When she can't, she reaches into her phone, bloodstained fingers unlocking it to dial 999.

Her hand shakes as she waits for the call to be answered.

'Emergency, what service do you require?'

'It's my son.'

'Is he injured?'

Pause.

'No... no, he's not injured.'

'Okay. Is he there with you now?'

'Uh... yes. Yes, he's here.'

'Could you tell me what your emergency is?'

Silence.

'Caller, are you still with me?'

'Yes, I'm here.'

Pause.

'It's my son... He's killed someone.'

A sob bursts from Jo's chest. She looks up at Toby from where she crouches beside Freya's body, praying for a contradiction, willing from him an explanation that this is all some kind of terrible mistake. Instead, Toby continues to stare forward, frozen, his mind absent, his body left behind.

She is told by the operator to stay on the line, and although she doesn't hang up, she doesn't keep the phone near her face. She rises, her knees almost buckling beneath her, and her hand falls to her side as she takes in the details of the scene, one she already knows she will never be able to erase from her consciousness. She has walked straight into a nightmare, a parallel universe where the worst thing she might have been able to imagine is a reality, the terrors of the unthinkable laid out before her like the staging of a horror movie after filming has been cut. Only there is no slap of a clapperboard to pause production; no chatter of crew to slice through the hellish silence that has frozen the room.

'Toby, please. You need to talk to me before they get here.'

There is blood on her son's wrists. It is smeared on his fingers and there are splatters across his knuckles and up the pale green cotton of his hoodie sleeve, the yellow Carhartt logo smudged with red. There is a pool on the wooden flooring, a crimson river leading to a red sea.

'An ambulance is on its way,' she says, and she hears the futility of her words like thunder rippling through the silence, their echo remaining even in their absence. An ambulance is no use to anyone now. But the police, she thinks. The police will have greater purpose here.

For a moment, it occurs to Jo that maybe she should have done things differently. She should have taken Toby away from here, cleaned him up, helped hide any evidence. They could have got into the car and driven for miles, tied the stone elephant to a brick and thrown it into a river. She could have been his alibi. They were watching television. He never left the house this evening. She could have protected him. Is this what a different, better mother might have done, protected her child no matter what?

She looks at Freya and a rush of bile rises in her throat, the taste and texture of it sickening her. This is not who she is. This is not who they are. They don't tell lies. They don't try to hide from things, no matter how difficult. She has raised her children to be honest and true, to face their mistakes and the consequences of them.

She looks at Freya's blood-spattered clothing. A mistake. No one could ever believe this was a mistake.

Freya's dress is raised over her hip, the string of her barely-there underwear showing. Jo feels an urge to reach down and cover her up, to protect her modesty, to stop her from getting cold. A thought rushes in, intrusive and grotesque. What has Toby done to her? Just what was he doing before she walked in?

When she looks at her son, he doesn't so much as flinch beneath her gaze. She's wrong, she tells herself. This isn't him. He hasn't done this. He hasn't done anything wrong. He would never hurt Freya. He would never hurt anyone. He has barely moved since she arrived at the house, his eyes wide, his body frozen with shock. There is another explanation to what has happened. There has to be.

'Toby,' she urges, gripping his sleeve. 'Please. You need to speak to me before the police arrive. We can work this out. I can help you. But you have to tell me what happened.'

They are running out of time. In just moments, the house will fill with people and panic. He has to speak to her now, before it's too late.

'Toby. Please.'

He doesn't try to shake her off, yet still he doesn't utter a word.

'I love you,' she says quietly to her son, not even sure whether he hears her. Her confusion and panic turn to tears, and as she weeps silently for the loss of two lives, she hears the distant sound of sirens.

EIGHTEEN

ALICE

She hears her dad's car pull onto the driveway. When she checks her phone, it's gone 9.30. He must have gone for a drink with Uncle Dan after their game, although Alice is no longer sure she trusts her father enough to blindly accept this is the case. She wonders where Eve might be this evening. Perhaps all these Mondays of squash-playing have been an alibi to hide their affair.

She goes to her bedroom window and glances across the street at the Harris house. Eve's car is on the driveway, although that doesn't mean she's home. Perhaps they met up somewhere and Eve walked part way there before Alice's dad picked her up. Maybe he's just dropped her off around the corner before coming back.

Stop it, Alice tells herself. You still have no proof of anything other than a conversation that may have related to something entirely different.

Yet for whatever reason, and no matter how much she might want to, she can't bring herself to believe that.

She goes downstairs to find him taking off his shoes in the

hallway. The camera she found in her parents' bedroom is now hidden in a shoebox beneath her bed.

'You okay?' her dad asks, looking up at her.

'Yeah.' She passes him and goes to the living room, expecting her mother to still be there watching television. But the room is quiet and there's no one there. It occurs to her now that there doesn't seem to be any noise from anywhere: no background chatter from the television, no sad tune rising from the keys of her mother's piano, no take-off rumble from the washing machine as its cycle approaches its end.

'Jo!'

Her dad has gone to the kitchen, her mother apparently not there either.

'Did your mum say she was going out?'

Alice shrugs. 'She didn't mention anything earlier.'

She follows him back to the kitchen, where he gets himself a glass of water.

'Where's Toby tonight?'

'No idea.' Alice struggles to keep the frustration from her voice. She isn't Toby's keeper. 'In his room, as far as I know. I don't think he came down again after he got back from work.'

Rob reaches into his pocket for his mobile. Alice assumes he's trying her mother's number, but it must go straight to answerphone, as he quickly puts it down on the worktop.

'Dad?'

'Yeah.'

'I need to talk to you about something.'

'Okay,' Rob says, meeting her eye. 'What is it?'

Alice isn't sure how she's even supposed to begin this conversation. It's bad enough that her father has put her in a position where it's even necessary. She shouldn't be made to feel she's being disloyal when she's done nothing wrong and didn't ask to be involved in anything he might have done, but this is how she feels. If she questions him, he's going to be pissed off with her; if she says nothing, she's letting her mother down. It seems to Alice that no matter what she does, she can't win. But now she's found that camera...

'Saturday night, at the party...'

He looks at her expectantly, waiting for the next part. But it never comes. They are interrupted by the sound of sirens. They both hear them, heads turning simultaneously towards the street. Rob leads the way back along the hallway and into the living room. He goes to the window and pushes the curtains aside.

'What the fuck?'

Alice isn't sure she's ever heard her father swear before. He's dropped the odd 'shit' sometimes, when he's smashed something or stubbed his toe, but the f-word has always been a no-go, and both she and Toby always knew as kids that there'd be hell to pay if they were ever caught saying it.

Past the curtains, she sees the pulse and ebb of flashing lights, and hears the sirens rise to a scream. She goes to stand by her father, and they watch as an ambulance pulls up outside the Harris house, closely followed by two police cars, a convoy taking up the pavement at the opposite side of the street.

'Where's Toby?' Rob asks again, though Alice has already told him she doesn't know.

Her father follows her as she rushes to the front door. She runs out into the street, panic powering her limbs as her heart thunders in her chest. There's a taste of sickness in her mouth. Her brother is in that house. Somehow, she just knows it.

'Toby!'

Before she can get to the Harrises' driveway, a policeman holds out an arm, blocking her from going any further. Suddenly there are police everywhere, some in uniform, others in plain clothes, and the sickness Alice had tasted in her mouth now tastes like something stronger. Fear.

When she turns to her father, she sees some of the other

neighbours already outside their homes, drawn as they were to the sound of the sirens. Paramedics are inside the Harris house, but Alice is unable to see past them. Someone is telling her to stand back, to get off the pavement, and she feels hands on her shoulders as her father pulls her back.

'Toby,' she says, quieter this time, the word barely audible.

'You don't know he's in there,' her father says. But she does. In her heart, she knows.

Alice can't be sure how long they've been standing out on the pavement; it could be ten minutes, it could be ten hours. Someone runs back to the ambulance. It's then that Alice sees Eve. She makes her way along the pavement from the entrance of the cul-de-sac, her walk picking up to a run when she sees the police cars and ambulance. She is wearing gym leggings and a tight workout top, her tanned skin slick with sweat in the fading light of the evening. She pulls the earbud from her right ear and stops on the pavement at her next-door neighbours', trying to catch her breath as she absorbs the scene unfolding in front of her. She freezes for a moment, stalled by the unexpectedness of everything. She doesn't seem aware of either Alice or Rob there, watching her.

Terrified back into life, she rushes to one of the officers standing outside her home. Something is said, though Alice doesn't hear what it is. But what follows is clear enough. The sound is blood-curdling, like something from a horror film, a roar like an animal, something Alice has never heard before. She watches as the officer catches Eve before she falls onto the driveway, crumpling forward, her screams piercing the evening air. Her body convulses as though she's having some kind of seizure, and a second officer rushes to help.

Alice stands rooted to the pavement, frozen with terror.

The front door of the Harrises' house opens. Eve screams

something inaudible, the words mashed and broken in a flurry of grief and panic and rage. She breaks away from the policeman who had held her, and when another uniformed officer appears on the doorstep, it takes two others to hold Eve back on the driveway.

Rob sees first what Alice doesn't. The officer blocks whatever or whoever is behind him, but she hears her father's sharp intake of breath, and the noise around her becomes bubbled for a moment, cutting her off from the rest of the world. A silence rises around her as her heart pauses. She sees Eve's mouth moving, the bones at her neck taut as she strains forward, shouting something that to Alice is now muted beneath her own fear.

Then she hears her father's voice, the whispered name contorted and muffled as though she's hearing it from underwater.

'Toby.'

Her brother appears from behind the officer in handcuffs, led towards a police car. Alice cries out his name. Nothing makes sense to her, but she knows that whatever they think he's done, they're wrong.

'Toby!' she cries for a second time, but he doesn't once look up from the pavement. He doesn't writhe to free himself from the hands holding him; he does nothing to protest his innocence. He allows himself to be led to the car, then put inside it, an officer's hand moving to the top of his head.

As her brother lowers himself into the back seat, Alice sees his mouth moving, but amid the tortured sound of Eve's screams, she can't make out the words. She looks at the open front door of the house and wonders at just what has happened beyond it. Chris left this morning for a work trip; she remembers Eve mentioning it yesterday. Dylan is in London. That means the only other person likely to be inside the house is Freya.

She looks back at the police car, but the windows are blackened and she can't see inside. When she returns her gaze to the house, her mother is standing in the doorway. She looks right at Alice, staring somehow through and beyond her, a woman broken, an empty hollow taking her place.

NINETEEN

JO

The room is small and sterile, with nothing but a table, a recording device and a cardboard cup of cold pale tea sitting between her and the two officers sitting opposite. She can't remember when she'd been given it, but at some point someone had handed her one of Rob's sweaters, the one she'd seen earlier that afternoon left hanging over the end of the banister waiting to be taken upstairs. Rob must have passed it to one of the policemen, she thinks.

She pulls the sleeves down over her hands, feeling cold to her bones, her thoughts consumed by the fact that her son has been issued prisoner's clothing, the shorts and hoodie he was wearing when she last saw him just a few hours ago bagged in clear plastic and taken away for analysis. They wouldn't let her see him after they took him from the house. The thought of him standing naked in front of strangers, stripped of his clothing and vulnerable beneath the eyes of these officers, sends a strange prickling sensation across Jo's body. He's just a child, she tells herself, but a second voice inside herself reminds her he is not. She pictures him standing over Freya's dead body, the hands at his sides slick with her blood. The paleness of his face. The whites of his eyes. It was the absence of him that had terrified her more than his presence.

'We can do this tomorrow if you'd prefer, Mrs Clarke.'

She shakes her head, declining the offer. Whatever needs to be done is better being done now, while her mind is still in the moment, while everything lives in her head as it was just a few hours ago, a living nightmare. There's no hiding from this, not for her and not for Toby. Not for Freya. A strange noise gargles in her throat at the thought of Eve's dead daughter. She thinks of Freya at the party on Saturday, young and beautiful and full of life, her whole future ahead of her. She feels a stabbing pain in her chest, a piece of her heart crumbling for Eve and Chris.

'Mrs Clarke?' the man prompts.

'I'm fine,' she tells them. 'I'd like to do this now.'

DI Paulson reaches for a file and takes out some paper and a pen.

'Can you take us back to earlier this evening, Mrs Clarke. You told one of our officers that Toby had come home early from work?'

'Yes, that's right.'

'Do you know why he was back early from his shift?'

'He...' Jo stops speaking, aware that anything she says now might make things worse for Toby. She contemplates telling a white lie: that the shop was quiet and they hadn't needed so many staff on at once. But she has never told lies. She has always believed that if you tell the truth, everything will be okay in the end. Honesty will see a person through. What a naïve and hopeless expectation that seems to her now.

They will find out one way or another, she thinks – if not from her, then from one of Toby's colleagues at the hardware store. They'll likely speak to everyone he had contact with over the past twenty-four hours, and if the police know she's lied, she might inadvertently make things even worse for him.

'There was an altercation with a customer.'

'An altercation?' the male officer repeats, an eyebrow raised.

'A disagreement. Nothing physical,' Jo adds quickly, regretting the words as soon as they've left her. She doesn't need to put ideas in their heads. They'll already have too many assumptions about her son that just aren't true.

'What sort of a disagreement?'

'I don't know exactly. He spoke to his sister about it, not me.'

'But you know that something happened with a customer at work, and that was the reason he'd been sent home early?'

She nods. 'Apparently a customer was rude to him.'

Jo's hands are resting under her thighs. Her fingers dig now into the backs of her legs, her rising frustration with the detectives making her bite her tongue to stop her saying something that might make things worse. Does it matter that Toby argued with a customer? She sees no connection between that and Freya's death.

'And how did he seem when he got back from work?'

'A bit quiet. He was obviously upset about something.'

'Is that normal for your son, Mrs Clarke... for him to be quiet?'

'Not abnormal,' she says, wondering where this line of questioning is leading her. 'I mean, he's never been loud or boisterous. He keeps himself to himself.'

Wrong thing to say, she thinks. She watches DI Paulson scribble something on her notes before glancing at her colleague. Jo knows what message the look silently sends. *It's always the quiet ones.*

'Where did Toby go when he got home from work, Mrs Clarke?'

'He went upstairs to his bedroom.'

'And did you see him again after that? Before you went over to the Harris house?'

Jo nods. 'I went upstairs to his room to see how he was, to see whether he wanted to talk to me about what had happened.

He didn't, so I didn't stay long. I could see he just wanted to be left alone.'

'And what time was that, when you went up to his bedroom?'

'Just before eight p.m. I remember because as I was coming back downstairs, the theme tune for *MasterChef* was coming from the living room where I'd left the television on.'

'Talk us through the next hour or so,' the male officer instructs.

Jo obliges. She omits the details about Eve's Facebook post, instead telling the officers that she'd spent some time scrolling social media and watching television. They ask where Alice and Rob were, and she fills them in on the details: that Alice was in her bedroom and Rob had gone to play squash with his brother, as he did every Monday evening. She doesn't tell them about her overheard conversation between Rob and Eve, or Freya's behaviour towards Rob on the driveway, not wanting to offer them further ammunition against her family.

The more she talks, the less real everything becomes. Her son is at home, upstairs in his bedroom, lying on his bed and scrolling his phone. He's playing a game online, his headset attached as he chats with his friends. He is out in the real world somewhere, on the brink of an adult life that holds brilliant and countless opportunities, all his for the taking.

Reality comes crashing down upon her as the door opens and a uniformed officer appears.

'DC Worth,' he says, addressing the officer sitting opposite Jo. 'Can I have a word?'

'Can I see him?' she asks DI Paulson when the two men have left the room.

The detective shakes her head. 'Not tonight. This morning,' she corrects herself.

Jo glances at the clock on the far wall. It is 1.15 a.m. She wonders whether Toby is warm enough in his cell. Whether he's been given a cup of tea or something to eat.

'Is Eve here? Eve Harris. Freya's mum.'

DI Paulson eyes her with contempt. She is guilty by default, Jo thinks. She raised this boy, this young man who now sits in a cell not far from here, accused of murder. A chill passes through her, snaking from her neck down to her legs. She doesn't want a single part of her to believe it could be true, yet she can't erase from her mind the image of Toby standing there next to Freya's lifeless body.

The detective hasn't answered her question. She can't imagine Eve *is* here, though she doesn't know where else she would be. Where does the next of kin of a murder victim get taken? Where does a murder victim get taken? Where would Freya be now, and are her parents with her? She can't imagine the pain Eve must be in. She wants to reach out to her, to call her, to go and see her, but she knows she can do none of those things.

The other officer returns, and the statement is written up. Jo is given it to read over, to agree that she's happy with what's been documented before she signs it. When she's taken out to the reception area at the front of the station, Rob is there waiting for her.

'Where is he? Have you seen him?' she asks.

He shakes his head. He looks exhausted. Broken. He seems to have aged a decade since she saw him just a couple of hours ago. 'Christ, Jo. What are we going to do?'

The question sails over her head. She was hoping he would be the one with the answer to that. 'Freya,' is all she manages to say, the girl's name barely a whisper. 'Have you seen Eve yet?'

Rob shakes his head, but she can tell he's lying. He doesn't want to tell her what he's seen. What he may have heard said about their family.

'I just don't understand. Toby...' But he trails off, unable to form the words.

'Where's Alice?' Jo asks. She feels ashamed now that she has only just considered her daughter, her thoughts consumed with Toby.

'She's in the car. She couldn't stand being in this place any longer.'

Jo turns to the bored-looking desk sergeant.

'When can I see my son?'

'Your son will be able to contact you later this morning,' he tells her, annoyingly speaking through Rob rather than addressing her directly. 'If he wants to,' he adds, and the extra clause rankles.

'What does that mean?'

'Your son has said he doesn't want to have contact with either of you.'

Jo feels the statement like a burn. Beside her, Rob's features have hardened.

'He doesn't mean it,' Jo says through gritted teeth. 'He'll change his mind. I'll wait.'

She throws her coat onto one of the plastic chairs fixed to the waiting room floor.

Rob places a hand on her arm, but she pulls away from his touch. She won't be persuaded, not by him or anyone else. Toby won't sleep a wink tonight, so why should she? Why should any of them?

And he can't mean it when he says he doesn't want contact with either of them. He's probably been terrified into silence.

'You need to rest,' Rob says quietly, turning his head from the officer. 'You're no use to Toby in this state.'

'I'm not in a "state".' Jo settles onto a chair. 'See you tomorrow. Go home... be there for Alice. I'll call you in the morning.'

'Jo, please.'

But Rob knows her well enough to know that once her mind

is made up, no one can change it, not even him. He sits beside her and leans in, reaching an arm around her shoulder. 'Just give me two minutes outside,' he whispers into her ear.

She waits for him to get up before following him out to the car park.

'I'll call Leon as soon as I get home.'

'It's two a.m.,' she reminds him.

'I don't care. I pay him enough.'

'He's a corporate lawyer.'

'But he'll know someone who can help us.'

Jo wonders whether her husband listened to a single word that has been spoken over those past few hours. Fingerprints. Motive. Circumstances. Their son had Freya's blood all over him. There was no one else in the house.

'Why won't he talk?' she asks him.

'I don't know.'

'But if he didn't do it—'

'If?' Rob's eyes narrow. He looks affronted, the fact that she has any doubt about their son's innocence assaulting him like a slap to the face.

'I'm not saying he did it deliberately,' she protests. 'But if they'd argued... if things had got out of hand...'

Her husband is looking at her as though he doesn't recognise her. 'I don't believe this. You think he killed her?'

It's easy for him to be this certain, she thinks. He wasn't the one who saw Toby there in that hallway with Freya's body. Perhaps if he had been, he might now share her doubts. Surely he must realise it's killing her to think of their own son in this way.

'I think anything can happen in a split second, even the most unthinkable thing.'

Rob shakes his head in disgust. 'It's unthinkable to me that you'd even consider him capable of this.'

'I'm here for him, aren't I? I'm not going anywhere.'

He scoffs before turning away, leaving Jo alone on the police station steps. In the space of just a few hours, their life is unrecognisable. How does anyone move on from something like this? she wonders. How does anyone ever get over the pain of losing a child?

She hears the echo of Eve's scream inside her head, the agony of the sound haunting her. She wishes she could change the workings of her brain, but she can't. She knows what she saw. The image will haunt her. Toby's silence will taunt her like a past sin that can't be undone. The guilt will eat her from the inside out, but she will have to live with that. Because she can see no explanation other than that their son is guilty.

TWENTY

ALICE

Alice sits in the car and waits for her parents. She doesn't know where they're going to go; as far as she knows, their home is being searched, and she has no idea how long it'll be until they're allowed to return. They don't have any relatives who live locally: her uncle Dan is an hour away, and her parents aren't going to want to be that far from Toby. *She* doesn't want to be that far from Toby.

The same issue of distance applies to her auntie on her mother's side, who moved to Birmingham a few years ago when her husband got a promotion with the company he works for. The only neighbours they've ever been that close with are the Harrises, but that relationship has been imploded by whatever happened behind that front door just a few hours ago.

She knows she can't contact any of the girls from school. She already lied to Amy about being unwell this evening, and she knows that as soon as the news of what has happened gets out, everyone will hate her. She thinks of that TikTok reel. Scarlet may have been the instigator, but none of her other so-called friends seem to have done much to try to stop it being shared. They already thought so little of her. Now, after this, everyone will hate her.

But she no longer cares what those girls think of her. All she can hope is that other people see things as she does: that Toby didn't do this. He isn't capable of what the police are claiming.

Her father doesn't speak when he comes back to the car.

'Where's Mum?'

'She waiting to see Toby.'

'How long will that be?'

'I don't know.'

They drive home in silence, the awfulness of everything sitting between them like an invisible ghoul, uninvited and feared intensely. All Alice can think is that there's been a mistake, and she knows she won't let that feeling fall from her. Toby will be proved innocent. The police will be proved wrong.

When they get home, the first thing she notices is the police tape strung across the entrance of the Harrises' driveway. She senses her father turning away from it, as though if he doesn't see it there, it doesn't really exist. Every window of their own home is lit, the lights throughout the house turned on. When they get to the door, they're greeted by a uniformed officer who had watched the car pull onto the driveway. There are police everywhere. Alice can hear them upstairs, scouring Toby's bedroom: opening drawers and looking beneath the bed, bagging his laptop and his clothing. A younger female officer has been stationed by the door, presumably to await their arrival home. Alice notices her offer a small smile, but only when Rob's back is turned. This is what she will get now, Alice imagines. Simpering looks of awkward pity. Either that, or she will be shunned entirely.

'Can we go into the living room?' she asks.

The officer nods. 'We're finished downstairs.'

When she goes into the living room, Rob stays in the hall-way. She senses him close the door so that whatever conversation is about to take place is kept private between him and the officer. Alice crosses the room and sits on the window seat. Her father had it built in when she was about eight years old, when she loved to sit there and read, always keeping an eye for Freya or Dylan coming over to them from across the road. If she closes her eyes and focuses, she can see them again now, small and innocent – Freya's skinny limbs racing to her door, Dylan with his messy mop of dark hair – just as they had once been.

Now she sits at the window and looks at the Harris house. A crime scene. There are forensic officers over there still, white-clad figures moving back and forth below the street lights, the road resembling a film set. None of what has been said makes sense. There must be some kind of mistake. Freya can't be dead: she saw her earlier, over at the house. She wishes so much now that it could have been under different circumstances. That reel doesn't matter any more. The university application doesn't matter. She wishes they could just go back and rewrite it all.

She had been so angry, so filled with rage that she'd thought it possible she could wring Freya's neck if she got her hands on her. The betrayal of the university application had been bad enough, but together with that TikTok post and the way Freya had flirted with her dad, it had felt like poison running through her bloodstream. She can't recall ever feeling that angry towards anyone or anything. Now, the memory of its intensity leaves her numb. They're saying her brother killed Freya, that he hit her over the head with something and now he's been arrested for murder. But Toby didn't do that. He couldn't have.

She wonders when their mother is going to be able to see him. Alice has no idea what happens after a person is arrested. Maybe neither of her parents will get to see him. He's eighteen now; she imagines they're probably able to interview him without a parent present. Is he in a cell on his own? Possibly even worse, is he in a cell with someone else? She hopes that wherever he is he isn't scared, and the thought leaves her feeling six years old again, terrified of the monsters hiding under her bed.

It occurs to her that tomorrow – later today, even – it will be so much more difficult to keep themselves from acknowledging the house across the road. They are never going to be able to avoid it, or to escape what has happened tonight. Not only that, but there will be other people around. It won't be like this dark hour in the middle of the night. Neighbours will be out from their houses. Rumours will be circulated. How can they stay here now, on this quiet cul-de-sac where nothing ever happens but everyone knows each other too well?

She hears her father's voice close to the living room door, still talking to the officer in the hallway.

'We can stay here tonight then?' she hears him ask.

When the officer tells him yes, Alice feels relief settle in her chest. She doesn't want to leave here. She doesn't want to be in anyone else's home or to have to go anywhere people will ask questions. All she really wants is to go back twenty-four hours... forty-eight hours... ten years. Any time when Toby was here and not locked in a prison cell accused of something she knows could never be true.

'Alice.'

Her father moves through the room quickly, heading towards her, but when he reaches her he stops sharply, as though he doesn't now know what to say or do. She tries to remember the last time they hugged one another, but she can't recall it. When was the last time she'd hugged her brother? Whenever it was, it was too long ago. She wishes she could put her arms around him now. Wishes she could tell him she loves him. That she knows the police are wrong about whatever they think happened.

'What are they saying about him?' she asks. 'What are they saying he did?'

She knows, but she needs to hear it from one of her parents, and with her mother not here, her dad is it. The voice of truth. The irony of it, she thinks.

'Freya was hit with an ornament,' he tells her, the words choked on tiredness and emotion. 'That elephant Eve kept on the hallway table.'

Alice can't bring herself to turn and look him in the eye. It feels that if she does, all of this becomes true, and for the moment she wants to cling to the possibility that she might have got something wrong somewhere, that a switch with be flicked and someone will leap in front of the window and shout 'Surprise!' at her through the glass. A sick joke.

'But Toby didn't do that,' she says. 'He couldn't have.'

She expects her father to say something in return, to agree with her, but he doesn't. Instead, he drops onto one of the sofas, defeated.

'You should go to bed,' he says. 'Try to get some sleep.'

Alice looks back to the window. As if she could sleep now. She doesn't think she'll be able to find any rest ever again.

It's exactly what she didn't want to do, but once the tears start, she can't stop them. Her father gets up from the sofa and comes over to the window seat, dropping to his knees in front of her and putting his arms around her, pulling her to him. She feels herself tense at his embrace.

'Why didn't you stop her?' she sobs.

'Stop who?'

'Freya, on the driveway. You know I saw it all. You didn't do anything to stop what she was doing.'

There's a moment of silence in which her father keeps her held close to his chest. Alice thinks he's about to react with anger, but he doesn't.

'She was trying to provoke a reaction,' he says eventually. 'It was what she wanted. I wasn't going to play the game.'

'What game?'

'That was all it was to her. Girls... *people* like Freya... it's about the attention. That was all it was. She wanted to taunt me. She wanted to see how far she could push me. She's just like...'

But he doesn't finish the sentence. He doesn't need to. Alice knows what he was about to say. *She's just like her mother*.

TWENTY-ONE

JO

At just before 8.30 a.m., Rob walks through the doors of the police station. Jo is still sitting on the waiting room chair, his sweater spread over her knees like a blanket. Despite the heat outside, the air conditioning manages to make the station feel cold. She feels sick with tiredness, but even more so at the not-knowing what is going on with Toby. The desk sergeant has barely spoken to her, and though she saw one of the arresting officers a few hours ago, he too refused to tell her anything more than that she needed to wait.

She notices that when her husband looks at her, he barely makes eye contact. He hates her, she thinks. He hates the fact that she can even consider it a possibility that their son might have killed a person. That he has killed the daughter of one of their friends.

He sits on the chair next to her and hands her one of the canvas bags she keeps for shopping. Inside there's a bottle of water, a banana and a couple of cereal bars.

'You need to eat something.'

Jo unscrews the bottle and drinks two thirds of the water.

She rejects the food, the mere thought of it making her stomach churn. 'Is Alice okay?'

Rob nods. Jo knows it's a lie. Alice and Toby are as close as twins can be; they always have been, ever since they were babies. This will have broken her.

'You need to go home and get some sleep,' Rob says. 'Look at you. You're exhausted.'

'I want to see my son.'

'*Our* son.'

Jo watches Rob get up and go to the front desk. She over-hears snippets of conversation as he asks for an update, wanting to know what the procedure is now in terms of questioning. When he comes back to her, he shakes his head.

'It's pointless waiting,' he tells her. 'It could be another forty-eight hours before we know what's happening.'

'Forty-eight hours? Surely that's not right.'

'Look, I've spoken to Leon and he's trying to get something sorted for us. He said he knows someone in Cardiff. I'm waiting for him to call me back.' He lowers his voice as a uniformed officer walks through the reception area. 'Come home and get some sleep. Please. Alice will be glad to see you. I'll have heard back from Leon by then and we can get things moving with whoever this solicitor is. You can't do anything here.'

Jo watches the uniformed officer tap his ID on a scanner before a buzzer clicks and the door unlocks to let him through to the station's holding area. Toby is somewhere through that door, possibly less than fifteen metres away, yet she's unable to see or talk to him. She just wants to know that he's okay. She just wants to tell him that everything is going to be all right.

But she'd be lying to him, she knows that. Lying about something catastrophic, life-altering. Right now, she sees no way that anything can ever be made right again.

She stands, finally yielding to Rob's persuasion that she can achieve nothing here, for now at least. She follows him out to the car park, a distance kept between them as they walk to the car. Neither of them speaks as they pull away from the police station, and by the time they reach home, the silence has trapped them inside a bubble Jo can feel sucking the air from her lungs. She stays in the passenger seat when he opens the driver's door, not wanting to move. The knowledge that the Harrises' house is directly behind her makes her feel like she's drowning.

They should have moved. Last year, when Rob started talking about downsizing, she should have just let him do it there and then. If they'd been gone from here, none of this would have happened. Toby would be in his bedroom or out with his friends. Freya would still be alive, both families intact.

'Jo,' Rob prompts her, sticking his head back into the car. 'Come on.'

She gets out and closes the door, keeping her head lowered. She's grateful it's still early, though not nearly early enough; there are curtains twitching at the house next door to the Harrises', and she feels eyes on her as she hurries into her home.

She stands in the hallway and feels her heart thunder in her chest. The house looks nothing like it did yesterday.

But that's it, she tells herself. Nothing will ever look the same again.

'That was the press,' Rob says, locking the front door.

'What was?'

'There was a man across the street, just down from Eve and Chris's. Didn't you see him?'

She hadn't. She'd been too focused on getting inside without having to look at the house. How are any of them going to leave again? By the end of today, everyone is going to know what's happened. They will all think their son is a murderer.

At the thought, Alice appears at the top of the stairs. She stands there like an apparition, gaunt in her light-coloured dressing gown, face pale and washed out. Sleep-deprived, as they all are.

'Alice.'

Her daughter rushes down the stairs and flings herself into Jo's arms in a way she hasn't done since she was about ten years old. When she sobs, Jo does too, and the two of them cry together, Rob standing silently behind them.

'Have you seen him?' Alice asks.

Jo shakes her head.

'But when?' Alice asks, looking desperately from her mother to her father. 'Why won't they let you see him?'

'It's a bit more complicated than that,' Jo says, but she doesn't want to explain any further. She doesn't want to admit to Alice that her own son doesn't want to see her or their father. 'You need to eat something, love,' she says, taking Alice by the hand.

'I'm not hungry.' But when Jo leads her to the kitchen, Alice doesn't protest.

Jo makes them all tea and toast, though she knows none of them are likely to touch it. How can any of them eat while Toby is locked up at that police station?

They stay together for a while in the kitchen, though they barely speak to one another. A realisation seems to have settled over them all that the life they had known is gone. Yet nobody wants to acknowledge it aloud, to accept it as fact in front of the others. Rob persuades Jo to go upstairs to get some rest. She manages to sleep, but it's for little more than an hour. When she wakes, she feels guilty for having been able to fall asleep at all. The reality of the past few hours strikes her in the face, making her wish she could go back to sleep and wake again to find things different, everything back as it was. Thick, silent tears roll from her eyes. Toby. Her beautiful, kind boy. The intelligent, thoughtful child everyone had loved.

She pictures the smashed glass on Eve and Chris's patio on

Saturday night. Her son's reddened face following that unheard exchange between him and Freya. She sees the ornamental elephant at the foot of Eve's staircase, Freya's body lying lifeless just feet away.

She shoves back the duvet, sweating in the late-morning heat. The bedroom window is open; outside in the garden, a bird chirrups incessantly, its cheerful call in stark contrast to the hopeless dull grief Jo feels in her chest. She yanks the window shut, blocking out the sound. Through the glass, she looks out at the garden. She sees the ghosts of the children the twins once were playing on the lawn, their tiny frames darting in between the tree trunks as they chase each other. She sees a paddling pool and a trampoline, balloon arches and birthday banners; a hundred memories racing back in full colour and sound and life. She hears their tinkling childhood laughs, the sound flung out from the recesses of her brain.

'Jo.'

She turns at Rob's voice.

'I was going to wake you. I've just spoken with Michael Chapman.'

'The solicitor?'

'We can go to his office in Cardiff this afternoon. Get showered. I'll make you some lunch.'

He leaves without waiting for a response. Jo stares at the space he's left. She doesn't blame him. He wasn't there last night. He didn't see what she saw.

She stands for too long beneath water that's too hot, purging herself until her skin is bright red and raw. Everything she does now, she does with thoughts of Toby. Has he been able to get any sleep, as she has? Will they allow him to take a shower?

She dresses and blow-dries her hair quickly, pulling it back into a messy knot. When she goes downstairs, Rob has made some chicken salad wraps that are waiting for her on the kitchen table. The smell of the cooked meat makes her stomach flip.

'Where's Alice?' she asks.

'In her room.'

'Does she want to come with us?'

Rob shoots her a look. 'I don't think that's a good idea, do you?'

'I just thought she might prefer it to being on her own.'

Rob goes to the sink and stands with his back to her as he washes the things he's used while making lunch. The food on his plate sits untouched, and when Jo looks at it, she feels sick to her stomach. She can't remember when she last ate anything.

'You need to eat,' he says, seemingly with eyes in the back of his head.

'I wonder if Toby's been given anything to eat yet.'

She sees Rob stop, the dirty plate in his hand poised above the bubbles that rise like a mountain from the sink. He's always used too much washing-up liquid, one of the annoying habits she picked up on when they first lived together after university.

She waits for him to say something, but instead he continues to wash the dishes. Once he's finished, he comes to the table and picks up the wrap from his plate.

'That reporter's still outside,' he tells her.

'Great.'

'He's not going to go away. We need to make sure Alice knows not to say a word to him.'

Jo feels as though she's been transported to an alternative universe, one where this conversation should make some sort of sense. She watches Rob as he bites the end from his wrap, feeling what she knows is an irrational rage at his ability to digest food. She gets a waft of the chicken again, and the nausea in her stomach rises to her throat.

'Have you already spoken to her about it?' she asks.

'No. I wanted to talk to you first.'

She supposes she should be grateful for that. He still wants to consult with her on their children's well-being; or on Alice's, at least.

'Rob. What I said about Toby. I just want him to tell the truth about what happened.'

Rob's chair scrapes across the kitchen tiles loudly and sharply as he shoves it back to stand. 'I'll go and talk to her,' he says.

Jo gets up to follow him, but he turns to stop her.

'Please, Jo. Just let me speak to Alice, warn her about that fucking reporter. We need to get going or we're going to be late.'

'The solicitor is going to ask us questions,' Jo says quickly. 'So many of them. About us... about them... our relationships. Are we going to be honest about all of them?'

Rob gives her a look she's unable to read. Over twenty years together, but he's still capable of leaving her feeling like she doesn't know him. She thinks of him and Eve arguing on the doorstep: the abruptness of his tone, the desperation in her voice. She sees again the way Freya flirted with him by the car. He didn't do anything to stop her. Why didn't he do anything to stop her?

She doesn't want to believe that he could lie to her in any of the ways the past few days suggest; she doesn't want to believe it any more than she wants to believe her son might have lashed out in a moment of red-mist anger. Yet here they are, and the doubt has crept in, insidious.

TWENTY-TWO

ALICE

While her parents are out meeting with the solicitor who will defend her brother, Alice sees Dylan arrive home. The man her father warned her about earlier, the one he claims is a reporter, is there to capture the moment, making no attempt to hide the fact he's taking photographs of the family. Eve shouts something at him as she climbs from the driver's seat of her Mercedes, but from behind the closed front window of the living room, Alice can't make out what she says. Chris is presumably back home from his work trip now too, although Alice has yet to see him. She wonders what she might say to any one of them when she encounters them out in the street. It's going to happen sooner or later, and she knows they'll have to move from this house. There's no chance of them being able to stay here now that everyone believes Toby is a murderer, although a part of Alice thinks the worst thing they could do would be to leave. Leaving would look like guilt: a silent, slink-away-in-the-night admission of her brother's crime. But her brother hasn't committed a crime, and she needs to find a way to prove it.

Dylan gets out of the passenger seat and hurries to the front door, trying to avoid the attention of the reporter. She sees his mop of dark hair and lanky frame as he ducks from the car, keeping his face turned from the street. Alice wishes she could go across the road to see him, though she knows she never wants to go into that house again. She doesn't want to be in this house either. Every memory, recent and distant, is now tainted with what has happened. Nothing will ever look as it did before.

She reaches for her phone where it's slipped down the side of the chair and goes to WhatsApp, looking for Dylan's name.

Are you okay? she types. The words stare back at her from the screen, an insult. She deletes them. Tries again. *Are you home yet?* No. That won't work either. She can't act towards him as though nothing has happened, like everything is the way it was when they last texted each other.

She taps out words and deletes them... taps out more words then deletes them too. And then she writes the only word that seems remotely appropriate.

Sorry.

That's it. She presses send before she has a chance to change her mind and delete again, then she waits for the two ticks and then waits for them to turn blue. They do so quickly. She imagines Dylan sitting in his bedroom, trying to avoid the downstairs of his house, which was only this morning still a crime scene, for ever now the place where his sister's life was ended. She pictures him sitting with the door closed, not wanting to see Freya's bedroom just along the landing. He opens Alice's message. Reads the single-word apology.

She feels a flutter of panic in her chest. She wishes that she could unsend the message, but it's too late now: he's seen it. She imagines how she might feel if this whole situation was reversed; if it had been Freya who had killed Toby. No, she corrects herself. If it had been Freya who had been *accused* of killing her brother. How might she react to the word *sorry* being sent as though it might make everything better?

She waits for a reply, but one doesn't come. She clicks her phone locked and shoves it back down the side of the chair, where she can try to ignore it. Eventually, after sitting there for what feels like hours, she begins to drift in and out of sleep. It brings harrowing nightmares and a raging temperature, and she is jolted awake several times by images of Freya's dead body, and her brother beaten up and broken on the floor of a prison cell.

After ninety minutes of broken and fretful slumber, she wakes up crying. There is cold sweat running down her spine, though her skin feels unnaturally warm. Her heart is racing, beating frighteningly fast. She gulps air as she tries to control her breathing, reminding herself that it's only a nightmare. That it isn't real. But when she looks out of the window and sees the Harrises' house looming opposite, she's reminded that every-thing is real.

Her thoughts run straight to Toby. Something must have happened to him at the police station. They have a sixth sense, each of them knowing when the other is upset or in danger. She feels his pain as intensely as she feels her own. He is drowning, alone, and her lungs fill with the enormity of it, the pressure of his helplessness and her desperation pulling her under.

She scrabbles about in the chair for her phone. She remem-bers now messaging Dylan, but when she checks WhatsApp, there is still no reply. She pulls up her mother's mobile number and calls it, and Jo answers within two rings.

'Mum. Have you heard from the police station? Is Toby okay?'

'What's happened?' Jo asks. 'Alice, calm down.'

But Alice can't calm down. She can't breathe. Visions from her nightmare are still in her eyeline, the images of Toby's beaten body taunting her over and over, like staring at a light for too long and then seeing a continuation of bright shapes every time she closes her eyes.

'We're on our way home,' Jo tells her. 'Just stay where you are, we won't be long.'

Alice hangs up. She needs to go to the toilet, but she doesn't want to move from the chair. This is where she stays now, her focus never far from the house across the street. She set up camp here once the police finally left; she has barely eaten, only getting up to go to the toilet. She sleeps in stolen snatches, when her brain grows too weary to keep her body awake, and when she wakes, she feels a guilt tear through her that she could find even a moment's peace when her friend is dead and her brother is incarcerated. An imagined scenario plays out in front of her: Toby walking into the Harrises' house through the back door, in the same way they've done since they were kids, Freya waiting for him in the kitchen. There's an argument between them. Freya starts it. Freya always starts it. But this time, when the row continues and he follows her from the kitchen into the hallway, it's Toby who ends it.

She snaps herself from the thought, not wanting to let it linger.

Time passes, but she has no idea how long. She sees her father's car pull up onto the driveway, and she watches her parents get out tentatively, paranoid about who might be watching them go into the house.

'Alice?' her mother calls as she opens the front door.

'I'm in here.'

Her mother rushes to her, puts her arms around her and pulls her close. It is only now that Alice is aware of her body trembling, her limbs shaking as Jo tries to hold her still.

'Are you okay, love?'

'I had a dream about Toby. He was hurt and...' She can't finish the sentence. She doesn't want to share the awful details with her mother, not when she knows Jo is already so broken.

'What's happened?'

Alice hadn't heard her father come into the room. She doesn't turn to him, keeping her face towards the window, unable to pull herself from the scene of the crime even when enclosed in her mother's embrace. It is unthinkable to her that she and her father stood at this window and watched as police officers and paramedics filled the street just a little less than twenty-four hours ago. She would never have believed that life could so quickly change beyond recognition.

'Nothing,' she says quietly. 'Just a bad dream, that's all.'

Her mother's body loosens from hers at the words, their irony hanging in the air between them all. If only, Alice thinks. If only all of this were no more than a bad dream.

She pulls herself from her mother's grip. 'Sorry. I didn't mean to panic you. What did the solicitor say?'

'He seems confident he can get Toby to speak to him.'

'You still don't want to let me try?' Alice says.

'It's not a case of us not wanting you to speak to him,' her father tells her. 'Toby's refusing to see any of us.'

Alice feels the words with a pain in her chest, a sharp twist that catches at her breath. She knows her mother feels the same pain.

'When did you last eat something?' Jo asks her.

Alice can't remember. She can't remember when she last used the toilet or when she last drank any water. All she can remember is sitting and waiting, sitting and waiting.

Jo stands from where she's been crouched in front of her. 'I'll make her something to eat,' she says to Rob, as though Alice isn't there. 'Would you like anything?'

Rob declines the offer. Alice watches her mother leave the living room to head to the kitchen. Her father moves closer to the chair and puts a hand on her shoulder.

'We're going to get through this somehow, love.'

'How?'

Her father has no response for this. Alice can't bring herself to look at him. He probably thinks her distance is a reaction to everything that's happened, that the shock is keeping her detached, that any show of emotion might break her. But really it's that she can't stop thinking that her father's involvement with Eve is somehow the cause of Freya's death, because there's no doubt in Alice's mind that Freya knew something. She'd been going to tell her something, just before Eve had burst into the room. The game her father had accused Freya of play-ing... could that have been an attempt to hurt Eve with the secret she'd uncovered? It was the sort of twisted thing Freya would have done.

There's no doubt in her mind that the scene played out in her head, over and over on repeat like a recurring nightmare, is a lie. Toby and Freya arguing... Toby lashing out in a moment of rage. It didn't happen; she knows it in her heart. She knows her brother better than anyone. She feels his pain now, piercing her skin like a thousand needles. He isn't a killer.

Yesterday, just before their lives were upended, she'd been about to ask her father about what she'd overheard at the party. The sirens had interrupted them. But there's no distraction from it now.

'What's going on between you and Eve?'

The hand slips heavily from her shoulder. Guilt, she thinks. Already, so soon into the conversation.

'Dad,' she prompts, turning to him. 'I heard the two of you talking on Saturday, at the party. Don't try to fob me off, please.'

'There's nothing going on between Eve and me.' He looks her in the eye when he says it, defiant and resolute. Of course, Alice thinks, he's not lying, is he? He can do this now; he can look at her and say these words, because they're probably the truth. There may have been something between them, but there wouldn't be now, would there?

'Then what were you talking about in the hallway? I heard you telling her she just needed to leave it. Leave what?'

'God, I don't know, Alice. We'd all had a few drinks. It was nothing. I don't even remember now.'

'Lies.' She meets his eye, challenging him to deny it again. She waits for him to reprimand her for speaking to him in such a way, but he doesn't.

'Alice, I don't know what you think you heard, but now isn't the time for this. Don't go making things worse for anyone than they already are.'

They hear Jo in the hallway and both fall silent as she walks into the living room. The smile she wears is forced, painted on with the sense of duty that comes with being Mum. The one who holds the rest of them together.

It can't and doesn't last for long. Jo looks from Alice to Rob as the veneer quickly cracks.

'What do we do now?' she asks.

Alice watches her father go to her mother, reaching out to hold her, as though she might collapse should he not break her fall.

'I don't know, love,' he says softly, speaking the words into her hair. 'I don't know.'

Alice observes the scene silently, trying to squash the resentment that rises in her chest. She's certain of one thing above all else. Her father is lying.

TWENTY-THREE

JO

Alice is up in her bedroom, but Jo knows she won't be sleeping. It seems impossible to believe that any of them will ever sleep again. Every time her phone makes a noise, she makes a grab for it, never leaving it more than a couple of feet from reach. Rob is in the shower when Michael Chapman's name flashes up on her screen. She answers quickly; she's been waiting for his call all evening, wondering what happened when he went to the police station to see Toby. She thought she would have heard from him by now. She still hasn't had a call from her son, and the more time that passes, the more she begins to fear that he is hurt in some way, injured by someone else at the station, or – an even worse thought – he's done something to hurt himself.

'Jo. Sorry to be calling so late.'

She doesn't care how late he rings. He can call her at two in the morning as long as he's giving her answers. Providing it makes her feel some kind of progress is being made.

'Have you seen Toby? Did he speak to you?'

'Yes and no.'

She feels a partial swell of relief grow in her chest, a rising hope that Toby might come to trust this man and confide in him. But the small bubble is quickly burst at the thought of what he might eventually have to say. Of what he might confess to.

'Jo, are you still there?'

'Yes. Sorry.'

She doesn't want to ask, too fearful to know what one-sided exchange might have taken place, and yet she knows she must hear it.

'I've advised him to plead guilty.'

The words seem to thunder past Jo's brain, echoing somewhere in the recesses of her head. They bounce between her ears, losing order and cohesion, making no sense.

'It's the best thing for him, under the current circumstances. He won't speak to any of the detectives, and he didn't say a word to me either. We know the evidence is stacked against him, Jo. He was the only person present, and his fingerprints were all over the murder weapon as well as on Freya's body. An argument was reportedly heard by a neighbour shortly before the estimated time of Freya's death. The fact that Toby didn't call for help and called you instead... It doesn't help him, I'm afraid. I'm sorry, I appreciate this must be difficult to hear. But like I told Toby, if he pleads guilty, we can try to run with mitigating circumstances. I need to know everything, Jo, any pressures Toby has been under recently, anything that may have been going on at home.'

Jo feels stung. Michael's words imply a suspicion that there may have been something going on among the family, something so terrible that it might have caused Toby to act in a way completely out of character. Her son isn't a violent person.

'What do you mean, anything that may have been going on at home?'

'I don't know. I just need you to think of everything. Anything might help.'

There's an uncomfortable pause in which Jo feels her

resentment grow. This man is supposed to be helping them, yet he's already decided her son is guilty, and now he's implying that she might be in some way to blame for it. She realises the irony of her thoughts. She too has found it difficult to doubt Toby's guilt.

And if she can barely believe in it, why should anyone else?

Rob appears in the doorway, hair still wet from the shower. 'Who is it?' he mouths.

Jo moves the phone from her face and puts it on loud-speaker. 'It's Michael,' she tells him. 'Sorry, Rob's here now.'

He comes into the room, closer to the phone so that Michael can hear him. 'Have you seen Toby?'

'Yes, I've seen him. But as I told Jo, he's still refusing to speak to anyone.'

'He'll have had the right to a phone call, won't he?' Jo asks. 'Why hasn't he called us?'

She doesn't expect Michael to be able to answer the question. As far as any of them know, Toby has refused his phone call. Jo had thought she'd be the first person he would want to contact, but his ongoing silence is crushing her hopes that he might confide in her about what happened last night. Does he blame her in some way? she wonders. She's no idea what she might have done wrong, but if there is something, she would rather he talked to her about it. She wishes he would just talk to someone. Anything would be better than this silence.

'No one can stay silent for ever,' Michael tells her.

Jo feels a desperation she has never felt before. She needs to see her son. She needs to hold him and tell him that somehow everything is going to be okay. Whatever happened, she is here for him. She will find a way to help him through it.

But it would all be lies. She has no idea where they could even start to work through any of this. And what about Eve? The pain she and Chris must be enduring is unimaginable. Life as the Harris family has known it is over for ever. Two families' lives were ended last night.

'I'm sorry,' Michael says. 'I did what I could today, but I don't think going in all guns blazing is the way to get Toby to open up to me. I've advised him that his case will be helped immeasurably now if he speaks to someone.'

'So he's still not uttered a word to anyone,' Rob reiterates. 'Not even to one of the officers at the station? Another inmate?'

The last word makes Jo's stomach flip. She doesn't even know whether people under arrest get to communicate while being held at a station. Perhaps he's spent the past twenty-four hours alone, having seen no one other than the police and the solicitor. Toby doesn't belong to that world. If he's charged and moved to a holding prison, she is fearful for his safety. Her son isn't streetwise; he didn't grow up in a city and has never belonged to a gang. She's not aware of him even having had to deal with any bullying. She's not sure he has the strength of character needed to survive life in prison.

'Not yet,' Michael tells them. 'But he will. Give it time.'

'He doesn't have time,' Rob says sharply.

'Is he going to be moved to a prison?' Jo asks, casting her husband a glance. This isn't Michael's fault. They need his help and, according to Leon, Michael is the best around.

'If he's charged, yes.'

'If?' Jo repeats, raising an eyebrow.

There's a pause at Michael's end of the call. 'When he's charged,' he corrects himself.

Jo looks down at the tiled floor and bites her lip. She doesn't want the solicitor to hear her get upset. She doesn't even want to get upset in front of her husband.

'Will he be sent to a young offenders' prison?' Rob asks.

'If there's room.'

'What do you mean, if there's room?'

'Look, this is unlikely to happen, but I have to be honest

with you about all possible outcomes. If it happens that Young Offenders don't have a space for him, Toby could be sent to an adult prison.'

'But he's eighteen,' Rob argues.

'Exactly. Which in the eyes of the law makes him an adult.'

Jo's jaw clenches. 'But there are cases of people older than Toby being sent to Young Offenders,' she argues. She picks up her mobile from the worktop, already prepped and ready for this conversation. Earlier this evening, while waiting for Michael's call, she'd researched teenage offenders and the protocol following a criminal charge against them. 'I've just sent you a link,' she tells him. 'Here,' she says, opening the news article she'd found and saved to her phone, holding it out to Rob to see. 'This boy... this man... was sent to a young offenders' prison just a couple of months ago. He's twenty. *Twenty*. How is that right?'

'It's not about right or wrong,' Michael says. 'Or fairness, even. Every case will be considered individually, but it basically comes down to the spaces that are available at the time.'

'This *man* raped a fourteen-year-old girl. A child.' Jo's knuckles are white around the phone. Michael says nothing, and the silence that settles between them all manages to say only one thing. *Your son has murdered someone.*

'I'm not saying I agree with it,' he says eventually. 'But the prison service can only work with the provisions in place.'

'For fuck's sake,' Rob mutters.

'There's nothing to say that this will happen in Toby's case,' Michael tells them. 'As I said, I just have to prepare you for all possible scenarios.'

Jo feels herself shaking. This man is supposed to be representing her son. He's meant to be helping him, yet here he is speaking as though Toby is already condemned; not a case of *if* but *when*.

'So he gets put with paedophiles and rapists because Young

Offenders have got no room at the inn?' Rob says. His voice is acidic, and she realises that in part at least, she is the cause of this. He can barely bring himself to look at her.

'Let's cross that bridge if we come to it,' Michael says. 'But look… there's been a development that has given the police a motive.'

Rob glances at Jo. 'What development?'

Michael's momentary silence leaves them both simmering in a stew of 'what-ifs'.

'The police have gained access to the phone records and text exchanges between Toby and Freya.'

'And?' Rob prompts him.

Michael clears this throat. 'I'm not sure whether either of you already knew about this, but they'd been sleeping together.'

TWENTY-FOUR
ALICE

Alice lies in a cold bath, wondering what it would be like to die. She thinks about whether she's brave enough to hold her head underwater, to stay there and inhale until her lungs fill with liquid and she loses consciousness. But she figures there are probably easier and less painful ways to go. Not for the first time, she finds herself immersed in thoughts about Freya's final moments and what they might have been like. She doesn't want to dwell on it, but the horror of it clings to her like a leech. She hopes she didn't suffer. She hopes that it was over quickly and that Freya didn't know what was going to happen to her, because Alice can think of nothing worse than knowing you're about to die, waiting and watching it happen, every drawn-out, painful second of awaiting an irreversible fate.

She can go barely a moment without thinking of Toby. Whenever she pictures him now, she sees him wearing prison-issue clothing, his face cut and bruised by the imagined assault that taunted her all afternoon. Although she's had it confirmed by her parents that he is safe and unharmed, there's still a part of her that doesn't believe it to be true. If it wasn't a moment of twin telepathy, then it must be a premonition of something yet to come. It wouldn't be unlike her parents to tell a lie to protect her. And Alice already knows her father is a liar.

She twists and reaches for her phone on the windowsill behind her. She goes to the Instagram app, knowing it's exactly what she shouldn't do. Social media is a drug, she realises that. She's probably addicted, but then so are eighty per cent of people her age. Not that that fact makes it any better, she tells herself. But in her case, especially now, any social media sites should be avoided. That TikTok reel that was being sent around just days ago now seems like friendly banter compared to what she knows she may face in the aftermath of Freya's death.

She has thirty-two notifications. She never has this many; she occasionally gets tagged on something funny, or on the rare occasions one of the girls from school posts a photograph of them all together, but she realises even before opening any of them that that kind of thing applies to none of this most recent attention.

When she opens the notifications, the first thing she sees is Freya's smiling face looking out at her. It's a photograph from the prom, of Freya in a floor-length cream dress, her thick hair cascading down her shoulders, her make-up professionally applied. Alice was there when this was taken, just to the left of Freya, but she's been sliced from the image, like a severed diseased tumour.

RIP beautiful girl #FreyaHarris #murdervictim #sickworld #withtheangels

Tagged in the post are several of the girls from school, including Scarlet and Amy. Alice wonders why she would be included among them. Do people not yet know of Toby's involvement? But they must do, she thinks, even this soon. Bad news travels fast, but scandal on social media is instant. She hasn't heard from any of her friends since the news of Freya's death broke, not even from Amy. She's being shunned for a reason.

The next tagged post throws the hope that Toby's name might not yet have been revealed straight out of the window. Another photograph of Freya, but this time the caption is far less subtle.

Murdered by a friend! #FreyaHarris #TobyClarke #murderer

Below the caption, the accusations and speculations abound.

Can't believe it – only saw her the other day. Going to miss her face.

Anyone know if the rumours going round about what happened are true?

No smoke without fire, that's what my nan reckons.

Toby tho! Shocking. Such a nice guy. Obvs not tho.

Anyone know why he did it?

Reckon @AliceClarke2006 will be able to answer this. Might be something to do with…

The author of the final comment has attached a meme created using Alice's image from the TikTok reel. It takes her a moment to realise what it implies, but when it hits, the blow lands with the force of a fist. Is this what everyone thinks: that

Toby killed Freya because of what was posted about his twin sister? He has always been protective of her, forever looking out for her at school when they were younger, but he has never so much as spoken ill of anyone, let alone shown the possibility of a violent streak. And it wasn't even Freya who uploaded the post.

Alice is shaking as she continues to read the comments. She doesn't want to be involved in any of this; she doesn't want people to assume she knows what went on in the Harrises' house last night. Most of all, she doesn't want people to think her brother is a murderer. But it's apparently too late for that now.

Like a form of self-torture, she continues to check through her notifications, reading every single comment on everything she's been tagged in. Some of the comments are vile, offensive; she wonders how people get away with posting such things on public spaces, although she realises this has never been a problem for her before, only now that it involves her family. Her face is wet with silent tears. She knows she should put the phone down, hide it from her sight, smash it with a brick. But she can do none of these things, drawn to the gossip like a moth lured to a flame that will singe its wings, sickened yet transfixed by all the awful things these people, some of them strangers, are saying about her brother.

Whole family should rot in hell.

She puts her phone back on the windowsill, her heart hammering painfully. This isn't going to stop, she thinks. There will be more comments. More hate. She leans forward and pulls out the plug, then rises from the bath, water dripping to the bathroom floor as she reaches for the towel she left hanging on the radiator. She dries herself hurriedly and wraps the towel around her before retrieving her phone and returning with shaking hands to Instagram, then to Snapchat, X and TikTok, in turn deleting every social media account she has. Whatever is said about her family, she doesn't want to read or hear any more.

This is her fault, she thinks, as she sits on the edge of the bathtub. If the assumption everyone's making is correct, she's to blame for all of this. If that stupid reel had never been created and posted, would Toby be here now? Might Freya still be alive?

Forcing back tears, she takes her phone with her to the bedroom, where she throws it onto the duvet. She dresses and blow-dries her hair, and when she's finished, there's a WhatsApp notification on her phone. A message from Dylan responding to the one she'd sent earlier. She hadn't expected to hear from him, not today at least.

You have nothing to be sorry about. This isn't your fault.

She reads the text for a second time and then a third, a bubble of mixed emotions bouncing in her stomach. There's a sense of relief she knows she shouldn't feel at the fact that he isn't holding her responsible by association, and she feels guilty for the feeling that had swept over her on first reading the words, no matter how brief it might have been.

And then there's the second sentence. Toby's crime acknowledged indirectly; the responsibility placed solely with him. She doesn't want to lose Dylan. She's already lost her brother and Freya, and Dylan feels in a way like the last remaining sibling, the last connection to a life that has been ripped away from them all. She is grateful that he has responded to her, though she has no idea what to say in return. God, she wishes they could just go back in time. All those years they spent more like cousins than neighbours, in and out of each other's houses, playing games and sharing secrets. The summer holidays together, the two families camping and cycling and enjoying the great outdoors that her father and Chris in particular love so much. It seems inconceivable to Alice that all those years have led to this, and she still can't bring herself to believe that Freya is really gone.

She thinks about not replying, giving him some space while she tries to work out what she's going to say to him, but she's already had long enough to consider the right words, and there are none.

I wish I could undo everything, she types, before adding, *but I know Toby didn't kill Freya.*

The longer she stares at the words, the more unreal they become. She shouldn't even be having to type them. She shouldn't have to think it. No one should be able to so much as contemplate the possibility of her brother being a killer, because it's insane; this is Toby, studious, quiet, kind Toby, the boy everyone says is just like his father.

The thought sends a chill through her. Rob isn't the man she'd believed him to be. She doesn't want to accept that the same might apply to Toby.

She deletes the second half of the message, knowing it isn't what Dylan will want to read. After racking her brain for something to add in the deleted space, she presses send, leaving just six words to say everything she wants to tell him. She doesn't expect a reply, but she sees the message ticks turn blue almost straight away, and within moments, Dylan is typing something back.

So do I. I don't know what to do.

Alice can't think of a way to reply to this, but she doesn't need to; within moments, she sees Dylan is typing again. Another message pops up on her screen.

Do you think we can meet up? Not today, but soon.

She can only imagine how Eve would react to finding out Dylan has even asked to meet up with her. She wants to see him, but at the same time she doesn't. She's no idea what she could say to him.

TWENTY-FIVE

JO

Michael Chapman was unable to offer any more information regarding Freya and Toby's relationship. Because of his age and his refusal to talk to anyone, the police are apparently under no obligation to share the details of the text message exchanges between the two. Until Toby speaks to her, Jo won't know any more than she does now. A part of her thinks it might have been better had she stayed knowing nothing. The frustration of having any further details withheld from them means her mind has been given free rein to run wild, and it has already taken her to places she doesn't want to go. According to Michael, Jo is still being considered a witness, despite the fact she didn't witness anything. Not until it was too late, at least. She wishes she could have got there sooner, that she somehow might have been able to stop what had happened.

'Did you know about the two of them?'

She and Rob are still in the kitchen, Jo at the table, Rob at the patio doors. He hasn't moved for the past five minutes.

'Of course I didn't,' she tells him. The news is as much as a surprise to her as it is to him. Freya and Toby grew up together like siblings, and it seems inconceivable that they might have come to think of one another in any other way.

'Well,' Rob says, his back to her, arms folded across his chest. 'It's given them their motive, hasn't it?'

She doubts he wants an answer to that, so she says nothing. She can't stop thinking about the party on Saturday night, about that smashed glass and the anger she'd seen in Toby's expression when she'd turned towards the noise. She had never seen him like that before, red-faced and hard-featured. He didn't look like her son. But perhaps she doesn't know him as well as she thought she did.

'I think we can assume Freya had called things off then.' Rob turns now. His face is pale, and he looks watery-eyed, and Jo realises that he hasn't had his back turned to her because he can't look at her; it's because he hasn't wanted her to see him. He has always been a strong man, resilient and quietly confident, but these past hours have broken through all the carefully constructed resistance he has built around himself.

'It would explain why Toby's been so quiet recently.'

'That girl was always a troublemaker.'

'Rob...'

'What? I can't tell the truth about her now she's no longer here? I'm sorry, Jo, but it's a fact. She was just like her mother – desperate for attention and completely uncaring of other people's feelings. It wouldn't surprise me if she'd strung him along, letting him think there was something between them, and then discarded him as soon as she'd had another offer.'

Jo can't believe what she's hearing. Rob is never this insensitive. 'So she deserved to die?'

He bangs the worktop with a fist, making her jump. His face is glazed with anger; she can't remember ever having seen him like this. 'That isn't what I said. Don't you wish I could undo everything and bring both those kids back home? If I thought for a second that anyone would believe me, I'd go to the station right now and confess to murder to get Toby out of that place. Freya didn't deserve to die, but Toby doesn't deserve to be locked in a cell like some fucking animal. I'm not the one who thinks our son is a murderer, remember.'

'I've never said that.'

'You've not said otherwise either.'

Jo is silent for a moment, burning in the heat of her husband's anger. 'You didn't see what I saw,' she says quietly.

'How could neither of us have realised it?'

'What do you mean?' Jo asks.

'Toby falls hard, doesn't he? Remember that holiday to Portugal a few years back when the twins were about twelve? That Scottish family we met... I can't remember their names now.'

Jo can't remember either. But she remembers that they had a boy and a girl of similar age to the twins. Toby and Alice had got on well with them, and the four children had spent the week together, playing on the beach and at the water park.

'Toby followed that girl around the place like a stray puppy, didn't he?' Rob recalls, joining Jo at the kitchen table. 'He was like one of those scrawny cats hanging around the restaurant waiting for scraps of food.'

She remembers the way Toby had lingered close to the girl like a shadow, his young heart obviously smitten but his pre-teen pride too embarrassed to admit to it whenever Alice had teased him about it. The memory stings. It should be one that brings her joy, a nostalgia for the innocence of the twins' younger years, that precious time so quickly evaporated, but instead all it manages to do is pierce her heart. She already sees where Rob is going with this.

'And look at what happened with Isobel. He'd probably chosen a ring for her.'

She needs no reminder of how heartbroken Toby had been when his first girlfriend had told him she just wanted to be friends. He'd been fifteen, and the experience had seemed to put him off girls; as far as Jo knows, there hasn't been anyone since. He's been on dates, and she's sure he hasn't been short of offers. He's popular and good-looking, and he'd treat a girlfriend with respect and kindness, all the things he's been raised with since he was a child. But he doesn't seem to manage heartbreak well, and she had presumed that by staying single he was protecting himself from another possible rejection.

'Is this supposed to be helping?' she asks.

Rob frowns. 'Can't you see what I'm getting at? The kid's a romantic. He was in love with her, or thought he was anyway. He was probably writing her poems and planning the seating arrangements for their wedding. The last thing he would have done was hurt her.'

There is a logic to everything he says. What if he is right and yet also somehow wrong? Fierce devotion might be translated as obsession. Protectiveness can be used as a shield for control.

God, she loves her son. No one will ever be able to make her doubt that. She would die for her children, and she will do anything and everything in her power to protect him, no matter what it takes. But she is also a realist. And as powerful as her love for him is, she also knows that people are capable of being more than one thing. It is this that terrifies her more than anything else. The possibility that Toby could be a young man capable of killing in a moment of rage and blinded fury induced by the rejection of someone he loved.

'I need to see him.'

'We'll try again tomorrow,' Rob says. 'But right now, you need to get some sleep.'

Later, Jo goes upstairs alone and lies in the dark with her thoughts. It seems to her that she should have seen something, some exchange between Toby and Freya that would have alerted her to the altered nature of their relationship. There was the incident at the party on Saturday night, but she had no reason at that time to look further into it, and it had seemed to everyone, including Eve, that the smashed glass was nothing more than an accident. Yet still Jo berates herself for not having noticed what was right in front of her. Had she done so, she might have been able to change the course of the events that followed.

At some point after drifting into broken and disturbed sleep, she is aware of Rob getting into bed beside her. He settles quickly to sleep, as he always seems able to manage, and Jo tries to push aside her resentment of that fact. She grits her teeth at the sound of his snoring, wondering how he's able to rest so deeply while their son is locked in a police cell awaiting a possible murder charge. Yet she knows she must try to do the same. She is no use to Toby while she's exhausted and barely functioning.

A while later, she manages to drift off once again, but her sleep doesn't last long. She wakes to a noise: one she isn't sure came from within or outside of her sleep. She shivers with a cold sweat, her heart beating erratically beneath the T-shirt of her pyjamas. The room is so dark she can barely make out the outline of the wardrobe doors at the foot of the bed. Beside her, Rob is still snoring gently. When she checks her phone on the bedside table, the screen tells her it's 4.32 a.m. She was awake less than an hour ago, then again just forty minutes before that. Her sleep, like everything else, is broken beyond repair.

She was dreaming. Well, not so much a dream as a nightmare. She was in Eve and Chris's hallway, Freya there with her. Freya was yelling something at her, her face shoved close to Jo's; so close that she could see the pores of her skin in defined detail and the mascara blobs that clung to her eyelashes like dew drops on branches. Her cheeks were red with anger, and as she screamed, tiny flecks of spit flew from between her lips. Yet there was no sound. Jo was deaf to her fury, unable to hear a word that was fired in her face.

Everything appeared in full colour and high definition. Jo saw the hallway table with its lamp and its neat pile of as yet unopened post. She saw the mosaic elephant, and then her hand as it moved towards it, her fingers gripping the base of a stone back leg. It all happened so quickly. It occurs to her now, as she sits up with the duvet pushed down to her knees, that this was how it must have happened in real life too: a sudden moment that once executed could never be undone. She saw the elephant as it was swung towards Freya's head, and for the first time she heard a noise: a dull crack of skull as Freya fell and hit the staircase. It was then that she'd woken up.

'Rob,' she whispers. She nudges him, remembering the unsettling uncertainty she'd felt on Saturday night, when she'd thought there was an intruder in the house.

'Rob!' She shakes him now, needing him to wake up. When she reaches across to turn on the bedside lamp, he rolls towards her, one eye half opened as he attempts to drag himself from sleep.

'What is it?'

'I heard a noise.'

They get out of bed; she hears the sigh that escapes him, the thought that she is being paranoid let slip with it. She pulls on the dressing gown that hangs on the back of the door. In his boxers and T-shirt, Rob sidesteps her to leave the room first. She follows him along the darkened landing, where both the twins' bedroom doors are closed. She has been into Toby's room once since the police searched the place for evidence, and she was only able to stay there for a matter of minutes. The room still smelled like him, his scent lingering in the hoodie that was left on the bed. As she'd stood in the middle of the carpet surrounded by her teenage son's uncharacteristic chaos, she had visualised the room as it had been during various stages of Toby's childhood: the blue and grey animal border she had put up when he was a baby, with its cute-faced lions and marching giraffes; the action-hero character stickers he had chosen for his sixth birthday; the glow-in-the-dark stars and planets they had fixed to the ceiling when he was a pre-teen. She had felt a rush of nostalgia that had hit her like a physical pain, a sharpness in her chest that had taken her breath away.

How had they come to this? Where had she gone wrong?

Now, passing his closed bedroom door, she wonders whether he is managing to get any sleep. According to the solicitor, a charge is now imminent. This might be Toby's last night at the police station; after this, he will be moved to a holding prison, and she can only imagine how different things might be there.

She follows Rob downstairs, where everything in the hallway is as normal. He checks the front door before going to the living room, putting a hand around the door frame to flick the switch and throw the room into brightness.

'Shit.'

She peers past him and sees debris from the living room window lying on the wooden floor. This was the noise; this was what she'd heard in her dream as the crack of a skull, in reality the shattering of glass. The centre pane of the window has a hole in it the size of a football, the glass around it splintered and patterned like an intricate design of snowflakes. Broken shards litter the floor, tiny fragments coating the chair in which Alice is so often found to be sitting, waiting there silently as though for her brother to return home.

Rob stoops and picks up the brick that sits in the middle of the detritus. There's an elastic band around it holding a piece of paper in place; he removes the page, glances at it, and shoves it into the waistband of his boxers without saying to word to Jo.

'It doesn't matter.'

'It does.'

She reaches and grabs the paper before he has a chance to stop her. In red pen, printed in bold letters, is the word MURDERER. Rob snatches it back and starts tearing it into shreds.

'What are you doing?' Jo grabs his arm as she tries to stop him. 'You're destroying evidence.'

'Evidence?' Rob repeats sneeringly. 'You think the police will care about this?'

He goes to the broken window and looks out at the street, but the place is silent. Probably kids, Jo thinks; more than likely someone from the twins' school. Someone who knows Freya and Toby.

She follows Rob when he goes into the hallway and opens the front door, but whoever was responsible is already long gone. She checks the lock three times before they return to the living room, where a mild breeze makes the curtains sway.

'What are we going to do?' she asks. They can't leave the place like this; it isn't safe. Even if they could go back to bed now, she knows neither of them would sleep anyway. 'Have we got anything we can board it up with?'

Despite being a property investor, Rob has an impressive lack of manual skills. He can just about put up a shelf, but that's the limit of his DIY repertoire. There's no shed full of power tools in the garden; just the kids' old bikes, a lawnmower and some gardening equipment.

'I'll call Dean in a few hours. He'll know someone who can replace the glass.'

Dean is a builder Rob has known for years, one of the earliest trade contacts he'd made, who had also turned out to be one of the most reliable.

'So what do we do until then?'

He shrugs. 'You go back to bed, try to get some more sleep. I'll wait here.' He puts the brick on the sideboard beside a photograph from their wedding day. 'I think we should take this as a warning.'

She doesn't need to ask what he means. Next time, it could be so much worse. Faeces through the letter box. A petrol bomb.

'We can't stay here, can we?' she asks quietly. A thought crosses her mind, though she would never say it: he's got what he wanted.

'I don't know.'

'It isn't safe for Alice to be here. Maybe we should send her to stay with my sister for a while.'

'Maybe you should ask Alice what she wants to do.'

Jo turns at her daughter's voice. She hadn't heard her come down the stairs, and she doesn't think Rob had either. Alice looks at the mess of glass on the floor, and then at the broken window.

'Who did this?'

'We don't know.'

'I don't want to go to Auntie Hayley's.'

'We need to make sure everyone stays safe,' Jo tells her. 'And it's not safe here, not at the moment.'

'Not at the moment,' Alice repeats. 'What's that supposed to mean? It'll all be okay once Toby's sent to prison on a murder charge? We can all live here safe as houses then?'

'Alice,' Rob says, his tone reprimanding.

'What, Dad?' The word 'Dad' is spoken almost sneeringly, and when Jo looks at Alice looking at her father, she doesn't understand the vitriol their daughter is firing at him. None of this is his fault, though it's only natural that tensions are running high. Amid all her worry about Toby, Jo realises she has barely spared time to consider the effect that all this might be having on Alice.

'It's never going to be any different, is it?' Alice goes on. 'Life is never going back to what it was. People are always going to hate us, even if Toby is found not guilty. And that's not going to happen anyway, is it? He's already as good as sentenced. We may as well pack our things and move out now. How can we stay here with Freya's family just across the street from us, right opposite? We are never going to escape what's happened.'

Her voice cracks, and she starts to cry. When Jo goes to put her arms around her, her daughter shoves her away.

'Don't. You think he's as guilty as everyone else does. Don't pretend you care about him when you think your own son is a murderer.'

'Alice—'

'I don't want to hear it,' she says, her voice rising. 'You're both as bad as each other.'

TWENTY-SIX

ALICE

That news reporter is outside the house again. Alice knows it's the same man who was there yesterday: her dad had cornered her on the landing and talked to her as though she was six years old, warning her to not say as much as hello to him or any of them; that anything she said would be skewed and misreported in the way the gutter press is so expert at. This same man keeps recurring; he's easy enough to identify, with his apparent self-appointed uniform of tight checked trousers and white shirt, the overall effect giving him the appearance of a sweaty estate agent. Right now, he stands and watches her father's friend Dean replace the glass pane of the living room window, presumably relishing the attack upon the house.

He looks up at the bedroom window, and Alice lets the curtain fall. She feels her heart pounding in her chest, adrenaline and anger making her pulse race. She wonders what Toby is doing in this moment. He isn't cut out for prison. He's too nice. Last night, unable to sleep, she imagined the worst things her brain could conjure: her brother's cell ransacked, his belongings set on fire, Toby beaten to a pulp by a gang of fellow inmates. She's still waiting to be allowed to see him.

She goes downstairs to the kitchen and flicks on the kettle, for no other reason than to give herself something to do. She will make yet another cup of tea, and she will take it into the living room and sit in the chair at the window, only she won't even be able to open the curtains now, because that man is standing opposite the house and there is no such thing as privacy for her and her family any more. Not here. Not anywhere.

She goes into the living room, careful to hang back so that the reporter doesn't catch a glimpse of her. 'Do you want a cup of tea?' she asks Dean.

She only offers because earlier, when he first arrived at the house, he could barely look at her. He doesn't want to be here; doesn't want to be helping the father of a boy who's been arrested for murder, no matter how long the two of them might have known each other. The offer of tea feels like a point that needs to be made.

'No thanks,' he says, still without looking at her. 'I'm almost done here.'

He continues his work without paying her further attention. Alice feels her face flush. She can't just leave it there. She needs to say something.

'Toby didn't kill her,' she blurts. 'What they're saying about him... it's not true.'

Even to her own ears, she sounds like a child. There's a desperation to her voice that she hadn't intended, an eagerness to be heard and believed that now sounds almost pathetic.

'I'm just here to fix the window.'

She hears the kettle click off and hurries back to the kitchen, grateful for the excuse to leave the room. She makes a cup of tea but leaves it on the worktop when she goes to sit at the kitchen table, the empty hours of the day stretching ominously in front of her. Her parents have gone to meet with that solicitor again. That's all they do now, meet and talk and meet and talk, as though meeting and talking are making any difference to anything.

Alice stays at the kitchen table, and a little while later hears Dean go. His van leaves the driveway, but she stays where she is, fixed to the chair, not wanting to move. Unable to summon the energy to do anything other than sit there. There's a noise at the front of the house, and she assumes he must have forgotten something. She hears voices, commotion, but when she realises it probably isn't Dean because she didn't hear a vehicle return-ing, she is too anxious to get up to look. At the sound of more raised voices, she gathers the courage to go and see. She unlocks the front door and tentatively pulls it open, knowing that the reporter is still likely to be on the other side of the street, standing outside the Harrises' house like he's been employed to guard the place.

He watches as she steps onto the driveway and looks around, but everything seems to be in order. It's only when she turns that she realises what the noise was. The red catches her eye first, the two-foot-tall letters sprayed across the front of the house.

MURDERER.

Nausea flips in her stomach. When she turns back to the street, there are suddenly more people than there were before, the neighbours emerging from their gardens like moles peering into the sun. Her skin burns with eyes on her, everyone's judge-ment resting on the backdrop that stands behind her. She looks for a reassuring face among them, for someone who might help her or come to her defence, but these neighbours have become strangers, and no one wants to so much as be seen on the same side of the street as her.

'How could you just stand there and let this happen?' she yells at the reporter. He says nothing, but she's sure there's a twitch at his mouth, the slightest glimpse of a smirk taking form.

'Did you take any photos?' she asks, trying to keep her voice from cracking. 'It's criminal damage!'

The reporter pulls his hands from his pockets, and for a moment Alice thinks he's about to show her something on the phone gripped between his fingers, some kind of evidence that he captured the moment the house was attacked while he was standing there doing nothing to stop it. Instead, she notices the twitch of his free hand, the way both move in front of him instinctively, readying themselves. Then she realises. He doesn't want to help her. He wants to photograph her like she's some kind of rare animal on display.

'Don't,' she says, the wobble of her voice betraying her.

She crosses the road to confront him. He has no right to be taking pictures. She hasn't done anything wrong.

'Stop it!'

He's already taken countless photographs of her. Alice feels violated. Vulnerable. She may as well be standing there naked while he snaps shots of her, all of which she knows will end up on the internet for everyone to see.

He takes another photograph. Something in her disconnects. 'I said stop it!' She makes a grab for his phone, clinging to his sleeve as he tries to wrestle free of her grip.

'Runs in the family,' she hears someone say.

She can barely see through the blur of her tears, but as she continues to grapple for the reporter's phone, she feels hands on her shoulders and a familiar voice telling her to stop.

She collapses into Dylan's arms, sobbing with adrenaline and fear. For a moment, she lost herself. She has no idea what she might have been capable of had Dylan not intervened.

'Did you get that?!' she hears the reporter shouting to the neighbours further along the pavement.

'Lunatic,' one of them replies. 'Just like her brother.'

'Come on,' Dylan says quietly, lowering his mouth to her ear so that nothing can be overheard as he leads her back across the street to her house. 'You need to get inside.'

Alice wipes a hand across her eyes. When she looks back at the reporter, she sees him adjusting his clothing, making a drama of what happened. Elaborating on the truth, just as her father had warned her. She notices a neighbour with her phone in her hand, having captured the whole outburst on camera. Both look at Alice as though she's the devil incarnate, the few moments blown out of all proportion.

And then she sees Eve. She has come out of the house and is standing on the doorstep, barely recognisable from the person Alice has known all her life. Her usually immaculate blonde hair is greasy and lank on her shoulders. Her skin looks grey, her eyes heavy with a need for sleep. Even from the distance at which she stands, Alice can see she's been crying. But for now, her tears have been replaced with a look Alice can only think to describe as disgust. Her lips are somehow sucked in, like there's something sour in her mouth, and her face is taut with fury.

'Get away from her,' she cries, making her way down the driveway. 'Get the fuck away from her!'

Dylan's arm drops from around Alice's shoulders. 'I'm so sorry,' he whispers, turning his head so that his mother can't lip-read his words.

Alice feels Eve's hatred like a live thing, like a wild animal that has been loosed upon her. She steps away, bitten, looking cautiously at the neighbours who stand outside their houses, all of them staring at her like she's a rare and dangerous specimen behind glass. Eve hates her, she thinks, but from the looks on the faces of these people, so does everyone else. She hurries into the house and locks the door behind her, trying not to think about the way in which those photographs might be used. They could be online as early as this afternoon. Sooner. She's let

everyone down, she thinks. She might have just made things
even worse for them all.

TWENTY-SEVEN

JO

Within twenty minutes of getting the call to say her son has requested to see her, Jo was at the police station. She sits opposite him now, and yet it isn't Toby. The colour has faded from him, the blood drained and the life inside him washed to a pale reflection of what he'd once been. She wants to reach across the table to touch him, to hold his hand, but physical contact isn't permitted.

'Michael has advised me to plead guilty.'

The first words he has spoken to her since she saw him on Monday evening, since their lives were ripped away from them and altered permanently beyond recognition.

Jo had been expecting this. Michael has spoken to her and Rob about reduced sentences, preparing them for the nature of the resulting trial if Toby was to plead otherwise. The thought that her son might spend the start – maybe half – of his adult life in prison crushes Jo's heart. There have been a million and one things she has wanted for her children. Now all she wants is to get him home. All she wants is to be wrong about what happened in that house that night.

'What do you want to do?' she asks him.

'I'm not pleading guilty. I didn't do it.'

A single tear falls from Toby's left eye, landing silently on his pale cheek. He wipes it away quickly with the back of a hand, embarrassed by the show of emotion. He glances around him, awkwardly checking that the slip wasn't noticed by anyone else. Jo's heart cracks a little further.

'Tell me exactly what happened.'

'I was upstairs in my room,' he says, keeping his voice lowered to barely more than a whisper. 'You already know that. I was stewing over what had happened at work. That customer was so rude to me, but it was me who got into trouble. It did my head in. Anyway, I got a message from Freya asking me to go over. So I did. I didn't say anything to you on the way out because I didn't think I'd be gone long. When I got there, the gate was open and the side door was unlocked. I went in through the kitchen and...'

He stops sharply, dropping into silence.

'She was on the floor in the hallway. I called out her name, but she didn't answer. I ran to her, kneeled beside her. Her blood was all over me before I even noticed it there, or that there was so much of it. That elephant ornament was beside her... I picked it up and moved it. I wasn't thinking straight. I kept saying her name, over and over, like she was just going to open her eyes and everything would be okay. I didn't hurt her, Mum. I was trying to help her.'

Jo bites the inside of her cheek, trying to keep her own emotions buried. 'Why wouldn't you speak to anyone until now? Why didn't you just tell us all this?'

'Who would have believed me? Even my own mother just assumed my guilt.'

The words are like a knife through Jo's chest. She knows that what he says is true, and though she's tried to justify it with circumstances, the reality of it stays the same. She saw what she saw. In an instant, she thought what she thought. Ever since, in the grip of yet another sleepless, nightmare-filled witching hour, she has sat silently with her thoughts, going over and over what Toby must think of her. She has tried to place together the possible pieces of that night in a different sequence, forcing the mismatched sides together to make an alternative picture of what happened. She has fought to crawl into her son's mind, searching for a switch that might have been flicked that night. An accident. It was an accident. But the word itself implies faultlessness, and it needs no detective to disprove the theory.

'She was already dead, Mum. I was too late. I knew it before I called you.' His voice cracks. 'There was so much blood. Too much blood from her head for her to still be alive. I didn't know what to do. I just froze. I held her on my lap trying to wake her up. I think deep down I must have known she was gone, but I didn't want to believe it was true. I loved her, Mum. She didn't feel the same about me, and I was trying to get used to that. It hurt, though. She made me feel used. But I'd have still done anything for her. I would never have hurt her.'

'I'm sorry, Toby. I am so, so sorry.'

She reaches across the table, forgetting for a moment that she isn't allowed to touch him. A guard steps forward from where he stands near the wall, and she holds up her hand in apology before returning it to her lap. The words are not nearly enough for the depth of damage that has been done. How betrayed he must have felt by her, that his own mother had assumed his guilt.

'Michael told you about the argument that was reportedly overheard coming from the house earlier that evening?'

Toby nods. 'That was nothing to do with me, I swear. The last time I saw her alive was at the party on Saturday.'

'I know. I made a mistake. When I walked into the house and saw you both—'

The mistrust in his eyes when he looks at her is painful. She means it now, that she believes him wholly, and the thought of ever having doubted him, even for a moment, makes her feel sick to her stomach. When she thinks back on that call he made to her on Monday evening, she hears his voice again for what it was: fearful; desperate. *I need you.*

'I'm sorry, Toby. Truly I am.'

He looks at his hands in his lap. 'What you said when you made that 999 call. "It's my son. He's killed someone".'

Jo sighs. She can't apologise to him again, not when the words sound so meaningless and empty.

'You were so adamant about it. You could have said a hundred different things... "something's happened", or "I think my son might have hurt someone". But you just said the words as fact. It was like there was no doubt in your mind.'

'We couldn't run away from it, Toby. We're going to get you out of this, I—'

'But if you don't believe I'm innocent, who else is likely to?'

Jo holds eye contact, allowing herself to see him for a moment as the child he once was, not all that long ago. She has always prided herself on doing her best for her children, for always having tried her best even when she'd felt she hadn't succeeded. Now, she knows she cannot fail him.

'I believe you, Toby. I should never have doubted you. And you may not feel you're able to, but I hope you'll forgive me. Your dad and I just want to help you out of this. You need to tell the police everything you've just told me,' she says. 'And Michael too. He's on your side. Don't miss out any detail, even if you don't think it's important.'

'What about you? Are you on my side?'

'Always,' Jo says, wiping tears from her eyes. 'I am always on your side, and we're going to get you out of this.'

This time when Toby cries, he allows himself to do so freely.

Jo knows she means every word, that she must cast aside her guilt at ever having believed her son could have been capable of hurting Freya. She doesn't have time for that now. She must focus on proving Toby's innocence. But she knows it's going to be difficult to do that when the police seem intent on hanging him out to dry. Proving her son's innocence is going to mean uncovering someone else's guilt.

TWENTY-EIGHT

ALICE

Her mother is in her bedroom packing things to take to the hotel her father has booked for them. After the attacks on the house, her parents have decided it isn't safe for them to stay here, especially with Toby still waiting to be charged. When he is, which Alice knows he will be, she imagines things will only get worse for the rest of the family. She knows her parents are right, yet being forced from her home feels unfair. She checks through the things in her overnight bag on the bed. She knows they'll be away from here for longer than just a few days, but for now she can't begin to think about that. She just needs to focus on the next twenty-four hours, and then the next, and then the next. One day at a time.

When she goes to her mother's bedroom, Jo is in the en suite bathroom. She continues what she's doing, presumably thinking Rob has come upstairs to do the same, but when she comes back into the bedroom, she looks surprised to find Alice there, sitting on the bed.

'Have you packed a bag yet?' her mother asks. 'Don't pack too much, just enough for a couple of days. If there's anything you forget, I can pick it up from the shops for you.' She stops talking when she realises Alice is crying. She puts her toiletry bag on the chair and goes to sit next to her on the bed, putting an arm around her shoulder. This time, Alice doesn't try to push her mother away. Instead, she sinks against her, her body sagging with a weight of sadness.

'I'm sorry, Mum.'

'If this is about last night, forget it. You've got nothing to be sorry about.'

She puts a hand to her daughter's head and smooths her hair in the way she used to when Alice was a child and was finding it difficult to get to sleep.

'It's not about last night,' Alice says, her voice quiet. She breaks away from her mother's hold and goes to the bedroom door, making sure it's clicked shut. 'There's something I need to tell you. I wanted to tell you before, but there never seemed a right time, but now I think I should have. I keep thinking that if I'd said something then Toby might not be in prison and Freya would still be alive and none of this would have happened, but I didn't want to hurt you, Mum, and I didn't want to say anything if I'd got it wrong and—'

'Alice.' Jo cuts her off. 'Just tell me what's happened.'

She's trying to remain calm, but Alice can see that her words and the rate at which they've left her have got her mother worried. Is she already half expecting what Alice is about to deliver?

'The night of the party, at Eve and Chris's house,' Alice says, returning to her side, 'I heard Dad and Eve talking. I didn't get it all, but...'

She's stalling in a bid to protect her mother. Her brain is screaming at her not to do this, especially not now while Jo is already going through one of the worst possible things that could happen to a parent. But there is no room for secrets between them now; they can't afford any more of them or the price they come with.

'I think there's something going on between them.'

She sees her mother trying not to react. She spies a twitch at her temple, but other than this, Jo remains unflinching. An act, Alice thinks.

'What did you hear?' Jo asks.

Alice gives her the details of the conversation, word for word as she remembers it. She describes her father's tone, and Eve's as well, and Jo listens silently as her daughter relays everything she heard that night.

'It could be something else,' Alice tells her hopefully. 'But I knew I had to tell you. I'm sorry I'm doing it now. I didn't want to hurt you, Mum.'

'Nothing can hurt me now, love.'

Jo takes Alice's hand in hers and holds it tightly, keeping her focus on the skirting board at the far side of the room. She doesn't seem to want to look at Alice, still trying to protect her from witnessing another piece of her crumbling.

'Tell the truth, that's what you've always said, isn't it? Even if you don't come out of it well. The truth matters.'

'The truth matters,' Jo repeats.

'I kept trying to tell myself I was reading too much into it. But I don't think so. I asked Dad about it, but he got angry with me, said I'd only make everything worse than it already is.'

Jo sucks in her top lip. 'Thank you for telling me.'

Is that it? Alice thinks. Doesn't she get it? Doesn't she want to know why Alice now believes that if she'd said something earlier, they might not be standing here having this conversation now, with Toby in prison and Freya dead?

'The thing is, Mum,' she says, 'I think Freya knew.'

'What are you trying to say, Alice?'

'Nothing. I don't know. But since Monday, my mind's just gone into overdrive. All that weirdness with Freya flirting with Dad... what if she was doing it to make her mother jealous? It was like she was trying to prove a point to somebody.'

She waits for her mother to react, but Jo remains character-
istically stoic, silently absorbing everything Alice says.

'There's something I need to show you.'

She gets up to fetch the camera, which is still in the shoebox
beneath her bed. But as she reaches the door, it swings open and
her father walks in.

'Everything okay?' he asks, looking from Jo to Alice. 'You
both packed?'

He makes it sound as though they're off on a jaunt, about to
go away for a nice family weekend rather than having to flee
their own home because of vigilantes who are intent on running
them off the street for a crime of which none of them is guilty.

Alice looks back at her mother, and a silent sentence passes
between them. This will have to wait until later.

It occurs to her that this was exactly what happened with
Freya on Sunday, just when she had told Alice there was something she needed to talk to her about. The conversation had
been interrupted, with Eve appearing at the door just at the
wrong moment. Now it is Rob's turn to intercept an imminent
revelation, although he hadn't reached them in time to stop her
telling her mother about the affair. It feels to Alice too much of
a coincidence that her father and Eve would both be so alert to
the possibility of secrets being shared behind their back.

She feels resentment surge inside her. The first thing he'd
asked was whether everything was okay, but she's starting to
think he doesn't really care. He's just trying to save his own
skin. His and Eve's. Alice had looked right at him, forcing eye
contact, but he had glanced away, averting his gaze to the carpet
between his feet. Shame, she thinks. Cowardice. She just hopes
it isn't anything worse than that.

TWENTY-NINE

JO

Rob has booked them into a generic chain hotel just off the M4 between Bridgend and Cardiff: a cheap, nondescript concrete block of a building that's close enough to the station where Toby's being held yet far enough away from their home village for them to hide out until the macabre interest in their family has died down. Jo wonders how long that might take. Now that Toby has begun to voice his innocence, his case will go to trial. It could be months before they even get to that stage, and then the process could take God knows how long. They can't stay hidden here for ever.

They booked two rooms, and Jo is grateful that she can use Alice's vulnerability as an excuse to get away from Rob. She has barely been able to look at him since her daughter told her about the overheard conversation at the party. She doesn't want to believe that an affair is even a possibility but, like Alice, she can't see an alternative explanation for the exchange. She knows her daughter wouldn't lie about something like that. And she knows that what she herself heard on the doorstep between Rob and Eve wasn't about Freya. Rob lied to her face.

'I'm sorry,' Alice says as she comes out from the bathroom.

She has showered and changed into pyjamas, her shoulder-length hair hanging in wet tendrils.

'What are you sorry for?'

'Telling you about Dad and Eve. Maybe it would have been better if I'd said nothing.'

Jo rummages in her bag for an oversized cardigan and puts it on; despite the recent warm temperatures, the air this evening is cooler and the recently switched-off air con has made the room feel almost chilly.

'You did the right thing,' she tells her daughter.

'There's something else, though.'

Jo feels her already heavy heart sink a little lower. 'What?'

'The night of the party,' Alice says, going to her overnight bag and lifting it onto the bed. 'You came into my bedroom and asked if I'd heard anything, do you remember? What was it you'd heard?'

'A voice,' Jo admits. 'I didn't want to worry you, though.' Since Monday, she hasn't given that voice a thought. Everything and anything that might have concerned her before that evening was evaporated by Freya's death. By Toby's arrest. Nothing else matters now other than uncovering the truth. She's just worried about how close to home the truth might bring her.

Alice rummages beneath the piles of clothing shoved inside the bag.

'What is it, love?' Jo asks, tense with nerves. 'What's the matter?'

Alice pulls something from the bag and passes it to her. Jo can't make out what it is.

'I heard the voice as well. It was this.'

Jo turns the device in her hand, not understanding what she's looking at. It might as well be a hand grenade, and despite not yet knowing what it is, she imagines it capable of having a similar effect. 'I don't understand.'

'It was fixed to the inside of your wardrobe. It's a camera, Mum.'

Jo tastes bile at the back of her throat.

'The battery was going,' Alice explains.

'Okay,' Jo says, swallowing the taste of sickness in her mouth and pushing the camera down into her own bag, covering it with a handful of underwear. 'Thank you for showing me.'

'Is that it?' Alice asks, incredulous. 'That's all you're going to say? You didn't know it was there, did you?'

'Of course not.'

Jo doesn't want her daughter to see her upset again. Alice has endured enough tears, her own and everyone else's; more in just a few days than most teenagers her age have had to experience in a lifetime. She doesn't want to subject her to any more of them.

'What are you going to do?'

I don't know, Jo thinks. She can't comprehend anything right now. She needs time and she needs answers, though she doubts she's likely to get either of those things.

'I'll sleep on it. You need to do the same. Don't go to bed with wet hair, will you?'

Alice looks as though she's about to say something but changes her mind, instead returning to the bathroom to blow-dry her hair. Jo goes to the window and pushes aside the curtains, looking out onto the concrete greyness of the car park. All she can think is that Rob put that camera there. It couldn't have been anyone else. But why would he do that? The thought is disgusting. She feels violated, her privacy invaded, her most intimate moments observed in the most deceitful and criminal of ways.

Unless, of course, she wasn't the woman he'd been recording.

When Alice comes out from the bathroom, they barely

speak. She gets into bed and Jo waits for her to fall asleep. With the television on, its sound muted, she sits on the single bed of the otherwise darkened room and looks over at Alice beneath the white duvet of the double, peaceful for now at least, her mind lost in slumber. After last night's wake-up call from the brick through the window, and the emotional tornado of today, she had been exhausted all evening, trying to fight the pull of sleep. Jo knows Alice feels as guilty as she herself does, that in relenting to sleep she is allowing herself to forget for a moment everything that has happened. She has told her so many times already that she mustn't punish herself for things that are beyond her control. Jo has always been good at dishing out advice she never heeds herself.

Her thoughts linger on the Facebook post Eve uploaded on Monday. Now more than ever, she believes it was intended for Rob. Their affair might have already ended, and perhaps Eve was trying to show him what he was missing out on. This is why Freya was the way she was, Jo thinks. Frivolous with people's feelings. Selfish and provocative. Learned behaviour. Is Alice right, and had Freya known what had been going on between them? Had she threatened to tell Chris? It isn't difficult for Jo to imagine Eve getting into a heated argument with her daughter. She'd been witness to their rows in the past, and if things got that tumultuous when they were in the company of others, goodness knows how volatile they became once they were alone.

She waits until she senses Alice in a deeper sleep before getting up from the bed and slipping out of the room, remembering to take the key card so she can let herself back in later without disturbing her daughter. Rob's room is three doors along the corridor. She taps at the door, knowing he'll still be awake. He might be a liar and a cheat, but she doesn't doubt for a moment his commitment to proving his son's innocence.

He comes to the door still wearing the clothes he was in

earlier, his hair dishevelled and grey shadows beneath his eyes. He steps aside without speaking, giving her space to enter the room. Like Jo, he hasn't bothered to unpack anything from his suitcase. It lies open on the floor near the desk chair, an array of chargers tangled upon a pile of clothing.

'Is Alice okay?' he asks once the door is closed.

'She's sleeping.'

'I feel fucking useless stuck here. We should be doing something constructive to get him released.'

He turns away from her in a vain attempt to hide his tears.

'I'm sorry for doubting him,' she says quietly. 'I wish there was something I could do to change it. If you'd seen what I'd seen...'

'I know. Let's just move on from it now, shall we? We need to stick together for Toby now. Be a team.'

Jo feels her jaw tighten. She checks his face for recognition of the irony, for some acknowledgement of the audacity of his words, but there is nothing. He either doesn't realise, or he is more brazen than she had ever imagined.

'Be a team,' she repeats. 'Togetherness... honesty... that type of thing?'

His face creases as he looks at her questioningly. 'What's going on, Jo?'

'Maybe you should tell me that.'

Panic crosses Rob's features. 'What's happened? Has something happened to Toby, is he okay?'

'This isn't about Toby. You and Eve. What's going on?'

He sighs and closes his eyes for a moment, but just before he does, Jo sees it flash across him. Guilt.

'Look,' he says, sitting on the side of the double bed. 'Alice and I already spoke about this. I don't know what she thinks she heard, but—'

'Don't bullshit me, Rob, please. We can't have any secrets.'

Before the weekend, Jo had never considered the possibility

that they might have any. The satisfaction of her belief that they had a transparent relationship and the kind of bond that was impenetrable no matter what life threw at them now seems to her an almost smug kind of self-delusion. How naïve she has been.

'How long has it been going on?' she asks.

'Jo, I—'

'How long?'

'It wasn't like that. It's not what you think.'

'You have no idea what I think. But I know you lied to me about that conversation on the doorstep.'

She sits on the single bed of the family room, opposite her husband. She can wait. She'll sit here like this all night if that's what it takes, because she deserves the truth, and there is no right time for it. The time is now.

'It just happened once,' Rob says eventually, too much of a coward to look her in the eye as he admits to it. 'I swear on the kids' lives, that's all it was. It happened, and as soon as it had, I wished it hadn't. If I could undo it, I would.'

'Oh. That's okay then.'

'Jo, please...'

She stands when he tries to touch her, recoiling from his hand like a child dodging a wasp. She moves to the window, where the curtains still hang open and the outside world is a darkened blur of concrete; she breathes in the night air that curls through the opened gap and wishes more than anything that this – this affair, this non-affair – was the biggest thing she had to worry about.

'I asked you what you'd been talking about. You could have told me then, but instead you lied to my face.'

Rob says nothing. He has no defence.

'Why did you do it?'

'She's always had a thing for me.'

Jo laughs bitterly. 'A thing?' she repeats, turning back to her husband. 'How old are you, Rob?' She stands with her back to the radiator, arms folded, hands tucked near her armpits to stop herself from digging her nails into her palms. 'How long?'

'I told you, it was only once.'

'I don't mean that. I mean how long has she had this supposed "thing".'

'God, I don't know. Since the kids were young. She told me once when she was drunk. That summer we all went camping together to Cornwall. There was that night we had the barbecue on the beach, do you remember?'

Of course Jo remembers it. The kids had played together for hours on the beach; it hadn't mattered how late it was, it was the school summer holidays. Those endless days of summer had been the best of Jo's own childhood. She'd wanted the same for the twins, for them to feel unrushed and carefree in the moment; for them to have the same experience of freedom among nature that her parents had allowed her to enjoy as a child. There was a barbecue, beach games, music. They had danced on the sand, the four of them; she remembers feeling envious of Eve's figure, toned and lithe beneath her summer dress, and berating herself for the futility of her momentary jealousy. Rob had danced with Eve. Jo had danced with Chris. They were friends, and the thought of anyone crossing those boundaries had been unthinkable to her, not when they were all so close and she trusted them unquestioningly.

How had she never seen that there was something more?

'What happened that night?' she asks, not really knowing whether she wants the answer. She had fallen asleep when the children had eventually gone to bed back at the campsite, she remembers that. She had drifted off between them, the three of them snug in their sleeping bags, exhausted by the fresh air and the freedom.

'Nothing happened. I told her it never would.'

'Something must have happened for you to get to that point in the conversation,' Jo says flatly.

'Chris had gone into the tent to see to Freya. She woke up crying, came out telling us she'd had a nightmare. When he didn't come back out, we assumed he'd fallen asleep with her. We finished our drinks, but then...'

'But then what?'

'Eve put a hand on my leg, that was all. She said she wished it could always be like that, just me and her.'

Jo feels the heat of betrayal crawl from her stomach up into her chest. All these years, for almost two decades now, Eve has been one of her closest friends. They've been through everything together: raising their families, navigating their careers, planning for the empty nests that had soon awaited them. The camping trip was a decade ago. The past ten years feel like a lie.

'I moved her hand away from me,' Rob tells her. 'I told her it was the drink talking, that I wouldn't say anything about it if she never did anything like that again.'

Jo smiles thinly. 'And then what? All those years later you had a change of heart?'

He presses his fingertips to his forehead. 'It was a couple of weeks after the break-in. Chris was away with work. Freya had gone to a friend's house for the night. Dylan was in London. You and the twins were staying at your sister's house for the weekend. Eve thought she heard a noise over at the house. She was still on edge after what had happened.'

Jo remembers that visit to her sister's house. Her dog had just died, and her sister was heartbroken; she'd had the dog for twelve years, her first and only baby. Jo and the twins had been a welcome distraction. She'd called Rob each evening while she'd been there, to ask about his day and let him know what they'd been up to. He'd spoken so normally, as though everything was as it always was.

'Poor Eve,' she says, her voice dripping with sarcasm. 'How

lucky for her that her knight in shining armour was just across the road.'

'I just went over there to check everything was secure.'

Jo smirks. She contemplates a smart-arse response along the lines of everything being secure apart from Eve's underwear, but there's no point in voicing it: the damage is done, and nothing Rob can say now will change it.

'Go on,' she prompts him.

'Go on what?'

She shrugs nonchalantly. 'And then what happened?'

'Jo, please.'

She raises an eyebrow, waiting for him to deliver the rest of the story.

'I'm not doing this,' he says.

'Something you could have said at the time.'

Rob looks at the floor like a reprimanded child. It's so pathetic it makes Jo want to scream, but she barely has the energy to remain here talking to him, let alone give form to her anger.

'I want to know what happened,' she tells him. 'How much worse can it get?'

He glances up at her briefly.

'Come on,' she says, losing patience. 'You checked all the doors and windows, made sure the bogeyman wasn't there... and then what? You slipped on a banana skin and fell into her bed?'

Rob gets up from the bed and stands just a few feet away from her, his arms folded defensively across his chest.

Jo hears her own words played back on repeat in her head. *Her bed.* Perhaps they hadn't made it that far. Maybe they'd done it downstairs, on the sofa or in the kitchen. She visualises herself in that house just this past weekend, sipping champagne at the island with Chris, the two of them oblivious to what idiots their spouses had made of them.

'Where did you do it?'

She has no idea why the answer seems important, but for some reason it does. She wants answers. She wants details. She needs to know what was going on in his head when he made the decision to betray her. To betray their family.

'It doesn't matter.'

'It matters to me.'

'Please, Jo,' he says. 'Don't make me do this.'

It shouldn't matter, she tells herself. It shouldn't matter now whether it was a one-night thing or a ten-year affair, not when they have a murder charge against their son hanging over them. Yet she still wants to know.

'Don't you think you owe me the truth? That's what we've taught the kids, isn't it? Always tell the truth, even if you don't come out of it well.'

His eyes are filled with tears, but in this moment, she feels nothing towards him. She cannot sympathise because she doesn't believe that those tears are for her. He isn't sorry he did it, she tells herself. He's just sorry he's been caught out.

And in this moment, she realises why he can't bring himself to answer her. This, she thinks, this is the part that will destroy them: not the fact of it, but the fact of where it took place. She'd assumed they'd done it at Eve and Chris's house. Now she knows she was wrong.

'Where?'

'Jo, does it ma—'

'Where, Rob?'

She feels sick. She knows what he can't bring himself to say because it's written all over his face in the look of guilt that sheens his skin like suncream.

'Did you do it in our bed?'

His silence answers the question for her. Jo laughs bitterly and heads for the door, not wanting to be around him a moment longer.

'Jo, please...'

'How, Rob?' she says, having to fight the urge to scream at him. 'You were across the other side of the street! A choice was made there. You had the time it took you to get into our house – our bed – to realise you were making a horrible mistake and to put a fucking stop to it, but you didn't.'

Through a blur of tears, she sees Rob crying. She doesn't care. She hates him for what he's done to her. For what he's done to their family. More than anything, she hates that everything now feels a lie.

'Jo...'

But she doesn't give him a chance to say whatever it is he wants to. She yanks the door closed and rushes back to Alice's room, sick with the thought of what that camera had been doing in their wardrobe. She could have questioned him about it, but she doesn't think it's the right time. No, tonight her heart is racing and she's sick with the thought of how any of this might link back to Freya, and to what happened on Monday night.

She opens the door carefully and quietly makes her way to the bed near the window. The idea that Rob is somehow involved in Freya's death trickles into her mind like poison into her bloodstream, gradual and insidious. Was Alice right, and had Freya found out about Rob and her mother? If so, there was a motive. Yet that doesn't explain the camera. He might be lying about it having been only one night. He's already lied, so what difference would one more make? He might have put it there to film him and Eve. Yet this isn't the person she has known for over twenty years. But does she know him really? She'd never thought him capable of being unfaithful.

She gets into bed and pulls the duvet to her neck, wishing for a moment she could be smothered beneath it – just a moment's respite from Freya's death and Toby's incarceration, her husband's lies and her friend's betrayal. She wants to scream into the silence until it all becomes undone: Freya home with her family, her son back where he belongs, her husband the person she'd always believed him to be.

She thinks of the camera in her bag on the floor. For the first time, it occurs to her that she doesn't know how it works; whether it carries its recordings on it or if they're streamed to a device somewhere. She presumes it to be the latter, the way of most things these days. Like a doorbell camera, she thinks, which can be accessed any time.

She gets up quickly from the bed and just makes it to the bathroom in time before she throws up in the toilet. Her head pounds with sleep deprivation and grief, and now, sitting on the cold tiled floor with her back pressed to the bathtub, she realises the obvious had yet to hit her. Rob isn't the only one with access to their bedroom. Eve has a spare key for their house.

THIRTY
ALICE

On Thursday, the three of them all wake early. Alice's parents
are going to the station this morning; after that, they're meeting
again with the solicitor who's representing Toby. They've not
yet told her much: they either think her too young or too upset
to grasp the ins and outs of what Toby faces, and though she
gets why they're trying to protect her, at the same time it pisses
her off. She isn't a child and doesn't want to be treated like one,
and if there's anything she can do that might help prove Toby
didn't kill Freya, she is prepared to do it in a heartbeat.

'We need to pop back to the house for something,' her
mother tells her as they wait in the hotel foyer for her dad. She's
only seen them together briefly this morning, for little less than
a minute. They could barely look at one another, and their
exchange was curt, her mother's words clipped and her father's
tone pathetic. Alice knows he's upset with her too. Perhaps he
expected her to keep his secret for ever, but he should have
realised she would never betray her mother like that.

When they get to the street, the reporters who've been there
for the past couple of days are gone, perhaps having learned that

the family has temporarily moved out and taking a break from their stakeout while there's nothing more to be seen.

'Wait in the car,' Jo tells them, and Alice watches as she goes up the driveway. There are still smears of red paintwork across the front of the house, despite her father having paid someone to clean it off. Perhaps it's a sign, Alice thinks. This stain on their family is permanent.

'I had to tell her,' she says quietly, once her mother has disappeared into the house. She waits for her father to say something, a reassurance that he's okay with her, that he understands why she did it. But she gets nothing in return.

A moment later, as Alice has her head down, scouring internet search results on how to help a family member after they've been charged, there's banging on the car window. She looks up abruptly to find Chris pounding the driver's window with his fist, Eve standing just behind him, her face pale and haggard-looking.

'Get out of the car!' Chris shouts.

Rob raises both hands as though he's got a gun held to his chest, and when he unclips his seat belt, Alice does the same. She gets out from the back seat just in time to see Chris punch her father in the face, the assault unexpected and more violent than she would ever have thought him capable of. Despite the speed of the incident, she sees in high definition the burst of her father's nose, the spray of blood that jets from his face like paint from an aerosol can. He does nothing to defend himself, just steps back against the car and lifts a hand to his face, unable to meet Chris's eye.

'You fucking bastard,' Chris yells, spit flying in her father's face. 'Protecting that piece-of-shit murdering scumbag!'

'Rob!'

Jo runs from the house and rushes down the driveway, pushing past Chris to get to her husband. Already neighbours have left their houses. It seems to Alice that no one on their street seems to work any more; since Freya's death everyone has stayed at home, a community frozen in grief, resolved not to miss the next update in the unfolding drama.

Jo reaches into the car and fumbles about in the driver's door pocket for a pack of tissues. She pulls out a handful and passes them to Rob, who holds them to his nose, trying to stem the bleeding. 'Jesus Christ, Chris,' she says, turning to him and Eve. 'This isn't going to help anything.'

'Fuck you, Jo. Fuck all of you. I hope your son rots in hell for what he's done to my family. For what he did to my girl.'

Alice can't watch when Chris begins to cry. She has rarely seen her own father cry: once, a decade ago now, when her grandfather died, and then again, more recently, when her grandmother was diagnosed with cancer. But Chris's grief is the rawest form of emotion she has ever witnessed from any man, like a dying animal, trapped and desperate.

'Chris...' Jo reaches out to him, and Alice moves around the car, instinctively protective of her mother. But instead of lashing out at her, he allows himself to be held, this six-foot-something rugby player of a man crumpled against her broken mother, the two of them crying, victim and perpetrator-by-association clinging to a mutual grief. The sound is so unbearable that no one – not Alice's father, nor any of the neighbours – can bring themselves to look at them, eyes cast to the pavement, where the grey blankness is safer. Eve looks away, face taut.

For a moment, it is all too surreal, like Alice has sunk into a different life where none of the past few days have happened. Someone somewhere will shout 'cut' at any minute. A curtain will fall, and this will all be over. And then just as quickly as the moment of strangeness descended, it ends. Chris pulls himself brusquely from Jo and straightens himself out, a flush of shame colouring his cheeks.

Her father and Eve have made no acknowledgement of one another. When Chris moves from Jo's embrace, Alice notices how her mother doesn't quite let go, her hands still resting on his arms, letting him know she's there for him. This isn't just about Freya, she thinks. This is about the four of them, and the lies that sit within their so-called friendship.

'Come on,' Chris says, reaching for his wife's hand. 'Let's go.'

Eve allows herself to be led away, neither of them looking at Alice as they pass her to leave the driveway. She goes to her father, his cheek and chin smeared with blood.

'You need to get cleaned up,' Jo tells him.

'I'm fine,' he says, pulling his arm away when she tries to reach for him.

They go into the house. Alice waits in the hallway as her parents go to the downstairs toilet. She hears her mother instructing her father, fussing with tissues and antiseptic cream, though each word is crisp and sharp, her former soft edges towards him hardened by his betrayal.

Her phone pings in her pocket. A text from Dylan.

Can we still meet today?

She wonders whether she'll be able to sneak away. Her parents don't want her going to the police station, and she knows they're keen to keep her as far away from their dealings with Michael Chapman as possible. She decides to say she's got a migraine and is going back to the hotel while they meet with the solicitor.

What time? she texts Dylan back.

'We need to go to the hospital,' she hears her mother say.

'It's fine.'

'Your nose is broken.'

'Then they won't be able to do anything for it, will they, so it's pointless going.'

Sitting on the staircase, Alice thinks back over what

happened on the driveway just a little over ten minutes ago. It was almost as though Eve and Chris had been waiting for them to return home, that somehow they had known they would be coming back to the house that morning. All Chris's fury had been directed at her father. True, it was only him and her there when he had first approached the car, but when Jo had turned up, he hadn't behaved towards her as he had towards her dad. There can only be one reason for that. Somehow Chris already knows about Eve and Rob too.

She feels her head begin to hurt from all the overthinking. No one looks trustworthy any more. Just what the hell happened at that house on Monday evening?

She hears her mother's phone ring on the other side of the downstairs toilet door, and Jo comes out into the hallway to take the call. Rob appears after her, his face still flecked with traces of blood, his nose visibly busted at its centre.

They both watch Jo as her face turns pale.

'It's Michael,' she says, sliding the phone from her ear to her chest. 'Toby's been charged with third-degree murder.'

THIRTY-ONE

JO

When they pull into the police station car park, Jo realises she needs to think of an excuse to keep Rob away from the place for long enough to give her a chance to speak to DI Paulson about the camera Alice found in her bedroom. It can't be a coincidence that it's been discovered there now, the same week Freya was killed. Somehow it's linked to all this, but Jo just can't yet work out how.

'Can you call Michael back?' she says.

'Why?' Rob asks, cutting the engine.

'I never arranged a time to meet him. I'm sorry... I wasn't thinking straight. Find out where they're planning on transferring Toby.'

Rob eyes her questioningly, but he takes out his phone, and Jo gets out of the car, not allowing him a chance to ask any further questions. She hurries into the station. The desk sergeants know who she is without asking for a name. Jo assumes that everyone in the town now knows their names and their faces; they are an enemy of the public, guilty by association. She is the mother who raised a killer; the woman whose son killed her best friend's daughter. No one wants to hear anything she has to say, but she must make them, for Toby's sake.

The sergeant at reception says something into the phone, but Jo doesn't make out what it is. Before she has a chance to take the camera from her bag to show him, DI Paulson appears at the double doors. She has her coat on.

'I need to talk to you,' Jo says breathlessly.

'I'm just on my way out.'

'Please. Just two minutes.' She glances behind her to the automatic doors. 'Not here.'

The detective sighs. 'Two minutes,' she says curtly. 'Follow me.'

DI Paulson scans her pass at the doors behind her, and Jo follows her down a now familiar corridor. She opens a door and ushers Jo inside.

'Alice found this in my bedroom.' Jo reaches into her bag and takes out the camera, which she's wrapped in a clear plastic bag.

'A camera,' the detective says, taking the bag from her. She glances at it briefly before looking back at Jo as if to say 'So what?'

'It was hidden inside my wardrobe. Alice found it there on Monday.'

DI Paulson hands the bag back. 'Okay,' she says casually, as though Jo has just asked her to open an investigation into a cheese sandwich. 'I'll make a note of this.'

Jo steps aside to block her path as she heads back for the door. 'That's it?'

'I'm not sure what else you'd like me to do, Mrs Clarke.'

'It can't be legal for someone to have done this, surely?'

'Well, no. Report it to the desk sergeant and he'll get it on record.'

Jo feels her heart rate increase. 'This changes everything, don't you see that? I should have explained better. My husband had sex with Eve Harris. I've only just found out. He claims it was a one-night thing, but it might have been going on for years. She has a spare key to the house – I gave it to her years ago. She must be the one who put this in my bedroom.'

'Or your husband,' DI Paulson suggests.

'Or my husband,' Jo agrees. 'But either way, don't you see what this means? Everyone's been assuming Freya was killed because of that reel about Alice that was put online. You think it was because of Toby's break-up with Freya. But this offers another possible motive. Alice thinks Freya knew about Rob and Eve. She said Freya was about to tell her something on Sunday, but Eve burst into the room and interrupted them before she had a chance to say anything. Why would she do that? This is the only thing that makes sense. Eve and Freya must have argued about the affair. Maybe Freya had threatened to tell her father about it. Eve could have lashed out.'

She inhales deeply, exhausted by the explanation and the betrayal she feels twisting in her gut like a tumour. This is the only thing that makes sense. She knows now that Eve is a liar. She has lied to Jo for half the time they've known each other, possibly even longer. If she can lie about her feelings for Rob and keep a secret as big as having had sex with him, just what else is she capable of lying about?

'If all this is true,' DI Paulson says, 'why didn't Toby just tell us he didn't do it? He could have said it as soon as we arrived at the house on Monday night, but he didn't, and his silence hasn't helped him.'

'He's saying it now, though,' Jo argues desperately. 'He was terrified on Monday night. He was in a state of shock. He loved Freya and he was grieving, and he knew what everyone's assumption would be once he was found with her body with blood all over his hands.' It was my fault, she thinks. If she hadn't reacted as she had, if she had allowed herself time to find an alternative explanation than the obvious, perhaps Toby would have spoken then and there. The shock would have faded, and the truth would have been told. Instead, she'd pierced his heart a little deeper, shutting him into silence. She should never have doubted his innocence, and she knows she'll never forgive herself for it.

'Toby's been charged now. You know this already. It's for his lawyer to put together a case before it goes to trial.'

Jo follows DI Paulson into the corridor. She knows that when she gets back to the reception area, Rob is going to be there waiting for her, wondering where she's been and why she's been talking to the detective without him. More lies, she thinks. More secrets.

She isn't going to mention that camera to him. She doesn't trust him, though she hates the fact. But while the knowledge of it remains just with Alice and her, she feels it gives her something to work on, some element of control to retain amid all the things her husband has taken from her with his lies. There will be a right time to reveal what she knows, but for now, she doesn't believe this is it.

THIRTY-TWO

ALICE

Alice hasn't yet learned to drive; she's never seen the point in doing so, not when her heart was set on Loughborough and there would be no need for a car when she'd be close to everything she needed. She can't meet Dylan in Cowbridge or even anywhere nearby, so she gets an Uber to Merthyr Mawr, a village twenty minutes away. She doesn't risk catching the bus, anxious that she might bump into someone she knows.

They meet in the quiet car park north of the sand dunes, a backdrop to miles of secluded woodland and coastal walks. When she arrives, she sees Dylan waiting for her near an old mile post that tells them they are three miles from Bridgend. The car park is sheltered, cast in shadow by the trees. The humidity hangs trapped beneath the overhanging branches, but despite the temperature, Dylan is wearing a hoodie. Alice stops before he sees her approaching. She shouldn't be here. Though she believes more than anyone else in Toby's innocence, he is still the person who stands accused. She can only imagine what Eve's reaction might be to finding out her son is here with her now.

Sickness rolls in her stomach. She can't do this.

He looks up and sees her, and it's too late: she can't turn back now.

He raises a hand slightly to acknowledge her. Alice approaches tentatively, with caution, as though pieces of Dylan might start to crumble from him if she makes any sudden movement, like a landslide disturbed by a bout of thunder. She stops a couple of feet from him, not knowing what to do. At any other time, he might have grabbed her in a headlock or dug an elbow into her ribs, some form of mock-rough, awkwardly affectionate sibling type of greeting. Instead, his hands stay shoved in his pockets as he looks down at the ground, barely able to make eye contact with her.

'I am so sorry, Dylan.'

His jawline tenses as he fights back tears. 'There's a café about a mile along the path this way,' he tells her, as though she hasn't just apologised. As though this is nothing more than a casual meet-up between a couple of friends.

She knows the place he means; she's been there before, years ago, with her parents. It's built between trees and decorated outside to look like a fairy house, and as a child she had been mesmerised by the small curved doorway her father had needed to duck down to get through, and by the multicoloured string lights that had hung in clusters at the tiny windows.

'I mean, I don't really want to sit in,' he adds, 'but we could get a coffee to take away or something.'

He turns to lead the way, and Alice walks slightly behind him, feeling herself unworthy of being here in his company. With his hands still in his pockets and his head lowered, he walks in silence, looking away from the few people who pass them by, oblivious to the now oh-so-strange relationship between the two of them.

'I'm guessing your mum doesn't know you're here,' Alice says eventually, when the silence between them has become almost too much to bear.

'God, no. She'd kill me.'

'Your dad broke my father's nose this morning.'

Dylan doesn't so much as flinch. Maybe he already knows. Maybe he thinks Rob deserved it. She wonders whether he knows anything more.

He stops and looks at her properly for the first time now. 'None of this is your fault, Alice. You've always been like a sister to me. I've already lost one sister... I don't want to lose another.'

He puts his arms out to her, and she allows herself to be pulled to his chest. They stay there for a moment, silent and alone, just the two of them on the path with the arch of over-hanging trees above keeping them sheltered from the sun. He holds her there for so long, so tightly, that Alice begins to feel claustrophobic.

'I've fucked everything up,' he says, finally pulling away from her. 'Everything in London's a mess. My parents hate me. They probably wish it was me who was dead instead of Freya.'

'Dylan. Don't say that.'

'It's true. I've seen the way my father looks at me. He misses her so much. She was always his favourite.'

He sounds like a twenty-year-old child, thinks Alice, but she supposes that under the circumstances, she's in no place to judge. She's never lost a sibling before, although in so many ways, Toby's arrest has felt like a bereavement. If he's found guilty of murder, he'll get a life sentence. He'll be in his thirties by the time he's even considered for parole, and neither of their lives will bear any resemblance to the ones they'll have left behind.

'They're in shock,' she says. 'They're grieving. Nothing makes any sense to anyone right now.' Except my brother's innocence, she thinks. That will never stop making sense.

'I know Toby didn't kill her,' she blurts. 'I know my brother better than anyone. He isn't capable of it.'

'Did he tell you they'd been shagging?' Dylan asks, though it's clear he already knows the answer to this.

Alice shakes her head.

'Don't know him that well then, do you?'

He starts walking again, and Alice follows him, his defensiveness sizzling in the air between them. 'I'm sorry,' he says eventually. 'It's not your fault.'

Except it might be, she thinks. If only she'd said something about what she'd overheard that night at the party, perhaps none of this would have happened.

'I keep getting the feeling I should do something for her, to commemorate her life in some way,' she tells him. 'But no one's going to want that now, not coming from me.'

'There's a vigil being held tomorrow night,' Dylan tells her. 'I thought you might have seen about it on your socials.'

'I've deleted all my accounts. There was too much being said.'

They reach the café, and Dylan offers to buy her a drink. She waits outside while he goes in and orders two coffees, trying to pull herself from the memories that have assaulted her at the sight of the place. She'd forgotten it until this moment, but she can remember the four of them here now, she and Toby on scooters they'd had for Christmas. Their parents had bought them ice creams and they'd sat on one of the wooden picnic benches that have since been removed, undeterred from their sweet treats even when the rain had set in.

She's close to tears when Dylan comes out with their drinks. He asks her if she's okay as he passes her a cardboard takeaway cup, and she nods yes, then leads him to a grassy patch beneath a huge oak tree.

'Where's the vigil being held?' she asks as they sit down.

'We're starting at the house and walking up to the playing fields near the school. Freya always loved that place.'

He doesn't need to remind her of this. As soon as they'd

become teenagers and had been given a bit more space and freedom to roam from the confines of the cul-de-sac, this had been a favourite meet-up spot for many of their year group. Secrets were shared there, gossip was spilled, first kisses were exchanged and friendships made and broken. It seems fitting to Alice that they've chosen to hold the vigil there.

'Your suggestion?' she asks.

Dylan nods. She moves a hand across the grass and takes his in hers, squeezing his fingers for a few moments before letting go.

'I need to apologise to you for what happened in London.'

'What?' Alice says, though she knows what he's referring to.

'In the club. I should never—'

'It doesn't matter,' she tells him. 'That's gone now.'

They sit in silence for a moment.

'What do you think happened on Monday night?' Dylan asks.

'I don't know. I thought for a while that maybe the house had been broken into again, that it was just random – Freya interrupted an intruder and they lashed out – but then that text she sent to Toby meant that couldn't have been what happened, not in the time between him receiving it and getting over to your house.'

'So what do you think now?'

'I really don't know,' Alice lies.

Because for whatever reason, she can't bring herself to tell him about that camera she found in her parents' bedroom. It might be completely unrelated to Freya's death, yet it seems too much of a coincidence for it not to be connected somehow. Now that her mother knows, she has the feeling she should keep it between the two of them. For now, at least.

And she can hardly tell him that she thinks his mother is guilty of murdering his sister.

THIRTY-THREE

Jo can't stop thinking about Toby's transfer to a holding prison. There's some reassurance in knowing that there was a place available to him at a young offenders' prison, and that's he's been spared from having to share his cell with a murderer or a paedophile, but she's only able to take a moment's consolation from the fact. The situation remains the same: her son is awaiting trial for murder. And for now, it seems there is nothing she can do about it other than put all her faith in Michael Chapman.

She has spent hours since they got back to the hotel this evening scouring the internet for similar cases in which people have been found not guilty. Cases where the real perpetrators were revealed while the accused had been awaiting trial or the trial was ongoing. She believes that at some point she will find something that will help them with Toby's case.

She doesn't want to be around Rob, but she knows that for now he is her only lifeline. They need to stay strong for Toby, so when Alice falls asleep, Jo goes to his room, knowing he will still be awake.

'Look at this,' she says, waving her phone at him. 'This man served two years before new evidence came to light that proved he wasn't guilty.'

She pushes the door closed and presses play on the YouTube video before gesturing for him to sit down beside her on the bed. When he doesn't, she pauses the video and looks at him expectantly. 'What? What is it?'

'You're torturing yourself.'

'I'm trying to help our son.'

'And so am I, but watching videos of unrelated cases isn't going to help Toby. It's completely irrelevant to what's happening to him. I'm sorry, Jo. I know you mean well. But all this is going to do is make you ill.'

'At least I'm doing something.'

Rob bites his lip, holding back a response. 'There's something else you should see, though.'

He goes to retrieve his own phone from the desk beneath the television before joining her on the bed. She notices the way he keeps a careful distance between them, making sure their hips don't touch when the mattress sinks as he sits. She wonders whether it's respect for her or because he doesn't want any contact. Either way, she still can't bring herself to look at him for long. Every time she does, she pictures him with Eve, and the images taunt her, staining every memory she has of her and Rob.

'I'm going to speak to Michael about it first thing in the morning,' he says, passing her the phone. 'They surely can't be allowed to get away with this.'

When Jo looks at the screen, a weight tugs in her stomach.

ACCUSED'S SISTER IN STREET BRAWL, the headline reads. Beneath it, there's a photograph of Alice taken just outside their home. She's mid run, face to the camera, features contorted in a snarl. It appears as though she's about to attack the person taking the photo. It looks so unlike their daughter that at first glance Jo might not have believed it to be her.

'Was this that reporter who's been hanging around since Tuesday?' Jo asks.

Rob nods. 'The bastard probably provoked her.'

Jo doesn't doubt it: this was exactly what he was looking for, and he must have thought he'd won the journalism lottery when Alice played right into his hands by reacting like this.

She reads the report, dated yesterday.

Alice Clarke, 18, twin sister of Toby Clarke, the teenager accused of murdering his 18-year-old neighbour, Freya Harris, was today involved in an altercation with the press outside the family's home in an affluent area of Cowbridge. Reacting to a comment on her brother's arrest, Alice Clarke was seen engaging in abusive behaviour, which was witnessed by several neighbours. Toby Clarke was arrested on Monday evening at the Harrises' home after his mother called 999 to report the murder. Freya had been struck with a heavy ornament inside the family's hallway and received a fatal blow to the head. Toby Clarke has been charged with third-degree murder. A vigil for Freya will be held on Friday evening at St Asaph's playing fields in the family's home town of Cowbridge, close to the comprehensive school attended by the children of both families. The reporter caught up in the incident outside the Clarkes' home today will not be pressing charges against Alice Clarke.

'Oh, how noble of him,' Jo says between gritted teeth. She thrusts the phone back at Rob, apologising when she catches the back of his hand.

'I knew this would happen. Look how they try to skew things, making out like violence runs in the family. These people are sick.'

'Did you install a camera in our wardrobe?'

Rob shifts on the bed beside her, turning to face her. 'What?!'

Jo's heart is racing at the sound of the words, at having them finally leave her mouth. 'Alice found a camera in our wardrobe. I'd heard a voice a couple of days earlier, but I didn't know what it was. It was the camera, warning about low batteries.'

Rob's mouth hangs open. 'What the fuck? I swear to you, Jo, I know nothing about this. Why the hell would I do that?'

'I've no idea. To film you and Eve having sex?'

Rob stands from the bed. 'Are you joking? It was a one-off with Eve, I've told you that. I know you've got no reason to believe me, but it's the truth. We never had an affair, and even if we had, what sort of bloke do you think I am if you can believe for a second that I would plant a camera to film someone in secret? Do you really think I'm capable of something sick like that?'

'I didn't think you were capable of cheating,' she replies flatly.

Rob folds his arms across his chest and goes to the window. He puts his palms on the windowsill and exhales loudly, trying to rid himself of his frustrations. Jo doesn't know what to make of anything any more, but in her gut, she believes him, despite everything else.

'I've shown it to DI Paulson.'

'Is that what you were doing this morning, when you asked me to make that call to Michael?'

Jo almost apologises, but stops herself. She has nothing to say sorry for. 'Yeah. She didn't seem interested in the slightest, even though it's a possible motive for Freya's murder.'

Rob returns to the bed. 'What do you mean? How?'

'Well, if you didn't put that camera there, then someone else must have. I know it wasn't either of the kids, so that leaves only one other person.'

Rob shakes his head. He's forgotten, Jo thinks. He doesn't

realise Eve still has a spare key to their home, given to her years ago when they went abroad for a holiday. It was supposed to be for emergencies only, in case anything happened while they were away.

He stays silent as she explains her theory – the only explanation to Monday night that now makes any sense. Freya must have planned to tell her father. She'd somehow found out about Eve's night with Rob, and she was going to expose them.

'We've both seen how volatile their arguments could become. What if they'd argued about the affair and Eve had lashed out.'

'But the camera... I still don't understand why Eve would do that.'

'To blackmail you? Or me. Like you said about Freya, who knows what goes on in that head of hers.'

'I don't know, Jo. It just seems so extreme.'

'She wouldn't have meant to kill her. In the same way the police don't believe Toby intended to. They argued, she reacted. Then she panicked and framed our son.'

Once the words have left her, Jo feels herself weaken. Tears pool in her eyes, and when Rob reaches out to hold her, she lets him.

'We just need to prove it,' she says through sobs. 'I need you to help me.'

They lie down together, his body curved to the shape of hers, and she allows herself to be held by him as she cries, her grief an audible, tangible thing, until she eventually subsides into an unsettled sleep.

THIRTY-FOUR

ALICE

Alice wakes with a jolt. When she checks the phone on the bedside table, the screen tells her it's 11.20. She has a feeling that something's happened. Toby, she thinks. Something's happened to Toby. Once her eyes have adjusted to the darkness, she looks over to the single bed at the far side of the room. The duvet is flat; her mother isn't here. She must be in her father's room, and the thought brings with it mixed reactions. She has felt guilty at being the cause of their potential separation, yet at the same time, her father doesn't deserve her mother's forgiveness. If he's lied about this, it makes her wonder what else he's capable of lying about.

She checks her WhatsApp to see whether either of her parents have been online, but neither has since over two hours ago. If anything had happened to her brother tonight, they would have been notified. If there had been an emergency, she would have been told about it by now.

She lies awake for a while, wishing she could get back to sleep. It's no good; she can't, and she knows she doesn't want to. She needs to be doing something. Something that will help Toby. She needs to go home.

As she hurriedly pulls off her pyjamas and replaces them with leggings and a sweater, it occurs to her that despite the police searching their house, they were only looking for evidence of Toby's guilt. It seems fair to her to assume then that anything that might prove his innocence has been overlooked, and if the police aren't going to bother to look for it, Toby needs someone else who will. She has let him down all week with inactivity and weakness. Now, she knows she needs to do better by her brother.

She orders an Uber and goes down to the hotel foyer to wait for it. She gets into the back seat and gives the driver the address, and then she turns on the tracker on her phone. She's not an idiot. She's read enough stories of young women abducted by psycho taxi drivers to know she needs to leave a trail in case anything happens to her.

Thankfully, the taxi driver turns out not to be a serial killer. He isn't chatty either, something else she's grateful for. When he pulls into the cul-de-sac, she hopes he doesn't realise this is the street where Freya Harris was killed, the teenager whose photograph has been plastered all over the news and social media for the past few days. She hopes he doesn't realise she's the sister of the boy accused of Freya's murder.

But she has been a coward for long enough, hiding behind her parents, her brother, her friends – waiting for things to happen to her instead of making them happen for herself. It wasn't Freya's fault she didn't get onto that course at Loughborough, was it? If she was good enough, she would have been offered a place. For once, for Toby now, she needs to be good enough.

She goes quickly to the door, not wanting to be seen in the street. On a normal night, she wouldn't believe anyone would be around at this time, but nothing is normal here any more. She doubts Eve has slept since Monday evening. She pictures her pacing the kitchen in the darkness, not wanting to go into the hallway where her daughter's life was ended. She wonders whether she's argued with Chris about what happened in the street this morning.

The house is dark and eerily quiet. Alice doesn't want to put on any lights; she doesn't want anyone to know she's here. She uses the torch on her phone to guide her upstairs, where she goes straight to Toby's bedroom. Using the phone as a night light, she props it against the lamp on the bedside table and sits on the bed for a moment, wondering now what she's doing here. A surge of bravery has been replaced with a doubt that has crept in like a parasite, making her question herself. She doesn't know what she's hoping to find. She just needs to do *something*.

She starts beneath the bed. It occurs to her that this is where she herself hides anything that matters; it was the first place she'd thought to put the camera she'd found in her parents' wardrobe. Yet a thought strikes Alice now: that if Toby is innocent, as she knows he is, he will have nothing hidden, not here or anywhere else. This might all be a waste of time, yet she felt something pulling her home, in the same way she is drawn to the thought of her twin when she knows there is something wrong. She had known on Monday that he was inside the Harrises' house. Now she knows there must be something she can do to help him.

There is little under the bed: some old trainers, a box of old 45 singles Toby had bought with his pocket money a few years back when he'd gone through a record-collecting phase, and a pile of textbooks from his A-level studies that he's yet to get rid of. Alice sits in the dimly lit corner of the room and flips through his annotations, feeling closer to him just by being among his things and looking at his too-perfect handwriting.

She pulls herself from her reverie when she realises how little time she has. Her mother will wake at some point – she hasn't slept for more than a three-hour block since Monday evening – and when she does, she will be likely to return to their room to check that Alice is okay. Alice needs to be back in bed before this happens, so neither of her parents will ever know she left the hotel.

She moves to the desk now, looking for Toby's laptop. It's usually to be found there, but there's no sign of it, not even in the drawer below. Might there be an email, she wonders, or something else to prove he was online at the time Freya was murdered? She knows the police will already have investigated it, but she doesn't trust them entirely. There have been plenty of times they have settled on an easy option, overlooking potentially relevant details when a convenient scapegoat has been available.

Her body freezes at a sound that comes from somewhere outside the bedroom. In the darkness, the noise is thrown, making it impossible to tell which direction it came from. Had it been a windy night, it might have been something blown over outside, a wheelie bin disturbed or an unlocked shed door banging shut. But the night is peaceful: outside, at least.

A chill creeps through Alice's limbs as she hears something that she knows this time came from downstairs. The front door clicking shut. A movement in the hallway. There is someone in the house. She goes to the bedside table and carefully, quietly unplugs the lamp from the wall socket. With its lead looped around her fingers, she grips it tightly, thinking of what happened on Monday night, that stone elephant swung at Freya's head with a force that had been enough to kill her. Might she be capable of the same if someone were to attack her now? Under the wrong kind of circumstances, she assumes everyone is capable of anything.

She moves tentatively to the bedroom door, waiting a moment before opening it a fraction. The landing is so dark that she is barely able to see a few feet in front of her. She treads quietly on the carpet, careful not to make a sound. Yet she feels her heartbeat like a klaxon in her chest, and she's sure it must be audible. She stops outside her own bedroom door. There are footsteps on the stairs, someone coming up towards her. She moves again, pressing herself into the shadows against the doorway, and when she sees a figure at the top of the stairs, she pulls the lamp back above her head.

'Alice!'

The lamp comes crashing down, but it is knocked to one side, smashing against the wall. Alice opens her mouth to scream, but it is stifled by a hand. She grapples and fights back, clawing and scratching like a wild animal as she tries to free herself from the man's grip. But when she hears his voice again, she realises who it is.

'Alice, stop. It's me. Please, stop.'

Chris releases his hand from her mouth, raising both palms in a gesture of surrender. Alice gulps down air, her lungs swelling as she tries to breathe in enough oxygen to calm her nerves.

'What the hell are you doing here?' she eventually manages to ask.

He glances along the landing, seeming to check that she's alone. 'I heard a noise. I saw a light from the bedroom. I thought... I just came to check everything was okay.'

Lies, Alice thinks, taking a step back. 'How did you get in?'

'We've got a spare key. We've had it for years, in case of emergencies.'

He turns to glance at her parents' bedroom door, and when he looks back at her, Alice sees in his eyes the answer to everything. She knows why he is here.

'It was you,' she says quietly.

'What was me?' he replies, his voice thick with panic.

She can't get to the staircase; he's blocking her only escape. She pats down her jacket pockets, checking for her phone. It must still be in Toby's bedroom, on the bedside table, but if she goes back for it now, Chris will stop her. She tells herself she needs to remain calm. She just needs to somehow talk him down.

'I know about the camera,' she blurts. 'I found it. If that's what you're here for, it's gone.'

She braces herself for an assault that never comes. Instead, Chris crumples in front of her. As she watches him slide to the carpet, his head in his hands as he sobs, she considers the fact that an assault might have been preferable. Once more his grief is unbearable.

'I can explain everything.'

'Maybe I'm not the one who needs to hear it,' Alice tells him.

'I thought it mattered,' he says, looking up at her pleadingly. 'I always knew she had feelings for him, and I'd learned to live with it. I never thought either of them would try to take it any further. But now Freya...' Another sob bursts from him, his chest heaving with the force of it. 'Nothing matters now. Not after this. I only meant for it to be there a while. I just needed to know if it was a one-off, or if there was something still going on. I'd intended to come back for it sooner, but...'

Alice stands just a few feet from this broken man, a man who was like an uncle to her throughout her childhood, and watches as his grief for his daughter expels itself in a spew of hot tears and unconcealed shame. She wonders how she's supposed to feel towards him, whether anger or disgust or confusion should take precedence at the front of her mind in the mirror of what he's guilty of, and yet she can feel none of these things, because all she is able to feel for him in this moment is pity. For all his success, his wealth, his physical strength, he is as fragile as anyone else.

She slumps to the floor opposite him and sits with her back to her bedroom door, waiting quietly as he weeps. She thinks back on what happened this morning, rewatching the memory of Chris assaulting her father. Eventually, he speaks.

'I shouldn't have done it,' he tells her. 'I was desperate... I wasn't thinking. I should never have done it. I loved her so much...'

The past tense rings in Alice's ears in the ensuing silence, and she wonders if he's still talking about Eve. She wonders whether when he says he shouldn't have done it, he's still talking about the camera.

THIRTY-FIVE

JO

Jo starts at the sound of the hotel room door. When Alice comes in, she rushes for her, gripping her in a tight embrace. A part of her wants to scream at her, to demand an explanation, but for now, she is just relieved to have her here, safe. It is 3.50 in the morning and she has been trying Alice's phone for the past half-hour.

'Where have you been?' she asks, holding her daughter by the shoulders and pushing her from her so she can look her in the face. She doesn't want Alice to lie to her. They can't waste any more time on secrets.

'Home.' Alice removes her jacket and dumps it on the double bed.

'What for?'

'I needed something.'

Jo shakes her head. 'Don't, Alice. We all need to be honest with each other about everything now.'

She wasn't expecting Alice to start crying, and when she does, Jo goes to her and puts an arm around her shoulders, guiding her to the bed. They sit side by side while Alice cries, and as she talks through what's happened over these past few hours, Jo listens intently, not speaking until her daughter has told her everything.

'What are you going to do?' Alice asks her.

'I don't know,' Jo lies. 'Don't you worry about this though, okay? I'll deal with it.'

'That's exactly what worries me.'

She puts a hand on Alice's knee. 'You need to get some sleep.'

She pulls the duvet back, and Alice gets into bed fully dressed, her eyes already pulling her towards sleep. Then she does something Jo is sure she hasn't done since she was about nine years old: she reaches for her mother's hand and rubs the back of it until she eventually stops, having fallen into slumber. It was something she'd done every night for years and years, a comforting ritual that had become a habit.

Jo moves to her own bed, but she doesn't sleep. She knows she wouldn't be able to even if she wanted to. Chris's strange behaviour towards her at the weekend now makes more sense. When he'd touched her, he'd meant for Eve to see it. He'd been trying to make his wife jealous.

She reaches for her phone on the bedside table and sends him a message on WhatsApp.

Meet me in the car park at the top end of Oldfields Industrial Estate at 7 a.m. If you're not there, I'm going straight to the police.

She waits for the message to double-tick, expecting to have to wait a while. Yet moments later, it does. Within minutes, Chris has read it. Jo doesn't expect him to respond. She has no doubt he'll be there.

.   .   .

Jo plans to leave the hotel at 6.30, but when Alice starts stirring half an hour before this, she quietly leaves the room and goes down to the car. When Rob wakes and they realise she's left, they'll probably assume she's gone back to the house, which is exactly why she's told Chris to meet her elsewhere.

She arrives with forty minutes to spare, and at 6.53 she sees Chris's Audi pull into the car park. She gets out, gesturing for him to do the same. She doesn't want to get into that car, and she knows this place is public, with plenty of CCTV cameras about.

'Did you give the spare key back to Alice?' she asks as he approaches her.

'Yes... Jo, I'm sorry.'

She nods, but says nothing.

'How long have you known about it?'

'I assume you mean Eve and Rob,' she says, and she sees him flinch at the mention of their names strung together in the same sentence. 'Only for a couple of days. Alice told me. She overheard them talking at the party on Saturday.'

'So something has happened between them then?'

Jo narrows her eyes. Does Chris not know about the night they slept together?

'Just the once, Rob says, but who's to say that's the truth. You didn't know whether something was going on then?'

'I suspected, but I wanted proof.'

'So you planted a hidden camera in my bedroom.'

His face flushes with shame. 'I never intended to hurt you, Jo. I swear to God I never looked at anything...' He fades into silence, too embarrassed to say it aloud. 'I just wanted the truth.'

The truth, Jo thinks, is something she already knows Chris won't be able to handle. She doesn't want to hurt him either – God, the man is already hurting enough – but he needs to hear what she knows.

'You can't protect her from this, Chris.'

His eyebrows furrow. 'Protect who?'

'Eve. I know what she did. What she's done.'

He tilts his head to the side, his eyes boring questioningly into hers. 'You mean this thing with Rob?'

'Not Rob. Freya.'

He can't even bear to hear her name. His jaw locks at the mention of his daughter, and his eyes darken, challenging Jo to say anything more.

'What are you implying?'

'Freya knew about Eve and Rob. She was trying to tell Alice something on Sunday, but before they could talk, Eve happened to conveniently interrupt them. And then the next day, Freya—'

She cuts herself short, not needing to finish the sentence. When Chris says nothing, Jo fills in the blanks for him.

'Eve must have known that Freya knew about her and Rob. I think Freya was planning to tell you.'

Chris clenches his jaw. 'You've lost your mind. Eve has been beside herself all week. I've had to remove anything from the house that she might be able to use to hurt herself with. A piece of us has died, Jo... Surely as a mother you understand that better than anyone? How dare you call me out here to accuse her. You should be ashamed.'

'I'm not saying she meant to do it,' Jo says, desperate to make him see sense. 'You know what Eve and Freya could be like at times. They'd argue like sisters. Remember the time Freya slammed the car door shut on Eve's fingers when they were arguing about that sleepover?'

'It was an accident,' Chris says defensively.

'Exactly. It was an accident... but someone still got hurt.'

His face is red now. 'You're in denial,' he accuses her, jabbing a finger in her face. 'I know you don't want to accept the truth, but your son is a murderer. Coming here and accusing Eve isn't going to change that fact.'

'My son isn't capable of murder.'

'So what about you then, Jo? Are you capable of it?' He takes a step towards her. 'You had every motivation to hurt her. You were upset about the way she'd treated Alice. So where were you on Monday evening?'

'At home,' she responds flatly, but she realises as she says it that no one would be able to confirm this. Before Toby had gone over to the Harrises' house that night, he'd been upstairs in his bedroom. Alice had also been upstairs. 'But this isn't going to—'

She doesn't get to finish her sentence. Chris grips her by the shoulders, shaking her so hard that her head jolts back. 'Listen to me. You keep your filthy little lies to yourself, okay. Your family has broken mine. You stay the fuck away from us, or I swear to God, Jo, I don't know what I'll be capable of.'

He lets go of her and Jo stumbles back in shock as she watches him return to his car. Even after he has left the car park, she remains fixed to the spot, stunned by the reaction of a man she had once thought she'd known. Last night with Alice. Yesterday with Rob. Now this. Jo had thought Eve the dangerous one, yet now she's not so sure. She never really knew Eve. Now she realises she may have never known her husband either.

Her phone starts ringing, and when she takes it from her pocket, she sees Rob's name on the lit screen.

'Where the hell are you?' he asks. 'You need to get back here. It's Toby. He's in hospital.'

THIRTY-SIX

ALICE

Her parents have given up on the idea of trying to keep her protected from what is happening, so when they go to the hospital where Toby has been transferred, Alice goes with them. None of them know whether they'll be allowed to see him: he's still in police custody, and they have no idea what the rules are regarding a situation such as this. No one has even told them what his injuries are, only that he was assaulted at the holding prison and is in intensive care. Intensive care means badly injured. It means life-threatening.

In the car, they speak with the solicitor, the conversation coming through the speakers so that everyone can hear it.

'How the hell was this allowed to happen?' Rob demands. 'He's only just been moved there. Surely he shouldn't have even been exposed to the other inmates yet?'

Inmates. The word sounds so alien and inappropriate in the context of her brother.

'There was a security breach,' Michael tells them. 'Look,' he adds when he hears Rob swear, 'I'm dealing with it. You just focus on Toby.'

'You need to get the police to reinvestigate the murder,' Jo tells him. 'Eve and Chris Harris. They're hiding something, I know they are. I saw him this morning,' she adds, a fact of which Alice and Rob were both until now unaware. 'He's violent. You know what he did to Rob yesterday.'

'I'm doing everything I can to prove your son's innocence.' Michael attempts to reassure them, but Alice can hear the doubt in his voice, that even he doesn't believe he stands much of a chance.

'Will we get to see him?' Rob asks.

'I don't know. I'm on my way. I'll meet you at the hospital.'

Rob cuts the call and immediately questions Jo. 'What the hell were you thinking seeing Chris this morning? Where did you go?'

She tells him, but he is less than impressed. 'For Christ's sake, Jo, anything could have happened.'

They pull into the hospital car park. It takes twenty minutes to find a parking space, and when they get to the ICU, they're refused entry.

'For fuck's sake, this is ridiculous,' Rob snaps at the intercom of the unit's locked double doors. 'I just want to see my son.'

'Sir,' the woman at the other end of the intercom says, 'your son is under police watch and is still in custody.'

'And he's also in intensive care,' Rob shouts. 'You could let just one of us see him. Just let his mother see him.'

Jo's top lip is sucked in to stop herself from crying. She puts a hand on his arm. 'It's not her fault,' she reasons. 'She's just doing what she's told.'

Rob curses again loudly and kicks the door with frustration. A moment later, a uniformed officer appears at the door. 'I'm going to have to ask you all to leave.'

'I want to see my son,' Rob snarls, red-faced.

'You need to leave now, or you will be arrested,' the man says, churning the phrase out like a robot taking direction from a preprogrammed chip.

'Please,' Jo says. 'Let's go. We'll wait outside for Michael. He'll be able to help us.'

Rob stares at the officer with contempt, but allows himself to be pulled away from the doors. Jo continues to fight back tears as they head towards the lifts. Alice feels like crying too, but she doesn't want to do it here. Why won't anyone just tell them how Toby is?

When they get down to the concourse area where the shop and restaurant are, she makes an excuse about needing fresh air. Her parents are so engrossed in their argument that they allow her to leave without following her like a pair of bodyguards. Outside, she takes out her phone to call Dylan.

'Hey,' he answers, just as she is about to end the call and send him a text instead.

'Hey. I just wanted you to know I'm thinking about you. I know it's the vigil tonight. Are you okay?'

'Yeah.' The sound is muffled for a moment before he speaks again, his voice lowered. 'Sorry, I've just moved into a different room.'

'I was thinking about what we talked about before,' Alice says, remembering their conversation yesterday. 'I'm here for you, okay? No matter what.' No matter that I think your mother's guilty of your sister's murder and your father is a messed-up pervert, she adds in her head.

'Thanks, Alice.' There's more background noise.

'Are people there already?' she asks. It's not even midday yet.

'Yeah. It's been like this all week. Everyone will forget about us after the funeral, though, so I've been told. Look, I'd better go. Can I message you later?'

'Any time.'

He says goodbye and cuts the call, and Alice stays outside for a little while, contemplating the irony of the smokers outside the hospital doors. She watches people pass, patients, visitors, and staff: some on crutches, some in uniform, some being pushed in wheelchairs. She looks up to the tall grey tower-block building of the hospital, trying to work out which floor her brother is on. She imagines him behind one of those sky-high windows, unconscious and alone, his mind still active in a shut-down body. She hopes he isn't aware of where he is, or of the fact that he's alone.

Her thoughts roam to Dylan and the Harrises' house, people bustling in between rooms, making cups of tea in a bid to be useful. Amid them all she sees Eve, a woman who has built a life and a persona on appearances, still striving to be perfect even in grief; still hiding behind a pretence of what she really is. Perhaps Eve – a woman capable of striking her own daughter with an ornament in a moment of blind rage – has never been the mother she'd liked to portray herself as. Things can always be different behind closed doors.

Closed doors, Alice thinks. A locked front door. She needs to get into that house, to find out what they're hiding. The spare key to her own home that Chris gave back to her in the early hours of this morning is with her mother now. But Alice is sure that Jo was also given a spare key for Eve's house, for emergencies. As far as she's aware, it's still in the drawer of the hallway table. She needs to go home and find it.

She turns at the sound of her name. Her father is standing near the hospital main entrance, his eyes wet with tears.

'What?' she asks cautiously, unsure she wants an answer. 'What's happened?'

'It's Toby,' he says, coming over to her and pulling her to him. 'We've found out what happened at the prison. He was stabbed.'

THIRTY-SEVEN

JO

It is gone 7 p.m. when Michael advises them to go back to the hotel. Despite all his requests, access to Toby has been denied, and Jo is left with the torture of not knowing whether her son will make it through the night. But she isn't going anywhere. She's not leaving this hospital until she's been given permission to see her son.

'Take Alice back,' she tells Rob, but he doesn't want to leave either.

'She needs to go back to the hotel. Please.'

'I'll come back later,' he tells her, but Jo shakes her head.

'Stay with her, please. After what she did this morning, leaving the hotel like that...'

'She's not a prisoner,' Rob reminds her, before adding, 'Okay. I'll stay with her.'

After they've left, Jo walks the corridors of the hospital for what seems like hours. She goes back outside as the light of evening begins to fade, and is incredulous at the thought that she's so near her son and yet so far removed. The sky is slipping into darkness when she goes inside and finds a bench in a corridor few people seem to pass through. She sits silently for a while as she contemplates the long stretch of night ahead, and the agony of the not knowing. She thinks of Freya's vigil this evening and looks online for any details, but nothing much has yet been uploaded.

Every now and then her iPhone creates photo montages of the twins together. She's not sure how it does it – facial recognition, she supposes – but there'll be the occasional photo or video that will stop her in her tracks, flooring her with the reality of just how quickly time passes. She returns to one of these collections now – a series of images that's been given the title 'Together Over the Years'. The music selected is a tune she knows how to play; she learned it years ago as a student, though she can no longer remember the name of the piece.

Tears fill her eyes as the screen moves from shot to shot, a succession of photographs capturing the twins' childhoods together. Toby and Alice on the beach at Newquay, up to their ankles in the sea. The two of them playing snooker on a table so big they were barely able to reach up to manoeuvre the cue. Their tenth birthday party at an outdoor laser tag venue, later declared by Toby to be the best birthday ever. A Christmas dinner table, a paper crown on every head. A city break to Rome, the twins posing at the Trevi Fountain. Certificates from school. A sports day. The montage ends with a recent photograph of them together on the night of their Year 13 prom before it returns to the first image of the collection: two five-year-olds snuggled on the sofa in their pyjamas. Their lives played out in under ninety seconds.

Her body aches with longing to have that time back, to feel the warmth of their small bodies cuddled against hers; to press her face to their hair and smell the strawberry scent of shampoo that would circle them in an invisible cloud when they were fresh from the bath. They would each pick a story from the bookshelves in their rooms, and take them to the 'big bed' in Jo and Rob's bedroom, Toby sitting beneath the duvet and browsing the pages as Alice had her hair dried. There had been some evenings Jo couldn't wait for them to fall asleep. She would skip words, entire sentences, and rush them towards lights-off, torn by thoughts of the mess in the kitchen or the admin she hadn't completed or the pile of ironing that was waiting for her in the basket on top of the washing machine. There never seemed to be enough hours in the day. Now, their little faces staring up at her from a phone screen, captured in a moment stolen by time, she wishes she'd stopped more often. Breathed in that shampoo scent a little harder. Pulled them to her just that little bit tighter.

As she moves through the photographs in her phone's gallery, she comes across Eve's Facebook post from Monday. The sultry selfie she had taken in her living room, claiming herself victim of a two-day hangover. Jo had taken a screenshot of the post with the intention of showing it to Rob, though there had never been a chance to. No matter what his real reaction to it, she realises now that he would have kept it concealed behind a facade.

She's about to swipe to the next image when something makes her stop. She taps the photograph and uses her index finger and thumb to zoom in on the image. Just behind the snuggle chair where Eve is sitting, there's a long wall-hanging mirror. The side of the living room doorway can be seen in its reflection. She hadn't paid it any attention before as she hadn't been looking for anything untoward; she had been distracted by Eve's provocative pose and the embarrassing nature of the post. But now she notices something else. A flash of colour in the reflection. Someone passing by the door.

There's an arm. A sleeved arm with a distinctive logo, the same logo she recognises from the clothing Toby wears. A blue Carhartt hoodie, a brand seemingly so popular once again among teenagers and young men. She knows who the hoodie belongs to; she saw him wearing it in the street just a couple of days ago. Dylan. Only this photograph was taken on Monday, before Freya had been killed, and according to Alice, Dylan hadn't come home until Tuesday morning.

A lump forms in Jo's throat, stifling her air. Now she knows exactly what Eve has been hiding.

THIRTY-EIGHT

ALICE

Back at the hotel, her father tries to persuade her to eat something.

'I'm not hungry,' she tells him. She can't face even the thought of food. How could she eat while Toby is lying in that unit, fighting for his life? No one has really told them much about what happened, or how an inmate at the holding prison had managed to get his hands on a knife from the kitchen. All they know is that Toby has a single stab wound to the stomach. He hadn't even spent his first night at the prison. How is he supposed to get through the next God knows how many years?

Her thoughts take a change of direction. 'Actually,' she says, 'there is something I could manage.'

'What's that, love?'

'A cheese toastie.'

Rob smiles sadly. The memory of Toby and his cheese toasties settles between them, a silent ghost delivering a reminder of a life so recent and yet already so long past. 'That's what you fancy?'

Alice nods.

'I'll see what I can do. I'm sure I might be able to persuade the restaurant to rustle one up for you.'

'Thanks, Dad.'

As soon as he's left the room, she takes out her phone and orders an Uber. Then she pulls on her trainers and goes downstairs, careful to avoid the bar and restaurant opposite the main reception. She goes into the car park and sits behind a bush, hiding in case her father comes out to look for her. Five minutes later, she sees the car she's waiting for arrive. She gives the driver her home address as he pulls away from the hotel.

On the motorway, she taps out a WhatsApp message to her father.

Sorry, Dad – I just want to be close to Toby. Mum shouldn't be on her own x

She knows that her father will assume from this that she has left to return to the hospital, and as she reads it over again after pressing send, she reassures herself with the fact that it isn't exactly a lie. Her father will head straight for the hospital, and her mother will no longer be alone. She can't have him follow her, not with what she's about to do. No one can know where she's gone.

When her father tries to call her, she switches her phone to silent. Within half an hour, the Uber driver is pulling into the cul-de-sac. It is dark, already gone 10 p.m. She'd expected there to be people in the street – reporters and photographers, Freya's schoolfriends gathered for the vigil – and she hadn't thought through how she was going to get into her house without being seen. But she realises now that they've already moved on and will be making their way towards the playing fields on the other side of town. The cul-de-sac is deathly quiet. She pays the driver and gets out of the car.

She knows exactly where to look for the keys. There's a

table in the hallway similar to the one Eve and Chris have near their front door, the table upon which sat the ornamental elephant that was used to kill Freya. All the keys are kept in the drawer of this table, including spares and those for emergency use only. Alice rummages around in the drawer and removes three that could potentially belong to the Harrises. As she slips them into her pocket and leaves the house, she realises there has never been a greater emergency than there is tonight.

Jo knows that the vigil for Freya that's taking place tonight is being held in St Asaph's playing fields, not far from the secondary school that both her and Eve's children attended. She gets the taxi to drop her off outside the school, and crosses the main road to take the shortcut through the housing estate behind it. By the time she gets to the railed boundary of the playing fields, she can see the lights of the torches and candles carried by the mourners, a sky of stars illuminating the stretch of grass that surrounds the bandstand.

There are a couple of uniformed police officers present, and she wonders whether the investigating officers may also be among the crowd, there to keep a check on anything potentially untoward. This is what they do in murder cases – keep an eye on friends and family, watching for suspicious behaviour. Yet they've already got their man, she thinks bitterly. Why would they be here now when as far as they're concerned Toby has already been found guilty?

She feels herself shaking as she crosses the grass. There is someone standing on the raised platform of the bandstand, but from this distance she can't yet see who it is. She can't make out

Chris or Eve, and she wonders whether Dylan is here. He must be. He won't want to do anything that might draw attention to himself, and not showing up for his sister's vigil would be bound to raise eyebrows.

A song is being played through a set of speakers somewhere. Jo doesn't recognise it. A female voice, breathy, the lines almost whispered rather than sung. Lyrics about leaving behind someone they love.

Despite the warm summer days and mild evenings that have been the pattern of these past few weeks, she feels cold to her bones. She stops and watches as the man on stage, who she recognises now as Eve's brother, takes a microphone from someone else. The music fades as attention turns to him.

'Thank you, everyone, for being here tonight,' he says, his voice trembling as he speaks. He clears his throat. Jo continues to search for Freya's parents among the crowd, but she still can't see them.

'On behalf of all of Freya's family, we'd like to thank everyone for being here this evening, and especially Freya's friends who first approached her mother with the idea.'

Jo pushes forward, weaving between those lingering at the back of the throng of people surrounding the bandstand.

'Freya would be in awe of this,' her uncle continues. 'We all know how much she loved to be surrounded by people, to be in the limelight, so all of you being here tonight for her would have been right up her street. We just wish we could be celebrating her for different reasons and under different circumstances.'

His voice breaks and he moves the microphone from his mouth, his hand flying to his stubbled jaw as he tries to with-hold his emotion. Jo follows his eyeline as he looks out at the crowd of faces, and it's then that she sees Eve and Chris, propped against each other, keeping each other upright.

It's okay, she sees Eve's brother mouth to her.

She hears a few mutterings as she continues to push her

way through the crowd. Attention is beginning to turn upon her, with people recognising who she is. She tries to shut herself off from what is said, but she hears the expressions of disbelief at her showing up – *tonight of all nights.*

Eve turns. She sees her. Jo stops pushing forward. To her left, she spots Scarlet, who looks her up and down before turning to the young man next to her and whispering something in his ear. Scarlet edges back as though she might spontaneously combust if she stays too close to Jo, and the young man puts an arm around her and pulls her towards him, protecting her from the imminent danger Jo's presence seems to threaten.

She is surrounded by actors. Perpetrators presenting themselves as victims.

'Freya's life,' her uncle continues, 'may have been short, but during her time with us, she filled our lives with joy.'

Eve says something to Chris, who turns and looks at Jo. He shakes his head slowly, a silent plea for her not to cause a scene. Jo wonders if he might still consider her guilty, or whether it was his anger that spurred the accusation. Perhaps he presumes she's here because of that stupid bloody camera, but she couldn't give a damn about that any more. He doesn't know what his wife is hiding, she thinks. Chris had already left for his trip to Leeds when Freya had been murdered. Unless that was also a lie, it makes sense that he might not even know his son had been home on Monday.

There's a commotion behind her, people jostling and shoving, voices raised. Freya's uncle's speech is cut short just as Jo feels a hand on her arm.

'I'm going to have to ask you to leave.'

She looks at the police officer, one of the uniformed men she'd seen when she'd first arrived at the fields. 'Take your hand off me,' she says calmly. She knows she must stay composed and in control if she wants them to listen to her.

'Go home, Jo,' she hears Eve say. 'You're not wanted here.'

'Because of this, you mean?' Jo taps out her passcode and brings up the screenshot of Eve's Facebook post. She thrusts it at Eve before holding it in front of the officer. 'She posted this on Monday afternoon. Her son was in the house – you can see his arm in the reflection in the mirror! Alice told me he came home on Tuesday, because that's what Dylan told her, but he was lying. This is Dylan. Dylan killed Freya.'

There is a collective gasp among the watching crowd, and then someone shouts at her, telling her to go home. Others are quick to join in, trying to hound her into silence. Someone grabs her by the shoulders, but a second uniformed officer pulls the person away.

'Mrs Clarke, if you don't leave this minute, I will have you arrested.'

She looks past the officer at Eve, her faced turned deathly pale above the glow of candlelight. She knows the truth, Jo thinks. She knows what's she's done, what she's lied about. She knows she's been found out.

'How dare you,' Chris says, his voice shaking. He moves past his wife and jabs a finger in Jo's face, in much the same way he had that morning. 'We're saying goodbye to our daughter. The daughter your son stole from us.'

Despite everything his wife and son are guilty of, Jo's heart breaks for Chris. His eyes are wet with tears and the strong man she has known for the past two decades, successful and well respected in his career, is broken to a shadow of his former self. Grief has cut through everything he was. He doesn't know, she thinks. He doesn't know a thing about the secret that Eve and Dylan have been hiding.

She steps back and raises a hand in surrender, the image of Eve's screenshot turned to the braying crowd. The faces of the mourners are stamped with looks of indignation and outrage. How dare she come here and do this. How dare she even show her face here today.

'Mrs Clarke,' one of the officers says warningly.

'I'm going,' Jo says, shoving her phone into her pocket. 'I think DI Paulson will be interested to see this.'

She holds Eve's eye and sees the panic in her face, and it's now that she realises. He's nowhere to be seen. She scans the sea of faces in front of her before turning back to his parents.

'Where's Dylan?'

FORTY

ALICE

The house is unnaturally quiet. Alice wishes she could enter through the side door, but the gate is closed and she only has a key to the front. When she goes in, the first thought she has is of Freya, her body lying on the tiles in front of her, her head resting in a pool of blood. The spot on the hallway table where the white stone elephant had once stood is now empty. Alice hears the echo of a thud, and then a long, cold silence, as though the sounds of Monday evening have been trapped inside the house, haunting it for ever.

The rest of the family won't be able to stay here now, she thinks. How could anyone live within those memories, having to pass through the scene of the crime as part of their everyday routine? Eve might be brazen, but even Alice doesn't believe her callous enough to be able to stay living in the house where she killed her own daughter, painting on the face of victim with the same precision with which she applies her mask of make-up, lying to her husband and son every day about who and what she is.

Alice heads carefully up the stairs, using the torch on her phone to guide her way. She tries to keep her thoughts from what happened in the early hours of the morning, when she'd been confronted by Chris on the landing in her own home. But she knows that for now, at least, everyone is at the vigil. She's on limited time, but she must use what little she has. She can no longer hang around doing nothing but grieve.

In Chris and Eve's bedroom, she searches through drawers and cupboards, desperate in her search for a clue. She doesn't care about the mess she makes or the tracks she leaves; they can call the police and report her if they like. Both Eve and Chris are criminals in their own way, both guilty of their own sins, and she doubts either will want to have their secrets made public. If either of them threatens her, she is armed with ample ammunition, and she won't think twice about using it.

Thoughts of Toby accompany her as she goes from drawer to drawer, desperately seeking a sign of Eve's guilt. Over these past few hours, she has tried to convince herself that everything is going to be okay, an inner voice attempting to console her with a similar mantra her mother would use when Alice had been a child, after a bad day at school or a fall that had left her hurt. Toby is strong; he's going to be all right. But the adult that exists beneath Alice's naïvety is realistic enough to know this is likely not to be the case. Toby is in intensive care, fighting for his life. Since finding out earlier exactly what happened to him, she has run internet searches on the survival rates of stab wounds to the stomach, and the odds don't seem to be in his favour. None of this was meant for him. Whether the assault was an intentional attack upon his supposed crime against Freya, or simply a case of Toby having been in the wrong place at the wrong time, someone else should have been there instead of him. It shouldn't be her brother lying in the ICU.

Alice gasps to catch her breath, realising now just how wet with tears her face is. She runs the heel of her hand over each eye in turn, her vision clearing to offer her renewed focus. But as her desperate and directionless search of Eve and Chris's bedroom continues, she realises she isn't going to find anything here. Eve is thorough and calculated, too clever a liar to have left anything incriminating lying around where it might easily be found.

There is a framed photograph on the bedside table: the Harris family posing at a marina, a yacht moored behind them. Freya looks younger, maybe fourteen or fifteen, and when the image was taken, Dylan's skin was still marred by the teenage acne that had erupted a couple of years earlier. He'd always been self-conscious about it, his awkwardness no doubt made more difficult by his mother's attempts to treat it. Alice still remembers being in their kitchen one evening with Freya, and watching Eve try to persuade Dylan to wear some of her concealer before he went out to see his friends. For Eve, everything has been about appearance, even when it's come down to her own children. Now, because of her insistence on maintaining the pretence of a perfect life, Freya is dead and Toby is fighting for his life.

She takes the frame from the bedside table and hurls it across the bedroom. It smashes against the wall, the glass shattering to pieces on the carpet. Her heart thunders in her chest as she looks at the broken image on the floor, the breaks in the glass splintering across the family's faces.

On the other side of town, the night sky is being lit by a constellation of candles. Music might be played. Prayers might be said. Softly spoken words of sorrow uttered by family members and school friends, each with an anecdote to share or a memory to be resurrected. Eve will stand among it all, pale-faced and broken. She will stand and play victim while Alice's family falls to pieces.

There is nothing to be found in this room, and Alice is running out of time. She goes out onto the landing, doubtful for a moment that she has done the right thing in coming here tonight. But she is here now. She must do something.

Dylan's bedroom door is ajar. A lamp has been left on, and the soft glow pulls her towards the room. She pushes the door open gently, observing for a moment the chaos of the place. Dirty mugs litter the desk; clothing lies abandoned on the carpet. The wardrobe door is open, spilling shoes and bags and sports equipment onto the floor. The bed is unmade, the duvet thrown back, the sheet half pulled away from the mattress. The place is a pit, a room inhabited by despair. Dylan's grief can be witnessed in the uneaten food left to grow stale on a plate on the bedside table; it can be smelled in the fetid air that lingers here like a cloud.

And yet Alice knows Dylan well enough to know that this was what he was like before Monday, before his sister's death. His depression is at least a year old now, possibly older. She feels pity for him, and yet she can't afford room for sympathy, not now.

Does he know of his mother's guilt? A stab of betrayal spears her in the gut, that Dylan might have lied to her so blatantly when they'd met on Wednesday. She doesn't want to believe there could be a chance it might be true, yet it seems to her that she can no longer trust anyone, and that anything is possible. He might not have known then, she reassures herself, but there's always the possibility that he has found out since. She wonders whether he would lie for Eve or turn a blind eye to protect her.

She begins to trawl through Dylan's things, ignoring the sliver of doubt that warns her she has gone a step too far. She pulls books from the bookcase and shakes them out; she opens gaming boxes and sports bags and unopened envelopes she finds stashed in the drawer of the bedside table. At the end of Dylan's bed is an overnight bag, still unpacked since his return home from London. She roots in it and finds his passport shoved among underwear and toiletries. There's an outside pocket, zipped shut. When she opens it, she finds nothing but a train ticket. She shoves the bag away from her, but something makes her go back to it.

She pulls the ticket from the bag and takes in the details. London Paddington to Cardiff.

The air leaves her lungs.

The ticket is dated 1 July. Monday. The day Freya had died. Yet Dylan had told her over WhatsApp messages that he'd got home on Tuesday. She'd seen him arrive home in the car with Eve after his mother had collected him from the station. She stares at the date, checking it over in case she's made a mistake. But the print can't lie. And no one else would have taken that train route other than Dylan.

She gets up from the carpet at a sound from downstairs. She puts a hand on Dylan's desk, steadying herself, her other hand still gripping the train ticket. She waits a moment, and then hears something else. Footsteps on the stairs.

She knows it isn't paranoia, or the memory of what happened in the early hours of this morning when she'd found Chris in her home. There is someone on the landing. She turns to the door, her hand clenched into a fist. Her body tenses as the footsteps draw closer to the bedroom, as the door is pushed open, and she finds herself no longer alone.

Dylan stands in the doorway wearing the bright blue Carhartt hoodie he loves so much. He looks at the hand in which the ticket is now concealed.

'Alice,' he says. 'What are you doing here?'

FORTY-ONE

JO

Jo runs from the playing fields and heads back towards the school. There is little traffic, and few of the street lights are on. Through the darkness and the blur of tears and anger that blinds her, she is barely able to see the stretch of pavement that lies ahead of her. When she checks her phone, she finds three missed calls from Rob, as well as a string of texts asking where she is. And a final one: *Alice has gone. Call me.*

She stops on the pavement and tries to catch her breath. When she calls Rob back, he answers on the first ring.

'Where is she?' she pants, breathless from adrenaline and panic.

'I don't know. She texted me saying she was going back to the hospital, but when I got here, I couldn't find you anywhere. Where are you?'

The dark road on which she stands is a ten-minute walk away from the cul-de-sac. Half that if she runs. What if Alice is there? And then a worse thought hits her. What if Dylan is there with her? They've always been close, and Alice has no idea how dangerous he is.

'I need you to come home,' she says, picking up her pace into a run again. 'The house. I think Alice has gone back there.'

'Where are you now?'

'Five minutes away. I went to the vigil. It was Dylan. Dylan killed Freya.'

There is a silence so long she thinks one of them has lost signal. 'Rob?'

'I'm still here.'

'Did you hear me?'

'Yeah,' he says. 'I don't understand. I thought—'

'I can't explain now,' she says, struggling for breath. 'Just get home.'

She cuts the call and breaks into a sprint, wishing that she was fitter. She tries Alice's phone, but it rings through to the answerphone. As she approaches the main road that runs through the small town, she passes a group of women leaving a restaurant, laughing as they make their way to the bus stop. The next pub along is filled with people enjoying their Friday evening, either oblivious or unthinking of the event taking place a little less than a mile down the road from here. This is the tragedy of life, Jo thinks – that everything moves on regardless. Or perhaps in some ways it is a blessing.

She leaves the main road and cuts through a street of terraces before she reaches the path that leads into the estate just beyond where they live. By the time she gets to the cul-de-sac, her legs and chest are burning, her lungs tight with fear and exertion. She goes into the house, where the hallway light is on.

'Alice!' she shouts. She searches downstairs, then up, calling out to her daughter as she enters every room. But the place is empty, and her cries go unanswered. By the time she reaches the last of the bedrooms, she is forced to accept that Alice isn't here. When she tries to call her again, it does the same as last time, ringing through to the click of the answerphone.

Jo stands in the hallway, at the living room door, and looks in on the silent room, this heart of their home that seems suddenly so alien to her. She hears shouting from the street, and when she goes to the window, she sees Eve on the driveway of her own house, banging on the front door.

She can't get in, Jo thinks. She must be locked out. Dylan must be in there.

With a sinking feeling in her heart, she remembers what happened in the early hours of this morning. She thinks of Chris here in her home, intimidating Alice, an intruder on the landing. The spare key.

At the hallway table, she yanks the drawer open and flings out packets of batteries and spare light bulbs, all the crap she'd at some point planned to sort through but had never got around to. There are spare car keys, the keys to her sister's house, several copies of keys for Rob's business properties, each marked with a green fob to separate them from the rest. Always for emergency use only, but there just in case. When the locks had been changed at the Harrises' house following the break-in, Eve had given Jo a spare key to replace the one she'd had for years.

But as she gets to the bottom of the drawer, Jo realises the key she's looking for is missing.

Alice is on the wrong side of the street. She is there in that house, and Dylan is with her.

FORTY-TWO

ALICE

'I thought you were at the vigil,' Alice stammers.

'I was.' Dylan glances at her hand, at the corner of orange ticket that pokes from between her fingers. 'What's that?' he asks.

Alice takes a step back, though there's nowhere to go. She's small enough to get through the window if needed, but there's a twelve-foot drop to the patio; she would probably break all her limbs, if not worse. Right now, with the ticket in her hand that taunts her with the likelihood that this man she thought she'd known is a liar, it seems a preferable option.

'What are you doing here?' he asks again.

'I... I just thought...'

'You just thought what, Alice?'

They stand in a face-off, Alice wondering whether Dylan knew when he came back here that he would find her in the house. But how? She hadn't told anyone else what she planned to do. She can't understand why he's left Freya's vigil when everyone else is still there. Unless he could no longer stomach the guilt.

'I thought you'd come home on Tuesday,' she says, her hand

quivering beside her. 'But this...' She uncurls her fist. There's no point in trying to hide what she knows from him, not when she has nowhere to go. And this is Dylan. He would never hurt her.

'Were you here?' she asks. 'Were you home when Freya died?'

She braces herself, part of her expecting him to retaliate, but he doesn't. Instead, he breaks down. His jaw tightens as he starts to cry, and he looks at her desperately, his eyes pleading with her, already begging for forgiveness before his mouth has a chance to form words.

'I didn't mean to hurt her,' he insists. 'I swear to you, Alice, it was an accident. I never meant to hurt her.'

There is a rush of blood in Alice's head, a tide of red turning in front of her brain, blurring her vision. Not Dylan. She has suspected Eve... she has questioned Chris... but never Dylan. She would never have thought it possible.

'She was going to tell your father, wasn't she?' she says quietly.

Dylan nods. 'I begged her not to. She was angry... she wasn't thinking straight. I don't think she realised how much it would change everything.'

Alice closes her eyes for a moment, trying to make sense of everything. Dylan is close to his mother, but no closer than he is to his father. Not so close that he would keep the secret of an affair from Chris, allowing him to live in ignorance.

'The argument that was reported to the police by one of the neighbours on Monday evening,' Alice says. 'That was you and Freya.'

'She promised me she'd keep quiet. She'd already known for long enough... I couldn't see how a little longer would make any difference. She became fixated on it, saying she couldn't keep lying to Mum. She came down from her bedroom on Monday and said it wouldn't wait any longer. She didn't want to keep secrets from anyone.'

'Tell me what happened,' Alice says quietly, because although she doesn't want to hear the details, she needs to. She needs to know all the things that she's known all week Toby was never a part of.

'I told her she wasn't thinking straight,' Dylan says, still crying, 'that it would affect us all. That everything would be ruined. But she was so angry, Alice. She wouldn't listen to reason. She tried to push past me. I shoved her back. She went for me, like a wild animal. I just wanted to stop her. It all happened so quickly.'

Alice listens silently, her heart fracturing with every word. That text, she thinks – the one sent from Freya's phone to Toby's. Dylan had reacted in temper and panic. Had he then been calculating enough to get Freya's phone and send a message to Toby as though it was from his sister?

They are both startled by a banging downstairs, someone pounding on the front door. They glance at one another, neither knowing what to do. Another succession of frantic knocks ensues, the doorbell pressed repeatedly. Fear and panic rip through Alice. She was confident she could keep him talking while she planned a way to escape, but now he knows there's someone outside, he might not be so easily persuaded.

'Does your mother know what you did?'

Dylan sobs, and the sound is so pathetic it makes Alice want to slap him. She looks at his reddened, stupid face, and all she can think is that he set her brother up, allowing Toby to take the blame for a crime Dylan has known all week he is innocent of. And now her brother lies alone in hospital, possibly dying. No family permitted to sit beside him, no one there to hold his hand. No one to tell him they love him.

Dylan ended a life, and he was willing to end a second. He was willing to see Toby sentenced for a crime he didn't commit. Alice hates him with every fibre of her being, but she can't let him see it in her eyes, not while she's alone in this room with him and no one knows where she is. Her phone is in her pocket. It rang several times earlier, and each time she'd ignored it. Her battery was on red when her father had tried her, and then later her mother. Her heart sinks at the thought that it's probably now dead.

'Does Eve know?' she asks again.

It's now that they hear Eve's voice, shouting for her son through the letter box. 'Dylan! Dylan!'

'Does she know?' Alice repeats slowly, through gritted teeth.

'Yes! She came back from her run... she found us in the hallway.'

'Oh my God. That text to Toby, from Freya's phone. Eve sent it.'

She doesn't need a response from him. She has known Eve all her life; she has seen through the exterior that seems to blind everyone else to what the woman truly is. She takes another step back, her calf knocking into the bed frame. There's no way she can get to the bedroom door; Dylan is blocking her only exit, other than the window that still waits behind her.

'Why did it matter to you so much whether your dad found out?' she challenges him. 'You don't live here any more. It wouldn't have affected you if they'd argued over it. If they'd got a divorce, even.'

Dylan's eyes narrow. 'I'd have lost everything.'

Alice shakes her head, angry with herself that she has never seen him for who and what he really is. He is just like his mother, though she hadn't realised until now; their house, their lifestyle, their money are all more important than their morals, or the people they harm while taking what they want.

'My mother knows,' she tells him.

Dylan's features crumple. 'What do you mean? How does she know?'

'I told her. I overheard your mother and my dad at the party on Saturday night.'

'Rob knows as well?'

Alice tastes bile in the back of her throat. She studies Dylan's face, his dark eyes searching hers desperately, and she realises they're not talking about the same thing. Whatever Dylan is referring to, it isn't an affair.

'What are you talking about, Alice?'

'What are *you* talking about?'

Dylan hesitates for a moment before realising that all hope of keeping secrets now is lost. He pulls the sleeve of his hoodie over each eye in turn before exhaling slowly, expelling any reluctance as he prepares himself to tell her what he seems to believe she had already known.

'The break-in last year,' he says. 'It was me.'

FORTY-THREE

JO

Jo runs into the street, shouting Eve's name. Eve ignores her, still trying the front door. She stoops to the letter box and calls her son's name, and Jo feels a wave of dizziness at the knowledge that all her fears are coming true. Dylan is in that house with her daughter.

'Is he in there?' she demands.

'I'm afraid he might do something stupid.'

Jo grits her teeth. 'Alice is in there with him.'

As Eve stands, Jo sees the front of her T-shirt, emblazoned with a photograph of Freya taken on prom night. The words *Justice for Freya* are printed beneath it.

'What? No... she can't be.'

'The spare key. It's gone.'

'Why would she be in there?'

'I don't know. Because she doesn't trust you. Because her brother's innocent and she's desperate to find something that proves it.'

Eve starts to pound on the door again, pummelling her fists on the wood as she calls Dylan's name on repeat. Jo takes out her phone and dials 999, asking for the police.

'My daughter's locked inside a house. She's with my neighbour... he might be armed.'

She ignores the look that Eve gives her. All this time she's protected her son knowing who he is and what he did. She was prepared to sacrifice Toby to save Dylan, and Jo knows she will never forgive her for it. She will not let this family take another child from her.

She gives the call handler the address, and they tell her the police are on their way. Ignoring Eve, she goes to the side of the driveway and pulls one of the wheelie bins over to the fence.

'Help me then,' she says, waiting for Eve to make the right decision for once. Eve hesitates for a moment, and then goes to her. 'What are you going to do?' she asks.

'Whatever it takes. With or without your help.'

Eve's eyes glisten in the darkness. 'I'd do anything for my children,' she says quietly.

'So would I.'

For a moment, Jo thinks Eve might try to assault her; instead, she helps Jo pull herself up onto the bin. From here, she can reach the top of the fence, and she heaves herself over, not thinking about the drop on the other side. Climb like a child, she tells herself. Without fear or caution.

'Jo!'

But Jo doesn't wait to hear whatever Eve wants to say to her, and she doesn't want her to join her on the other side of the fence. She drops to the path at the side of the house and rushes to the door that leads into the utility room. Like the front door, it is locked. When she goes around the back of the house to the kitchen, the bifold doors are also locked, just as she'd expected them to be. She runs down the garden to the shed. It's never been locked in the past, but when she reaches it, she realises security here has changed since the break-in.

'Shit.'

The door has a padlock. Jo shakes it uselessly before taking her phone from her pocket and turning on the torch. She holds it at arm's length, moving it back and forth across the wide expanse of garden in search of something that might help her. But of course, Eve and Chris's garden has a similar appearance to the rest of their life as it had been before Monday: all perfectly ordered, with everything in its place. There are no bricks lying around; no tools left out.

She scans the garden again, desperate now. Outside the summer house, there are stone pots with lilies in on either side of the painted door. She runs and picks one up, grimacing beneath its unexpected weight. She carries it down to the shed, where she uses every bit of strength to lift it to the padlock. She brings its weight down once, twice, three times... and on the fourth attempt the padlock yields and bursts from the lock.

She drops the pot to the ground, narrowly missing her feet. It smashes on the concrete path as she yanks the shed door open. Inside, she quickly finds what she's looking for, and she takes the hammer with her to the house.

'Jo!'

She hears Eve's voice from the other side of the fence, and there is someone else with her now. It might be Chris, it might be one of the neighbours roused from their home by the noise. She doesn't know, and she doesn't care. As she swings the hammer at the utility room window, all she cares about is reaching Alice before the unimaginable happens.

FORTY-FOUR

ALICE

'Why?' Alice asks, her voice quivering. 'Why would you do that to your own parents?'

She glances to Dylan's desk, searching for something she might be able to use as a weapon. There's nothing heavier in sight than a hardback book, useless if he was to do anything to her. Dylan claims to have never meant to hurt his sister, but Alice doesn't trust that he wouldn't react in the same way again.

'I told you when we went for that walk that I'd got into a mess in London,' Dylan reminds her. 'But I've never told anyone just how much of a mess I've made of everything. I'm in so much debt. And I don't mean bank loans. I mean things I should have never got myself into. People I shouldn't have got involved with.'

Alice notices Dylan's hand move to his back pocket, resting just out of sight. He notices the way her eyes follow it, and he quickly returns it to his side. But it's too late. He has something waiting in his pocket, she thinks – something he's ready to use. She feels any earlier courage she might have had melt away from her as easily as ice cream in the sun.

'Your parents would have helped you, though. You would have only had to ask them.'

Dylan shakes his head. 'Not this time. Dad warned me ages ago that he was done with me – he wouldn't bail me out again.'

'You must have been worried the police might work it out, though? The forced lock, the whole set-up of the thing.'

'I was desperate, Alice.'

Alice glances to her side, still searching the room for a potential weapon. 'Your grandmother's things,' she reminds him, knowing she needs to keep him talking for as long as she can. 'Your mother was heartbroken. Those things were irreplaceable.'

'I know. And I'm sorry. I didn't know what else to do.'

'There are people who can help you,' she tries to reassure him. 'Mitigating circumstances. If you've been having problems, people will understand. The university might be able to vouch for your character.'

But even as she speaks, she knows he can see through her lies. They both know there are no mitigating circumstances for what he did on Monday evening.

'I didn't mean to hurt her, Alice... I swear to you I didn't.'

He begins to weep again, and for a moment so strange it takes her by surprise, Alice sees the boy he once was, a much younger Dylan standing in front of her, as though all these years and all this tragedy have somehow been erased. She might hold his hand, offer him some last comfort, pity him. If not for Freya. If not for Toby.

They hear glass breaking somewhere downstairs. Dylan turns to the door, and Alice takes her chance. She stumbles across the room, ready to shove past him to get to the landing, but he is quicker than she is, and he pulls something from his back pocket, a flash of silver illuminated in the air between them. A knife. She stops sharply, little more than a foot away from him.

'Dylan,' she mouths, the word barely audible.

'I'm sorry, Alice. I'm sorry about Freya. I wish I could go back to Monday and undo it all. I wish I could go back two years and un-fuck everything up. I'm sorry about Toby. No one was ever meant to get hurt.'

There's a noise from downstairs, something knocked over in the kitchen. Dylan glances to the door as he raises his hand, the knife held in front of him. 'I'm sorry, Alice. You've always been like a sister to me.'

There are footsteps on the stairs; she hears her name. She takes a deep breath and holds it, waiting for the pain. She'll know what Toby felt now, she tells herself. She'll live the same experience; she'll feel his pain in the same way she has for most of their lives.

But the pain never comes. Dylan's raised arm is lowered sharply, his face contorting as he plunges the blade into his own stomach.

'Dylan!'

He takes a couple of steps back and slumps against the door frame, his legs giving way beneath him. Alice rushes to him, crouches beside him; stares in horror as a patch of crimson spreads out across his hoodie like a blossoming rose.

FORTY-FIVE

JO

Jo reaches Dylan's bedroom doorway to find Alice crouched beside him. A knife handle juts from his stomach. Her daughter looks up at her helplessly, her features racked with panic, and Jo finds herself transported back to Monday night like some macabre déjà vu forcing her to relive her worst nightmare.

'Alice.' She almost falls into her daughter as she pulls her to her feet, gripping her so tightly that she might squeeze the breath from her. 'Thank God you're okay.'

'I didn't do it, Mum.'

'My God, I know you didn't. I know.'

Jo pulls away, then takes out her phone. 'Ambulance,' she says. 'Young man with a stab wound. Self-inflicted.'

She glances at Alice, not needing her nod of confirmation. Her daughter would never be capable of this, even had her life depended on it. She has raised her children to be honest and true, and this is what they are: both Alice and Toby. She should never have doubted her son's innocence.

Jo relays the details of the incident and the address to the call handler, taking directions on how to attend to Dylan. As she crouches beside him, she hears someone rushing up the stairs. A moment later, Eve is there with them.

'Dylan!'

She drops to the carpet beside him and puts her hands either side of his face. 'What have you done? Oh God... what have you done?'

She glares at Alice and then at Jo.

'Mum...' Dylan starts, but through the pain he is unable to utter anything more.

Jo tries to block out Eve's sobs. She continues to listen to the call handler's instructions, Dylan's blood marking her hands as she follows the steps that might help him survive. Because whatever this boy and his mother are guilty of, she will not become like them. Behind them, Alice has dropped to the bed, exhausted by her ordeal, watching silently as the two mothers sit alongside each other with the shared aim of saving a life.

'There's nothing we can do now,' Jo says, getting to her feet. 'The ambulance won't be long.'

Eve's face is wracked with despair as she holds her injured son. Jo doesn't expect gratitude for trying to help save Dylan's life, but there's something else Eve must do for her before either of them leaves this room. She retrieves her phone and pulls up a name from her contacts list, holding the screen out to Eve for her to see.

'You need to do it now.'

She expects resistance or argument; instead, Eve nods, resigned. She squeezes her son's hand before letting him go, telling him everything is going to be okay. Then she stands and moves towards Jo, who taps her phone screen with her thumb. She moves the phone to her ear and waits for DI Paulson to answer.

'It's Joanne Clarke,' she says, though she doubts she needs introduction. 'I'm with Eve Harris. She needs to speak to you.'

She passes the phone to Eve, who takes it with a shaking hand. Outside, sirens can be heard approaching.

'It's my son,' Eve says. 'I need to...' She falls silent. 'Yes, I'm still here.'

There is a pause. A single tear runs down Eve's cheek as she looks at her son's blood oozing through his clothes . She glances at Jo, making eye contact now for the first time. Something unspoken passes between them, a mutual acknowledgement of the other's actions. That they might not agree with them, but they understand.

'It's my son,' she says. The tear slips to her lip and is swallowed by her words. 'I need to report my son for murder.'

FORTY-SIX

ALICE

Eight months later

Alice rests on her knees and wipes the dirt from the stone. The recent spring months have brought terrible weather, winter prolonging its assault of ceaseless winds and rain. She hadn't told anyone she planned to come here today. For the past eight months they seem to have moved silently through the motions of life, each of them avoiding an excess of words for fear of hurting someone they love. Things have gone unsaid that should be spoken. Perhaps one day they might find the words for them, but not yet.

The engraved lettering of Freya's name is already moss-coloured, no one having been here to tend to the headstone. Alice vows to come back with something she can clean it up with, and flowers to help brighten the place up a bit. She imagines Freya as she might have been now, in a life cut short by greed and fear. Perhaps she would have pursued that degree course at Loughborough, the one Alice had had her heart set on; or maybe she would have already quit, setting her sights on something else.

Chris has yet to forgive his son for what he did. Perhaps he'll never be able to bring himself to do so. But Alice has learned at still so young an age that forgiveness is not for the person who has done wrong but more for the person who has been wronged. Resentment towards Freya had changed her temporarily, in the same way her anger towards Scarlet had for a while made her a person she didn't recognise. She feels lighter for having forgiven them, for knowing that whatever might have been done to her, she can choose how she moves on from it all. And she will move on eventually, because really, what other option is there?

She glances across the graveyard to where the other head-stone stands grey and unimposing. She will go there after she's finished here, but for the moment she can't bring herself to do it. God, she hadn't realised just how much she would miss him.

She pushes herself up from the sodden grass and moves across the graveyard. The ground is wet and boggy, the recent rainfall relentless in its prolonged assault. Yet Alice doesn't notice the cold as it seeps through the knees of her jeans.

She misses him more than she would ever admit to either of her parents. It was only when he was no longer there that she realised just how intertwined their lives had been, a childhood spent together, just like siblings.

The extent of Dylan's financial struggles were revealed a few weeks after his death. Too much partying had been the least of his problems, and his intention to prove himself inde-pendent of his parents had resulted in decisions that had led him down a path that would eventually cost him his life. He'd been running errands for drug dealers in London and taken loans from the kind of people who didn't hold much patience with late repayments. The jewellery and antiques he'd stolen from his parents had been sold on for a couple of thousand pounds – just a fraction of what they were worth, and a drop in the ocean of what he'd still owed.

If only he'd just spoken to someone, Alice thinks as she adjusts herself on the ground, her knees pressing into the damp earth. If not his own parents, then maybe hers. Someone would have been able to help him. All this might have been avoided.

Chris had refused to have his children's graves beside one another, by all accounts considering it an insult to Freya's memory. Alice doesn't know what to make of anything. She's still to decide whether Dylan's final act was one of bravery or cowardice: if by hurting himself in the way he did he exposed himself to the same suffering that had been inflicted on Toby, or if he saw the act as a way of escaping justice for what he'd done.

She runs a palm across the engraved lettering of his headstone: *Dylan Harris, 18 March 2004–10 July 2024*. There is nothing else: no *beloved son* or *adored brother*. Just the facts: a life that existed and was ended too soon.

She feels a hand on her shoulder, a familiar grip, and she smiles sadly. She should have known he would come here. That he would know somehow, instinctively, that this was where he would find her.

'I'm sorry,' she says, without turning.

'You've nothing to be sorry about.'

'I shouldn't be here.'

'Says who?'

No one, actually. Neither of her parents has ever said that she shouldn't remember the good times, the happier times – because they did exist, once, regardless of what came after. She still remembers the four of them as children, the long summers spent playing until the sun had gone down; the Boxing Days on which they'd all gathered to admire the new toys Father Christmas had brought for them.

She swallows a lump of sadness, feeling it stick in her throat. No one then could have imagined in even their worst nightmares that this would be how things ended.

The fingers on her shoulder tighten their grip for a moment

before letting go. Toby kneels beside her, and Alice tilts her head to rest it against his arm, the soft lining of his coat hood rubbing her cheek like a kitten nuzzling her face. She feels safe in the moment. Loved. Protected. Despite everything, so very, very lucky.

'Twenty-one today,' Toby says, running a finger along the engraved date.

Alice spares a thought for Eve and Chris, their lives now so very different. Dylan had died in hospital five days after stabbing himself. He might have survived the injury had it not been for the infection that had attacked his organs. Just a week after her son was gone, Eve was charged with perverting the course of justice. She is currently serving a five-year prison sentence. With the house up for sale, Chris has gone back to his parents' home, where he grieves both his children and the life that has been lost. Jo didn't press charges about the hidden camera installed in her bedroom, and Alice has never said a word to anyone. Chris has already been through enough.

'Do you think he meant to do it?' she asks.

'Do what?'

'End his own life.'

Toby is silent for a moment. 'I don't know.'

She glances at her brother. Beneath the thick winter coat and the sweater that he wears underneath it, a five-inch scar runs across his stomach. His battle wound, as they refer to it. His daily reminder that he is strong enough to get through anything. He rarely speaks about things, keeping his experiences to himself, but Alice realises the psychological wounds will take far longer to heal than the physical.

'I don't think he'd have been able to live with it,' he adds.

'The guilt?'

Toby nods.

'And then you.'

He shrugs. They fall into silence, but Alice knows that her

brother's thoughts have taken him to the same place as hers. Eve has never apologised for her involvement in what happened. She admitted everything, but she has never once said she's sorry for any of it. Given the same circumstances all over again, Alice suspects her decisions would be no different.

When she'd thought back on those days that had led up to Freya's death, Alice had remembered her WhatsApp exchange with Dylan on the night of his parents' party. *There's something I need to tell you.* She has wondered since whether this was it, that he'd wanted to confess to her that he was responsible for the break-in at his parents' house. If he'd done it then, while there'd been a chance, perhaps everything that had come afterwards might have been avoided.

'What now, then?' Toby asks, putting a hand on Alice's shoulder again, this time using it to push himself up from the ground.

'Lunch?'

He pulls a face as he helps her up. 'You know that wasn't what I meant.'

In truth, Alice doesn't have an answer to the question. She has no idea what comes next. Both she and Toby deferred their first year of university. Toby had no choice, needing until Christmas to recover from the multiple surgeries he underwent after the stabbing at the prison, and Alice could never have gone without him, instead staying home where she could help look after him. She got herself a job, which she enjoys, and university no longer looks like the be all and end all. Perhaps she'll go one day... perhaps she won't.

She slips her arm through his as they leave Dylan's graveside. 'Come on,' she says. 'Let me treat you to a cheese toastie.'

FORTY-SEVEN

JO

With most of their belongings packed in boxes or already moved to temporary storage, the house has never looked so bare. Jo stands at the door of Toby's bedroom, picturing what it had looked like years ago, with the sky full of stars dotted across his bedroom ceiling and the solar system duvet beneath which his little body would lie curled during sleep. A room full of memories, a house decorated with them, but she reminds herself that nothing is for ever. Rob wanted to move, and he got what he wanted, in one way or another.

She hears him along the landing, dragging boxes from the bedroom.

'Do you need a hand?' she asks, leaning back from the doorway.

He stops and puts his hands to his lower back as he tries to catch his breath. 'No thanks. Nearly finished.'

A moment passes between them, a hundred unspoken things rushing into a simple glance.

'Are you okay?' he asks.

Jo nods. She hears the clatter of the letter box as something lands on the doormat, and when she goes downstairs, there's an envelope addressed to her. The stamped mark catches her eye, pushing thoughts of anything else to one side. She doesn't have to open it to know who the letter is from.

She goes through to the kitchen and sits at the table, the envelope sitting in front of her like an undetonated bomb. By the time Rob comes down from upstairs, she still hasn't opened it.

'What's that?' he asks.

'It's from Eve.'

He stops what he's doing. 'Do you want me to open it?'

'No. Thanks.'

Jo rips the envelope open and slides out the single sheet that sits within it. She recognises Eve's writing from the party invitations that were pushed through the letter box when the twins had been little; from the meal-plan chalkboard that had hung near the fridge in Eve's kitchen when Dylan and Freya had been much younger.

Dear Jo,

I've been wanting to write to you for some time now, but I could never find the right words. I still can't. There are none. I just hope you'll make it to the end of this letter – that you'll allow me that time at least to try to explain the things that may seem inexplicable.

I know you may not be able to understand it (and I hope you never find yourself in a position where you are forced to reach such an impossible understanding), but the night that Freya was taken from us, I had a decision to make. There in that moment, with one child gone and another imminently lost, I had to make a choice. It wasn't about right or wrong or who was guilty of what. I was thrust into the rawest responsibilities of motherhood: to ensure survival and protection. I hadn't been there to help one child, but I could save another.

I prayed every night for Toby while he was in hospital (me... praying!). I am so, so relieved that he is now home safe with you.

I am sorry, Jo. I don't expect to ever receive your forgiveness; I know I don't deserve it. All the same, I am sorry.

I am sorry, too, for what happened with Rob. I fell in love with him gradually over the years, feelings that were never planned and were repeatedly fought against, but I always knew he would never be mine. He is a good man, Jo, despite the mistake he made, and I know to his mind that is all I was – a mistake he regretted bitterly. I should never have tried to do anything more than admire him from afar and envy you for everything you had.

When I leave this place, Jo, I have nothing to come out to. I suppose the universe gives us what we deserve. I wish your family a long and happy life, and I mean that from the bottom of my heart. You should never have been involved in our family's problems.

I love my children and would do anything for them. You, more than anyone, know how this feels.

From one mother to another,

Eve

Jo reads the letter again, and then again for a third time. Rob watches silently. She hands it to him when she's done, resisting the urge to rip it into pieces. She watches him as he reads it, and she wonders not for the first time whether they'll ever really be able to move on from what has happened here. She has forgiven him, but she knows she'll never be able to forget.

'Taken from us,' Rob says, quoting Eve's reference to Freya's death. 'Even now she can't bring herself to admit what her son did.'

Eve came home from her run that evening to find Dylan in the hallway, standing over Freya's dead body, in much the same way Jo had found her own son. She had acted quickly – there hadn't been time for deliberation. In her bedroom, awaiting her next hair appointment at a salon that only took cash payments, Eve had just short of £150. She gave it to Dylan and told him to check into a B and B or a hotel for the night; to keep his head down and not make conversation with anyone. She told him not to text or call her and gave him a time to meet her at the train station the following day, where it would seem he had just returned from London. Dylan had taken the overnight bag that he'd brought from London that morning, and had cut through the fields that backed onto the gardens on their side of the cul-de-sac. Eve had taken Freya's phone from her pocket. She sent a text to Toby, returned the phone to her daughter's pocket and had gone back out to rerun half the loop of her running route, returning to find the street awash with emergency services.

At some point, perhaps the police would have discovered that Dylan hadn't been where he'd claimed on the night his sister was killed. But no one had been looking at him over the days that followed, not in any way other than as a victim. Everyone had been so convinced of Toby's guilt that looking beyond him had seemed pointless.

The bitterness and resentment Jo feels towards Eve has faded over these past few months, giving way to feelings she would never have thought possible. When the truth was finally revealed, she hated her with such ferocity it had frightened her. This woman – her friend – had been prepared to sacrifice Jo's son to save her own. She had lied to everyone, to the police and to her husband, concealing the truth of her own daughter's murder. To save the family she had left. To stop herself losing a second child.

Would Jo have done differently? She likes to think the answer is yes, she would have, but the truth is that she doesn't know. How can anyone be certain of something so unlikely and so improbable? She doubts anyone can know for sure how they might respond to any given circumstances until they find themselves in that situation, struck with a split-second choice to be made.

'Jo—'

She raises a hand, stopping Rob's words before they're given time to be freed. 'We've talked about it all already. I can't do it again.'

He comes to sit by her and rests a hand on her arm, and they both sit in silence as Eve's letter lies in front of them, a million other unspoken words evaporating in the air around them. She might be a fool to forgive him, she thinks – to imagine their lives can continue somewhere else, the past pulled from beneath them as though it had never been there at all. A new home; a fresh start. Perhaps it won't be that easy. But she's determined to make it work. Above all else, she is a mother. She'll do whatever it takes.

A LETTER FROM VICTORIA

Dear Reader,

I want to say a huge thank you for choosing to read *The Mother's Phone Call*. If you did enjoy it, and want to keep up to date with all my latest releases, just sign up at the following link. Your email address will never be shared and you can unsubscribe at any time.

www.bookouture.com/victoria-jenkins

The idea for this book came after reading a transcript of a 999 call from a mother who was reporting her son for murder. It's a parent's worst nightmare, to be faced with the responsibility of having to 'shop' your own child, and Jo is caught in the dilemma of wanting to protect her son while being faced with a situation she could never have prepared for. Although the children of the two families are at the heart of the plotline, the book is very much a story of two mothers. When I first started writing, I knew I wanted the story to come 'full circle', with Eve having to make her own 999 call as Jo did at the start. I hope it raises questions over love, loyalty, and moral obligations, and how nobody can know how they might react to a certain situation until they're immersed in the awful reality of the thing.

I hope you loved *The Mother's Phone Call* and if you did I would be very grateful if you could write a review. I'd love to hear what you think, and it makes such a difference helping new readers to discover one of my books for the first time.

I love hearing from my readers – you can get in touch through social media or my website.

Thanks,

Victoria Jenkins

 x.com/vicwritescrime

instagram.com/vicwritescrime

ACKNOWLEDGEMENTS

Thank you to Jenny Geras, for sending me the 999 transcript that inspired the idea for *The Mother's Phone Call*. You have supported my writing career since my first book (fifteen stories ago now!) and I am forever grateful for the incredible and life-changing opportunity you gave me. To all the team at Bookouture, a big thank you for your on-going work in publishing, promoting and supporting my books – and thank you for the brilliant cover you gave me for this one. To the cover designer, copy editors and proofreaders – thank you for honing, polishing and making beautiful my often rambling efforts. And a massive thank you to my editor, Laura Deacon – I have loved working with you on this book, and I appreciate just how much you 'got' what I wanted to achieve with this story.

As always, thank you to my husband, Steve, who continues to encourage my crazy ideas, and to my two lovely little girls, who make being a mother my life's favourite story. I might not always get things right, but I'm always trying my best. Being a parent is the most rewarding, challenging, beautiful, exhausting job in the world – and for all the imperfect mothers who are trying their best, this book is for you.

PUBLISHING TEAM

Turning a manuscript into a book requires the efforts of many people. The publishing team at Bookouture would like to acknowledge everyone who contributed to this publication.

Audio
Alba Proko
Sinead O'Connor
Melissa Tran

Commercial
Lauren Morrissette
Hannah Richmond
Imogen Allport

Cover design
The Brewster Project

Data and analysis
Mark Alder
Mohamed Bussuri

Editorial
Laura Deacon
Sinead O'Connor

Copyeditor
Jane Selley

Proofreader
Liz Hatherell

Marketing
Alex Crow
Melanie Price
Occy Carr
Cíara Rosney
Martyna Młynarska

Operations and distribution
Marina Valles
Stephanie Straub
Joe Morris

Production
Hannah Snetsinger
Mandy Kullar
Jen Shannon
Ria Clare

Publicity
Kim Nash
Noelle Holten
Jess Readett
Sarah Hardy

Rights and contracts
Peta Nightingale
Richard King
Saidah Graham

www.ingramcontent.com/pod-product-compliance
Ingram Content Group UK Ltd.
Pitfield, Milton Keynes, MK11 3LW, UK
UKHW040841100125
4002UKWH00002B/92